THE SHADOW'S SON

THE WITCH HUNTER SAGA - BOOK THREE

NICOLE R. TAYLOR

The Shadow's Son (Book Three in The Witch Hunter Saga)

Copyright © 2013-20 by Nicole R. Taylor

Newly revised and edited - November 2020.

First Published August 1st, 2013.

This book is written in British/AU English.

www.nicolertaylorwrites.com

Cover Design: MoorBooks Design

Edited by: Silvia Curry

P aris, *Place de la Concorde*
     October 16, 1793

It was a fine day for a mass execution.

The square was heaving with human life, come to see justice done as much as to see the spectacle. The revolution was over, and the people were now in charge of France after prying it free from the hands of the greedy monarchy.

The country was bankrupted, its people starving and poor, but they were free to rebuild *a toutes les glories de la France.*

Anna was the name she went by in this life. There was this thing she had for the letter A. *Aeriaya, Aericura, Anastasia, Anwyn.* She'd had many names over the thousands of years she'd walked the Earth.

It'd been an exciting time in Paris, along with the

human revolution, there had been a lot of witchcraft that'd captured her attention. After all, it was why she continued living.

Once she'd dealt with the abuse of power, she'd remained in the city to see what would become of the uprising... but it wasn't long before she knew they were close again. Once more, her old enemy was at her heels.

As Anna stood in the crowd waiting for the first scent of blood, a vampire came to stand with her, just as eager for the spectacle of the guillotine as she was.

She didn't have to look to know her silent companion was a female and one she had met before. Glancing out the corner of her eye, Anna saw the woman was wearing too much finery for a public execution post-revolution, but the poorly dressed common folk that surrounded them paid no attention. If they could truly see her, then she would be beaten, robbed, and stripped of her fine dress.

"I know what you are," the woman said, not tearing her eyes off the gruesome sight ahead.

"I know," Anna replied, her gaze falling on the basket at the foot of the guillotine where the first head of the day had fallen, much to the delight of the crowd. "I also know who you are, Victoria."

The woman tensed but corrected herself quickly... but not before Anna noticed.

"Tell me," she continued, "when you were turned,

were you disappointed to find all your power was gone? That you were no longer a witch?"

Victoria smiled but remained silent. Anna had hit a nerve but had to give the Englishwoman a little credence for not taking the bait.

Just then, the crowd became excited, making Anna's skin tingle. The main spectacle was about to begin—the reason so many people had turned out to the square. A cart was approaching from the street behind them, followed by a strong contingency of guards who pressed the crowd back to allow them passage to the guillotine.

She watched without emotion as the cart came to a stop at the foot of the stairs that led up to the high platform. Despite her fate, the woman they'd brought to be executed stood proud. Her long tresses had been shorn off close to her scalp, her plain white dress meagre compared to the finery she'd once worn. Anna remembered her from the few balls she had attended at Versailles. It was hard to forget the once Queen of France, Marie Antoinette.

As she rose to the platform, the crowd began calling for her blood and she stumbled slightly, treading on the foot of the executioner.

"Monsieur, I ask your pardon. I did not do it on purpose," came the delicate, yet proud voice of the fallen monarch.

The executioner merely pushed her down and fastened the metal clasps of the stocks.

As the blade of the guillotine fell, the crowd let out a bloodthirsty cheer, but Anna didn't look away as the head of the Queen of France was severed, blood gushing from the open wound. It landed with a soft thud inside the wicker basket and the monarch was gone.

The lady Victoria still stood at her side, her grin most obvious. But Anna knew she was smiling at the thick scent of blood that lingered in the square, not because a greedy, treasonous member of the royal family was dead. Such was the curse of a vampire.

As the crowd jostled around them, she asked, "How is dear Regulus?"

Victoria tensed momentarily. "He is as well as can be expected."

Anna grinned. "I would expect nothing less."

The surrounding mob was dispersing, the show over for the day. Madame Guillotine would resume her duties in the morning with fervour.

Without looking, Anna knew the square was littered with vampires amongst the common folk— vampires in league with her old adversary Regulus. He was learning, at long last, how to corner and overpower her. In all the years they'd been hunting her, she hadn't been captured and didn't intend to break the cycle.

For the first time, Anna turned to Victoria and smiled. "Please give my regards to your maker." In one fluid motion, she was behind the young vampire, her head in her icy hands.

There was a snap as Anna twisted her head around, breaking her neck. A woman beside them screamed, pointing at the now dead Victoria who'd, crumpled to the ground, but Anna had vanished into the crowd as if she'd never been there.

Then all hell broke loose in the crowd of human commoners. They shouted and shrieked as human soldiers pushed their way through the throng towards the dead vampire.

It was all the distraction Anna needed to slip unnoticed from the square, the hidden vampires never noticing her departure. They were too busy rushing to Victoria's aid. Recovering her body was more important than following her. If they didn't, then their kind would be exposed.

Anna looked back over her shoulder as she slipped into the nearby *Jardin des Tuileries*. Catching sight of a familiar ominous form perched on the platform that held the guillotine, she cursed under her breath. Regulus' eyes locked with hers briefly, his furious gaze chilling her to the bone.

Before he could move, she disappeared into the manicured gardens, bound for Calais.

CHAPTER 1

A clash of steel rang out across the humid Louisiana swamplands as Aya came face to face with Zac, their blades locking together.

"You're such a showoff," she exclaimed, shaking her black hair out of her eyes.

"You're beautiful when you're annoyed," he told her, pressing his blade harder against hers.

He stood a head taller than her, his dark hair falling into his eyes as he grinned. He was young for a vampire—one hundred and seventy—but he was more than a match for Aya, at least where sparring with a katana was concerned. His green eyes pierced into hers and she couldn't help it when a wicked smile played across her lips.

Aya was a vampire, but there was nothing ordinary about that. Just shy of two thousand years old, she was the only one of her kind. A hybrid—half-Celestine, the race that'd founded the first witches, and half-vampire.

She had much of the intuition and power that came with being a creature of magic, paired with the predatory instincts and immortality of a vampire who needed blood to survive.

Her new family were the only people who knew the truth of who she was. The first she'd allowed to come close since the founding vampires—the Romans—had murdered her true family. Alex the kind-hearted human, Gabby the witch, Liz the newborn vampire, and the vampires known as the Degaud brothers, Sam and his older brother Zac composed her new family. And it was Zac who she'd fallen madly in love with despite all her efforts to the contrary.

Aya twisted away and Zac's blade came for her again in a long, swift arc. She arched backwards, barely avoiding her throat being slit. Grinning, she brought her katana around, parrying another blow, before kicking Zac in the stomach.

As her foot connected, he grabbed her boot, pulling her forwards. Landing heavily on her back, she rolled to the side as his blade sunk into the earth where she'd been only a second ago.

Sweeping her leg around, she kicked his feet from under him and he was on his back with a grunt. This time, her blade came down into the earth as he rolled to the side, cursing under his breath. He lunged upwards with an elbow out, but she was expecting his advance and came at him. Placing a hand on his shoulder, she used his momentum to vault over him.

She landed lightly, one knee on the ground, long black hair wild and unruly.

Sword play was her favourite combat style. She'd learned many techniques in her long life, from the last days of the Roman Empire, to the Crusades of the Middle Ages, all the way to Japan's Edo period in the 1600s, where she became a Samurai. When she'd mentioned her time in Japan and how much she enjoyed their style of fighting, Zac had somehow procured some well-made katanas. The curved, slender, single-edged blade always sat well in her long hands and wherever these had come from, they were sharp and well balanced.

Aya was teaching Zac what she could. He already knew how to use a sabre from his human days in the American Civil War and was quite good at it. He'd drawn her blood several times already, making her wonder how much she could actually pass on. He downplayed his intelligence so much that it put his opponents at ease, opening them up to their arrogance. He learned fast. In a fight with a vampire, age wouldn't matter where he was concerned.

Zac picked up the new guards and attacks she'd shown with little effort, and soon they were fighting with their strength behind them. They parried each other's blows, the clash of steel ringing out through the empty forest. When they both realised they could go for hours without a clear victor, the dirty techniques began. Tripping, biting, elbowing… all were met with laughter until Zac got the upper hand.

Pinning her against a tree, sword pressed to her pale throat, Zac's chest heaved as he stared into her strong, blue eyes. He dragged the blade gently across her skin, drawing a few beads of blood. She let out a low hiss as she watched his eyes change, her own responding in kind, blackness echoing the purity of her white. Running a thumb across the cut he'd inflicted, he put it into his mouth and let the coppery tang settle on his tongue. They dropped their swords at the same moment, their lips meeting in a hungry kiss, hands all over each other. It was like that with them— their attraction was so complete it took much will power to keep themselves under control. Fighting only made it unbearable.

Aya pushed Zac to the ground, straddling him, ripping his shirt open, running kisses up his hard chest. Grasping her waist, he flipped her over, allowing his weight to press her into the ground, the leaf litter clinging into her long black hair. He dragged his fangs along the soft skin of her throat, kissing a trail over the most sensitive veins, the echo of her hybrid blood shuddering through him and into her.

She arched her back, leaning her head away, silently giving permission for him to feed and he took it, but she knew he'd be unable to stop himself anyway. His fangs pierced the ivory skin in the crook of her neck, and he groaned as her blood flooded his mouth.

It'd stopped giving him dreams weeks ago, all Aya's potent blood memories having played out. What he hadn't seen, she told him about as she remembered things from her two thousand years as a vampire.

She moaned with pleasure as he drank from her, the feeling of blood leaving the wound in her neck painfully sweet. When he pulled away, Aya drew his face near and kissed him deeply while his hands roamed her body underneath her shirt. Then, she drew him up, kneeling in front of him, and let her fangs sink into his exposed jugular, her hand cupping his face.

This. This took her so completely, she was afraid she'd never come back.

Zac knew without a doubt that he would do anything for Aya. *Anything.*

She didn't have to let him feed from her to know that. If she refused him, he would still do whatever she asked. Fact was, she'd already done just that.

He wanted her completely, but as intimate as their blood sharing was, it was as far as she would let him go. It frustrated the hell out of him, but he let her. Of course, he did. He was madly in love with her.

Crushing her body into his, he closed his eyes as he felt the blood leave him. He let his hands find their way underneath her shirt, caressing the soft skin of her back, trailing their way up her spine to her bra, where he deftly unhooked the clasp. He wanted to be closer, skin on skin, as she took his blood.

Aya pulled away abruptly as his thumbs brushed underneath the curve of her breasts, gasping as a trickle of his blood ran down her chin. Frowning at her sudden coldness, Zac caught the trailing blood in a kiss.

"It's okay," he whispered as he pulled himself away, buttoning his black shirt back up. It wasn't really, but he couldn't broach the subject with her... she wouldn't let him. "It's getting late anyway. Alex and Sam are going to meet us at *Max's* soon."

She was on her feet, hands behind her back, clasping her bra. "Zac." Her voice was a whisper, full of uncertainty.

He stood and pulled her to him with his free hand, breathing in her scent. "I know," he said. "You're sorry."

After everything they'd been through in the short time they'd known each other, he'd never heard her say the word sorry so much. Until the day after their showdown with Arturius—the day after she'd used her power to kill her maker—he'd never thought it was a word that existed in her vocabulary. Now she never seemed to say anything else.

What had she to be sorry for? She'd saved them all from certain death many times over. She'd saved them from the founding witch Katrin, and she had rescued their human friend Alex from a deranged vampire. She'd saved Gabby from a fate worse than death, and had even gone after him when he'd flipped out after fighting with his brother, Sam. Then, when Katrin had cursed him that night in the cemetery, she'd given all her secrets and her life to save him... yet she still held herself back. Wasn't this all enough?

They knew every part of one another. He'd told her everything, every painful memory, every struggle he'd endured. He'd even told her the story of his first few horrible months as a vampire—something he'd never been able to share with anyone, not even Sam.

After all this, a wedge had still come between them.

Aya wasn't telling him the entire truth. Part of her still didn't trust him, and that hurt more than anything. Zac had no idea what to do, other than to wait and hope.

Letting her go, he let out a shaky breath. She threaded an arm through his and they walked back to the manor in silence, the rift that had unknowingly risen between them splitting even more.

Life was quiet and that made Aya restless. Life was never this easy for long, at least not in her experience.

Everyone was off living their lives as normal. Well, as normal as they'd been until she'd come along. Sam and Alex were still at the gardens working, Liz was at the coffee house until five p.m., and Gabby was off doing who knew what.

Ever since Arturius was killed, the witch spent less and less time with the vampires, and Aya had hardly laid eyes on her. She couldn't blame her with the lingering possibility that the last Roman, Regulus, would come looking for them one day. Gabby's power had increased significantly and that made her a target.

Since Aya'd expelled the darkness from her, the young witch had what she'd been craving—control. And now Gabby had to learn how to use her power again. After a lot of back and forth, Aya had finally convinced her to come to the manor in the morning to talk it through.

Aya almost jumped when Zac slid his hand onto her thigh under the table and she scolded herself for being so distracted. They were at *Max's*, the local bar and the brothers' favourite haunt. It was still early, and only a few tables were occupied, so they had a nice space to themselves. Sam and Alex weren't due for another hour.

"What are you thinking about?" Zac asked, a frown creasing his forehead.

"Nothing." She shrugged but tensed slightly as she felt something change in the air.

"No, really, what?"

"Someone's coming."

"Seriously? You're always avoiding my questions, Aya."

Ignoring the look Zac was giving her, she turned and watched the door. It was... No, it couldn't be. She hadn't felt that presence in a long time. And a long time to her was in the hundreds of years. In this case, six of them. Or was it seven?

The door opened, letting in the cool evening breeze and someone else. Aya locked eyes with a man who was undoubtedly a vampire. Mid-height, well-built, and with a head of unruly brown curls. He had muscled arms she knew were gained from years of wielding heavy weapons and hard fighting, and an impish grin that she remembered all too well.

He halted as recognition flashed across his face.

Standing, Aya walked towards the vampire with a smile on her lips. "Ser Tristan na Tri Tor. Here is a face I never thought I would see again."

"It's been six hundred and sixty years, Lady Arrow." He embraced her tightly, his thick Irish accent washing over her. "You're a hard woman to track down."

Drawing back, she placed a hand on her friend's face, smiling. Feeling Zac's hard glare on her back, she pulled Tristan towards the table where he was seated. "I want you to meet someone."

"Arrow," he whispered, glancing over her shoulder towards Zac. "I bring news."

She sighed. "I suspected as much, otherwise you wouldn't have sought me out."

Tristan tried to pull her away. "Arrow, I must insist."

"Tristan," she said firmly and gestured towards Zac.

"He knows everything, and I trust him with my life. Whatever news you have, you can share with the both of us. Now, don't be rude and come and say hello."

Zac looked none too pleased to see her so familiar with another male vampire, but her friendship with Tristan was just that. *Friendship*. He stood when they approached and extended his hand, ever the nineteenth-century gentleman.

"Zachary Degaud," he said stiffly.

"Ser Tristan na Tri Tor." He grasped the younger vampire's hand a little too firmly and shook.

Aya sensed the animosity between them over her and rolled her eyes. "Get over it."

Tristan sighed. "Always so astute, Arrow."

She glanced at Zac, then sat beside him. No doubt she'd have much to explain later. Grasping his hand under the table, she frowned at her old friend. "How did you find me?"

"You killed two Romans and ended the witch Katrin in a matter of weeks. News like that travels quickly," he said. "You made it easy."

Aya smiled wickedly. "I'm not worried about that."

"There is only one vampire you have cause to worry about."

"I know."

"He knows, Arrow. Arturius sent him word that you were dead. That your heart was torn from you." He shook his head in disbelief. "Yet, here you are."

She rolled her eyes. "Well, what a conundrum."

"If he has to imprison you for an eternity, he will, now that he knows how hard it is to end you."

Aya's eyes darkened and she hissed, "Not if I end him first. Regulus will die, whether it be today, tomorrow, or next century. He. Will. *Die*." She felt Zac's hand tighten around hers and she sat back, letting the tension ease from her body.

"I don't doubt it." Tristan shook his head at her sudden outburst. "But he is comin' regardless. And he will start here."

"Let him look. The moment I lay eyes on him, he is dead."

"I think he'll get more than he bargained for," Zac said, eyeballing Tristan with unmasked dislike.

"Likewise," the knight said, leaning forwards, elbows resting on the table.

Aya sensed the hostility coming from both the men and she stifled a groan of annoyance. Tristan's appearance was enough to rattle her, let alone Zac. He seemed to know a lot about Regulus and the thought crossed her mind that he might be in the Roman's back pocket. She would have to be careful with him, even though they'd shared a lifetime of sorts together... but that'd been centuries ago.

She glanced at Zac, who was watching Tristan with a hard jaw. He would have a lot to say about this later —another problem to add to the ever-increasing pile. There was enough going on with them without the appearance of a mysterious man from her past.

"And how do you know all this?" Zac asked, his lip curled into a sneer.

"I have my sources," Tristan replied, leaning back in his chair, his emotions carefully guarded.

"If you find it so necessary to warn us, then why not reveal how?"

"Arrow might know you, but I don't."

Aya slammed a fist onto the tabletop, the few empty glasses rattling against each other. Both men looked at her and she swore both of them were equally disappointed she'd interrupted their slanging match.

"Enough," she hissed. "Stop acting like children." She pressed her leg against Zac's and she felt the tension bleed from him. Eyeballing Tristan across the table, he shook his head and let out an exasperated sigh.

"I had thought more of you, Arrow," he said, keeping his voice low.

She clamped a hand on Zac's thigh before he could move and pressed her fingers hard into his flesh. "Be careful what you say to me, Tristan na Tri Tor. We may have been friends once, but that was a long time ago. I have torn greater men's heads from their shoulders for far less."

The knight laughed, the tension suddenly lifting from the table. "You haven't changed one bit."

"Arrogant bastard," she said, rolling her eyes.

"That's what got me the title of Ser in the first place."

"Ass," Zac hissed under his breath so quietly she almost missed it and apparently, Tristan didn't, either.

"Well," he said. "I see you have a penchant for arrogant men, Arrow. What were you, Zac? Military, am I correct? Were you a captain, major, or sergeant? A man as volatile as you would have some ambition, right?"

Zac let out a snort, his gaze measuring the knight. "Captain."

Tristan let out a slow whistle. "Good for you."

"I think you better leave, Tristan," Aya cut off their little bragging match. "We will continue this another time."

He chuckled, leaning towards her. "Oh, I am sure you have a barrage of questions, Arrow. Come and find me tomorrow... and leave your plaything at home." He took one last jab at Zac before standing, his chair scraping back against the floorboards. Glaring at the younger vampire, he said, "It was a pleasure meetin' you."

"I wish I could say the same," Zac replied, his voice dripping with sarcasm.

Aya watched the two vampires regard each other and didn't like what she saw. Tristan and Zac? That was a fight waiting to happen. And knowing both of their track records, she had no idea who would come out the victor.

CHAPTER 2

Zac let out a relieved breath when he finally walked through the front door of the manor, Aya's hand firmly clasped in his own. They made a beeline straight for the parlour. Today had completely screwed with his mind and despite her presence, he felt edgy. She had the uncanny ability to calm him down with a simple touch, but he was too tightly wound for that to work now.

Kneeling in front of the fireplace, he threw a few logs into the hearth and struck a match, lighting the kindling. Overly conscious of Aya's gaze on his back, he watched as the flames took, the flickering light beginning to fill the parlour with a dull orange glow.

This Tristan. He'd appeared out of nowhere, and Zac couldn't help his jealousy. He'd loved no one in the one hundred and seventy years he'd been on this Earth, and even though she'd told him the same, Aya had been around for two thousand years. Who knew half the things she'd done, and especially what'd gone on with this vampire?

Zac had sensed his feelings without having to witness them. The knight obviously felt he had some kind of claim over her, and it irritated the hell out of him.

Then there was the parts where Tristan seemed to know a lot about Regulus' comings and goings. It stunk of deceit. Whose side was he really on?

Zac knew Aya could read his emotions and when he felt her beside him, he shook his head, setting the poker to the side.

"What do you want to know?" When he didn't answer right away, she continued, "I know you have a million questions that you're burning to ask me."

"A million? Try a billion," he huffed, not bothering to mask his irritation.

She tugged on his arm, coaxing him to sit beside her on the sofa. "Start with the first one that comes to mind."

"What's with his name? It sounds like a circus act."

"It's Irish," she replied. "In English, it means Tristan of the Three Towers. His family were lower nobility and owned a castle that had three towers. They named things rather obviously back then."

"Back when?"

"1100."

He let his gaze linger on her as she watched the fire burn in the hearth, its glow flickering on the surrounding walls. They didn't need the heat on such a warm night, but the flames calmed her down—which was the only reason he lit it.

Sometimes Zac wished he could read her emotions as easily as she could his. She always carefully guarded her expression and it made him wonder what she thought about the possibility of Regulus coming to Ashburton. That's what Tristan had implied. They would have to do something about it sooner rather than later, and this vampire appearing only made him feel more on edge about it.

"So, he's about a thousand years old?" Zac asked.

"More like nine hundred."

"Why does he call you Arrow?"

"It was the name I took at the time. Ser Arrow. I was in England around 1180, give or take a few years. I pretended to be a man so I could pose as a knight, joined the Templars in England, and took part in the Third Crusade. Richard the Lionheart and the Church were trying to win back the Holy Land, though you would know it now as Jerusalem. I marched with them, as much to see a new part of the world as an excuse to fight," she said. "I didn't particularly believe in their cause. Christianity at that time didn't seem that holy. I mainly went because I was at a low point."

"A low point?" he asked, knowing full well what point she was talking about.

She sighed, rubbing her eyes. "A particularly messy low point."

Sensing her discomfort, he asked another question, "And where does he come into it?"

"Tristan was the only one who I never had to compel to forget I was a woman. He was a son of an Irish lord who sent him to England to squire for a man who later became one of the first Templars. He was made a knight just before we marched on the Crusade. I left right after the campaign failed, three years later, and he was still human. The last I saw him, he was marching back to England and I was off to what is now Turkey and beyond. It wasn't until fifteen years later that we met again. This time he was a vampire and in a right mess."

"How did he change?"

Aya sighed. "I think that's a story he should tell you... if he so chooses. He had a family in England. A wife and child, but he'd devoted himself to the cause of the Church and Crown all the same. He was a hero, in all senses of the word, until he was turned. He saw the atrocities his own people inflicted on the cities they claimed, and he tried to stop much of it. I saved him from a flogging more than once. He died during the Fourth Crusade, somewhere underneath the city of Constantinople. I found him years later in Europe and by that time, he was a true monster, but I owed him and helped him come to terms with his new life."

Zac snorted. It was an all too familiar story, so much so, it was becoming cliché.

"He had nothing, Zac," Aya told him. "That's why

he travelled with me for so long. When we finally parted, it was as friends. It was never anything more than that."

"He hunted witches with you," Zac whispered.

"Yes. And in turn, the Romans hunted him as much as they did me." She sighed, rubbing her eyes again.

"What's wrong?"

"It's been over six hundred years since I've seen him," Aya replied with a frown. "Just because we were companions once, doesn't mean I entirely trust him."

"Good," Zac said. He didn't, either.

"Tristan knows nothing about the Celestines," she said, caressing his face, making him shiver. "You're the first vampire, other than the Romans, who knows the entire truth. You, Sam, Alex, Gabby, and Liz. And you know I can compel a vampire if necessary."

"I know." He wasn't really convinced.

"Zac, what's wrong?"

"You were with him for one hundred and forty years," he murmured, a hint of anger in his voice. "That's my entire life. Forgive me if I don't understand, but I cannot fathom it."

Aya sighed and pulled his face her hers, kissing him with a need that unsettled him. When he moaned, crushing her to him, she whispered, "I never did that with him."

Zac stiffened and pulled away. "You're going to kill me, Aya."

"Of course, I am, because I won't let anyone else touch you."

She ran her hand up his chest and he pulled her close, kissing the delicate skin below her ear, her arms wrapping around his neck. When he eased her back onto the couch, his weight pressing into her, she turned her head away, obviously uncomfortable. Masking his frustration, Zac closed his eyes and tore himself from her. What wasn't she telling him?

Getting up from the sofa, he walked across the room, conscious of her gaze following every gesture he made. He wrenched open the liquor cabinet and poured himself a glass of the first thing his hand came in contact with.

The slow burn of whisky trailed down his throat, soothing his hunger

Leaving the glass on the sideboard, he went upstairs without looking at her again.

Perhaps it was childish, but he was at his wits' end. Aya was pulling away from him and nothing he said helped. It took him so much to get to this point, and he still didn't know what to do. It was glaringly obvious that she didn't trust him, and that hurt more than anything.

After everything they'd been through. After everything he'd shared with her.

Now this Tristan had waltzed into town and made things even more complicated. There was more to him than met the eye, that was for sure. The way he had looked at Aya hadn't escaped him, either.

Was this how she'd felt when Morgan had been at his side? Hell, was this how Morgan had felt seeing him with Aya? If it had been, then now he understood.

Thinking about Morgan brought back another ebb of emotion he'd been trying to forget. Morgan had helped him come back from one of his psychopathic rages and had fallen for him in the process. It was almost seventy years ago, but he remembered it like it was yesterday. When they'd finally met again a few months ago, she'd betrayed Aya to Arturius, hoping to get her out of the picture. Instead, Morgan was betrayed and ended up dead... all in the name of love.

Would this story play out the same way?

Zac had no idea where he stood anymore. He couldn't help but think maybe Aya was too much for him to handle.

Sometime later, after he'd finally fallen asleep, she'd found her way into his bed and he woke with her head resting on his bare chest. Her familiar scent washed over him as he dragged a hand through her hair.

If they didn't work this out... She was going to kill him, not Regulus. And it would be a slow, painful death.

Aya's mind was preoccupied a lot lately. She could use it as a reason for her coldness, but that was only an excuse and she knew it.

It'd been three months since she'd confronted and killed the founding vampire Arturius. And during the fight, he'd broken her body brutally, but she feared that he'd broken something in her mind as well.

He'd been the one to turn her all those years ago, and it was his vampire blood that ran with her Celestine. How was she to know what would happen if she killed him? When she had let her power flow into him, the blue fire had folded back on itself and shocked right into her mind.

It'd never happened before. *Ever.*

She was afraid it'd changed something inside her... something she didn't know yet.

Whatever it might be, she felt she had to keep Zac at arm's length. If she became unstable, she could tear him apart and not know what she was doing until it was too late.

There was no way of knowing if any of it was true. It was purely speculation.

Zac knew she was keeping something from him. He always knew. It was strange that he hadn't asked yet. He was less arrogant than when she'd first met him. Sam had told her that he was becoming more human, more like he was before.

She wasn't sure what to make of that.

Shoving *those* thoughts aside, Aya turned to other

pressing matters. The mystery that was Zac's blood. She could hear when he was near and if she listened hard enough, could even track him over miles. In her entire life, she'd never encountered blood that sang to her. There were no other words to describe it. Drinking his blood had awakened abilities that she'd thought were lost to her forever. It was an enigma.

In the weeks following the fight with Arturius, she'd tasted Sam's too, finding it had the same effect. Now she could hear Sam as well, but curiously, it was a slightly different song than Zac's. To her disgust and Sam's request, she'd even tried Liz's blood, but it was silent, her maker unknown.

They'd spent the last few months tracing Zac and Sam's family line, but so far had found nothing that would indicate a reason for their unusual blood. There was no witchcraft to be found in their ancestry or any hint of other supernatural intermingling that sometimes happened with humans. Not in the records that were available, anyway.

Aya's thoughts kept going back to her theory that it had to do with their sunlight spells. The same Mexican witch had cast the incantation that allowed them to walk in the day, and she knew that bruja practiced differently than others and didn't always use conventional means. Gabby made enquiries of her own and was told that a spell like that, even done by dark means, wouldn't affect blood.

The only avenue left to investigate was their

vampire heritage. Regulus turned Victoria and the brothers knew this. Arturius had implied it when Zac had confronted the Roman a few months prior. He was now dead, but that wasn't the Roman who would know.

Why had Regulus turned Victoria in the first place? Aya had neglected to mention to the brothers that she had been a witch—a particularly weak one, but a witch regardless. Aya knew that her power had disappeared once she was turned—she'd seen proof of that.

There was something else in play here.

Regulus didn't have a heart. He must have wanted something from her.

The more Aya dwelt on it, the more she knew it was Victoria's blood that had something to do with the brothers' strange vampirism. Their memories were sharper, and their blood was potent to her hybrid senses. If there were other benefits or disadvantages, she didn't know.

Eventually, she would have to track down Victoria's lineage, but for now, Aya was content with staying at the manor in relative peace and quiet. Their respite would be broken soon enough when Regulus deigned to retaliate for Arturius and Caius' deaths.

"Aya?" Gabby's voice broke through her silent reverie and she blinked hard.

"Yes?"

The witch frowned and said, "I asked you what I should do."

That's right, Aya had promised to help the witch with her power. She reached for the glass of scotch resting on the coffee table and sipped.

Since Aya had dispelled the darkness from Gabby, the young witch had hardly practiced at all. The fear that followed her hadn't escaped Aya's notice... she was overly sensitive to these things.

"You need to let your power back in, Gabby. That's the only way forwards."

"I know." She sounded reluctant, like she didn't believe her own words.

"I know it's difficult. I know all about power and control." Aya frowned as Gabby shook her head. "The darkness is gone. It's not coming back."

"I know that." Gabby shrugged. "It's just... It's too much responsibility. Being this." She gestured to herself with shaking hands.

"I never asked to be a Celestine, but I was born into it. And I never asked to become a vampire. You play the hand you're dealt, Gabby. It's all we've got."

The young witch was wringing her hands, her apprehension reverberating through her. "Yeah."

"You mightn't have asked for it, but you have it anyway. It's too great a gift not to be used for its true purpose."

"It's a lot, Aya. I can't just dive in headfirst." Gabby

seemed to know what she was talking about. All she had to do now was take her own advice.

"It's a start," she agreed.

Aya was quiet for several minutes. She'd seen this struggle Gabby was going through too many times to count. With great power came great responsibility, and not all who had it thrust upon them wanted it.

"You have a kind heart, Gabby," she said finally. "Whatever happens, I know you'll do what needs to be done."

"Whatever?" She sighed. "Even if I have to resort to doing something bad?"

"Sometimes you have to choose the lesser of two evils."

"But you'll be here to help me... right?" The struggle she was having with herself was clear from the look on her face.

Aya shook her head. "I won't always be here."

"What do you mean?"

"At some point, I will have to leave. You know that, right?"

"Yes, but..."

"There are no buts. Things might be..." She struggled to find the right words, "*different* right now, but I still have a duty."

Gabby nodded, seeming to understand.

There were other witches who needed to taste Aya's revenge and those who needed her help. Where that left this thing with her and Zac, she didn't know.

Perhaps it was foolish to hold on to this feeling of love, even though the witches had told her the opposite.

When she'd gone to see Sophia after Arturius had taken Gabby, the old witch had shown Aya a vision of her past. A moment in time she'd forgotten—when she'd first met Zac. He'd been entirely human, and she felt it then as she felt it now. She loved him. She loved him so much it hurt.

Aya couldn't help thinking that it was stopping her from fulfilling her twisted promise. She couldn't ask him to leave his brother and his home, not after everything he'd been through. Her life was all wrong for him. One day she would have to leave, and he would follow unquestioned.

She tried to ignore the thought that had been eating at the corners of her mind for the past few weeks.

Did she really want him to?

CHAPTER 3

Aya hadn't seen Zac all day.

When she'd woken that morning, he was long gone, and she felt strangely bereft.

She fought the impulse to seek him out, instead occupied herself with assisting Gabby and wandering through the forest, trying to sort out her own confused mind. Needless to say, she hadn't gotten anywhere.

She'd also avoided looking for Tristan, knowing anything he had to say wasn't going to be good and right now, she didn't want to hear it.

The only thing that was obvious was that she had a difficult decision to make.

When Aya could bear it no more, and when the sun had dipped below the horizon, she went to *Max's*, where she knew Zac would be.

Pushing through the door, she felt his presence immediately. It was more familiar to her than even her own family had been. He consumed her, and maybe that was part of the problem.

Looking away from where she knew he would be, she caught Tristan's eye. She hadn't noticed he was here, what with her silent pining over Zac. Walking towards him, he raised an eyebrow.

"I thought I would have seen you before now," he said, his hand clutched around a beer.

"I haven't come to see you," she sneered, not sitting down.

Finally, she looked up and saw Zac sitting at the bar with his back to them. Even if she couldn't feel his emotions, she would know exactly what they were.

His head hung low over his glass and his shoulders were hunched. Zac was a hard man and rarely showed anything other than annoyance or anger. Right now, it was the second of the two, and his posture meant he was trying to keep it to himself.

Aya knew that he'd registered her presence, but he acted as if she didn't exist. And he would know that she understood exactly what he was doing. He didn't know how to articulate what was on his mind, so this was how he acted.

"He's angry with you, Arrow," Tristan stated the obvious, taking a draught of his beer.

Aya knew she'd done something wrong, but something for the life of her she didn't understand. She could think of a few things and it could be any of them, but her gut was churning over one particular misdemeanour.

"You never were good at relatin' to people," the knight continued. "If you intend to keep him, you should do somethin' about it."

Shooting one last glare at Tristan, Aya walked over to where Zac sat and laid her hand lightly on his shoulder.

For a moment it looked as if he wasn't going to move, but he got up from the stool without a word, her hand falling away. He led her to a booth at the back of the bar, conscious that Tristan watched them out of the corner of his eye.

Sliding in next to him, she shot a warning glare at the knight, who shrugged and turned away, letting her know he wasn't eavesdropping. If Aya found out that he had, he'd regret it.

Zac stared at her with those unusual green eyes of his, like he was trying to think of the right words. After a moment, he said, "What do I have to do?"

She knew what he meant, but she asked anyway, "Do about what?"

He snorted and looked away with a shake of his head, knowing she was stalling. She could never get anything past him.

Aya frowned, not knowing what to say. Even she didn't understand why she couldn't just let go and give herself to him. All of herself. It wasn't like she hadn't done it before, but Zac was different. He knew things about her that no one else did, and he'd seen things that she would usually compel away. Then there was that moment with Arturius when her power had turned on her.

Zac turned back towards her, his jaw set. She felt the tension build as his leg pressed against hers. He grasped her hand with his right hand under the table, letting his left trace the inside of her thigh.

"Aya, I want all of you." He leaned closer, his lips brushing against the corner of her jaw. "Why won't you let me? What aren't you saying?"

"Zac," she said uncomfortably, "we're in public."

He pulled back sharply, breaking all contact between them, and she suddenly felt cold.

"We've been together for months. There hasn't been a moment we've been apart," he murmured. "I need some time to think about this."

"Come back to the manor with me," she whispered.

The faint trace of a sneer pulled at his lips. "And what?"

"We can talk without so many ears listening." She glanced across the bar where Tristan was talking to a pretty girl, but still had one eye on them.

Zac saw who she'd glanced at and rolled his eyes. "You know, I think Ser Lancelot is an idiot." Tristan's shoulders lifted as he let out a laugh at this, giving away that he was eavesdropping.

"Zac," Aya scolded. "*Please*. This isn't the place to be

talking about these things. Let's go and we can talk about it."

"That's the problem," he said. "Talking isn't working. I can't think straight around you."

She stood and held out her hand.

He sighed and took it, allowing her to pull him up. "You can talk your way out of anything."

"Not with you."

"*Especially* with me."

She led him by the hand from the bar, blindingly aware that Tristan's gaze followed their departure. She would have to question him later.

They lingered on the dark street around the corner from the bar, memories of her first night in Ashburton in a hundred and fifty years flashed through her mind. That lane to their right was where she'd saved Zac's life from a pack of werewolves that'd jumped him. She'd lost control and tore them into tiny little pieces.

"It's complicated," Aya said, breaking the uncomfortable silence that'd cropped up between them.

"Explain it to me, Aya, because I obviously don't understand." He used her name condescendingly and it hurt.

"How can I explain it when I don't understand myself? I love you," she said, almost pleadingly. "*Please.*"

"Really?" He shook his head. "I can't think straight for want of you, Aya. You drive me mad. Why won't you let me touch you? What are you afraid of? That I'm going to end up like the werewolves you so unashamedly ripped apart?"

"No!" Except, that was exactly it.

"Then what?"

She looked at the vampire she'd fallen so madly in love with and pushed away the uncomfortable thought that she was driving him mad, that their love was driving both of them mad. The pain and confusion on his face tore her apart and she didn't know what to do. She couldn't just give herself to him. All their problems wouldn't just magically disappear if she did.

"Your silence speaks volumes," he declared.

"You won't touch me again, will you?" she whispered as he looked away into the darkness. That was something she was afraid was going to happen, and it looked like it was going to anyway.

"It's not about that and you know it."

"Zac..."

"What aren't you telling me?" He snorted, shaking his head when she didn't reply. "What can I do if you won't say anything? Whatever it is, it's obviously screwing this up, Aya."

"I-I don't..." Why couldn't she just say it?

"You don't trust me."

She looked up at him with wide eyes. "Of course, I do."

"No. You don't. If you did, then we wouldn't be having this conversation. We would be *happy*."

He was right. For the first time in her life, Aya was lost for words. Zac was the only one who'd ever had the guts to call her out. She'd walked through two thousand years building a reputation for brutality and unrelenting chaos. She was someone who was feared and here was Zac, pulling her back down to earth. Aya had never felt so small in all her life.

And she deserved it.

"What's changed?" he murmured, his green eyes searching hers. "For the life of me, I can't work it out."

She opened her mouth to say something, anything, but nothing came out. A strange sensation stung her eyes and she realised she was fighting back tears.

Zac didn't seem to care and without a word, he turned and took a few steps, then disappeared into the night.

Deep down, Zac knew something had been wrong for a while.

Aya hadn't been the same since she'd woken after her wounds had healed from her fight with Arturius. He'd disregarded her aversion to their intimacy and trusted her to work it out. He didn't want to think about it. Instead, like the fool he was, he let it fester until it pulled them apart.

Lingering in the lane behind the bar, he sat on a step in front of a closed door, and cursed. He'd finally told Aya exactly how he felt, and she'd pushed him away. *Again.* He shouldn't be surprised, but it didn't stop it from hurting any less.

It wasn't about sex, not by a long shot—even he wasn't that much of an ass. It was about trust, always had been. She was hiding something and didn't trust him enough to confide in him. Whatever it was... *whatever*... he would stand by her, he'd help her. But what could he do if he didn't know?

Zac groaned when he felt Tristan approach. Of course, the Irish bastard would take the opportunity to sink in his boot right where it hurt. The knight's obvious claim over Aya hadn't gone unnoticed. In fact, he'd made it clear on several occasions and it'd only been twenty-four hours.

"What the hell is your problem?" Zac glared up at him when he neared.

"Just wanted to pass along a few friendly words of advice." Leaning against the wall, the knight shrugged.

Zac snorted and turned to face him. "I don't need your advice. You might be a billion, but I know exactly what I'm doing."

"Oh, I don't doubt it."

"Spit it out, Tristan. I haven't got all night," he hissed, not bothering to mask his dislike.

"We were companions for a very long time," the knight said with a note of mockery in his voice. "She can be unpredictable and manipulative, and she may say she loves you... but it hasn't been the first time she's uttered those words."

On his feet in an instant, he grabbed the front of Tristan's shirt and pushed him hard into the wall, his face inches away from the knight's. Scowling with an all too familiar fury, his eyes changed, the edges consumed with blackness, his irises still iridescent green as he tried to keep himself under control.

"*Calm down.*" Tristan held his hands up defensively. "No need for the theatrics, my friend."

Zac's breathing was heavy and his jaw clenched tightly as he held himself back. A minute passed before he roughly pushed Tristan away, turning to the darkness of the empty lot behind the bar.

"You're not welcome here, Tristan," he said as he composed himself. "As long as I'm here, you shouldn't be."

***

Aya tracked Tristan down to the motel on the edge of Ashburton later the next day.

The knight had a lot to answer for and she couldn't put it off any longer. She needed to know Regulus' intentions.

She was still agitated from the previous night. Zac hadn't come back to the manor at all, and she couldn't help herself when she'd cast her mind out, searching for him. She was worried he would do something reckless after their fight, but when she'd felt his presence on the opposite side of town, she knew he was at Alex's. What he was doing there was a mystery. They had never been that close, but perhaps Liz and Gabby were there as well. Liz—who he had once been in love with and now loved like a sister—would talk him down.

Standing outside the room she knew was Tristan's, she sighed. *Here we go again,* she thought as she raised her fist and knocked loudly.

The door opened and he peered out, not in the least bit surprised to find her standing on the other side. He looked like he'd just woken up, bleary-eyed and shirtless, and she knew it was for her benefit.

Rolling her eyes, she pushed past him and walked inside.

"Good mornin' to you too," he said in mock annoyance.

Surveying the room, she turned her nose up. It smelled like someone had pissed in the corner. The sign out front that said budget wasn't far off.

In one corner there was an old armchair clad in an offensive floral pattern, a double bed with a matching bedspread, and ugly mustard-coloured curtains. It reminded her of the motel she'd taken Zac to when she had tracked him after he'd fought with Sam. It only served to remind her of their precarious situation. That's where she first kissed him, after all.

Sitting in the armchair, she regarded Tristan coolly

as he pulled on a shirt and dragged his fingers through his tangled hair.

"What?" he asked when she only stared at him.

"I'm waiting for you to explain yourself." She tilted her head to the side. "It was you who said you wanted to speak to me."

"I want to speak to you about a lot of things," he said, sitting on a chair opposite her. "One bein' that vampire you seem so fond of."

"And what business is it of yours what I do, Tristan?"

"We have the same end game, Arrow. We can help each other, you know. So, I would say your attachment to him is my business if you want my help."

"Who says I want your help?" She let her lip curl up in a sneer. His assumption angered her more than she thought it would.

"He's a piece of work, your boyfriend." He grimaced, blatantly ignoring her question. "Very volatile."

"What did you do to him, Tristan?" she scolded.

"Just offered a few friendly words of advice."

"You had no right."

"It needed to be said, Arrow."

"What?" she hissed.

Tristan only shrugged.

"You don't get to mess with this, do you understand?"

"You really love him, don't you?" he asked like he

hadn't believed it until now. "I didn't think you had it in you."

Aya didn't want to get into it. She knew exactly what he would say, but she wasn't the same person she was a thousand years ago. Only a fool would presume that. Instead, she turned the conversation back to him. For her, there was only one question that he needed to answer. "What have you been doing for the last six hundred years, Tristan?"

"Lookin' for you."

Like she believed that. "Tell me the truth, knight, or I will rip it from your chest."

Tristan held his hands up in front of him defensively, trying to hide a grin. "Calm down. That was mostly the truth. After you left me in Austria, I wandered Europe for a while. Like most, I had many lives. Lived in many human societies. Then about two hundred years ago, I met a curious man named Regulus."

Aya tensed. "*Tristan na Tri Tor*—"

"Arrow," he cut her off before she could scold him. "I knew exactly who he was, even if you neglected to tell me about him. I recognised he was Cauis' brother and that could mean a way of findin' you. Yes, I did his biddin', but I did much more to undermine his efforts."

Her eyes narrowed as she watched Tristan explain himself. As far as she could tell, he was speaking the truth. Nothing other than arrogance radiated around him.

"Right now is a prime example. Consider this a defection," he said with a wink.

"Why did you work for him?"

He sighed, scratching the stubble on his chin. "Honestly?"

"Spit it out."

"All right, all right." He held a hand up. "I wanted to see you again."

She snorted. "Aren't I lucky."

"Aren't you pleased to see me?" Tristan asked with a chuckle.

"Under different circumstances, perhaps."

"Look. It was a chance to get inside. You know, like a double agent. I thought if I got close to Regulus, I could at least try to thwart his attempts at findin' you and be a thorn in his side. That's the honest truth."

Aya regarded him silently. All that time she'd known Tristan, he'd been a decent person. Apart from his unconventional beginning, he'd worked hard to become close to who he'd been when he was human. He'd taken his oaths as a knight seriously. *Vous ou la mort*, you or death.

"Then," she said, "how did you come to be here?"

"Regulus told me to come."

"He knows where I am?" She wasn't surprised, but it still annoyed her.

"Yes, but I expect he'd think you'd already be gone."

"You weren't sent to find me," she said, understanding his meaning.

Tristan nodded. "I was sent to warn you for a reason."

"And what reason was that?"

"No idea. But if there's one thing I've learned about him, is that he can be just as cunnin' as you. It could be any number of reasons."

"He wants to flush me out." That was the only logical reason and one they'd used before. If he confronted her here, she would have a greater advantage, but in reality, she would be the one with more to lose by staying.

"I would think so." Tristan nodded his agreement.

"What do you think I should do?" she asked. "You always have an opinion on that."

"I would go. No use stayin' here."

Aya grunted. She knew it would be his answer, so why did she even feel she had to ask? Ignoring his advice, she said, "Arturius said Regulus was looking for something. Do you know what?"

He frowned. "He's very secretive, Arrow. Probably even more than you. If he's searchin' for somethin', I have no idea what."

So, the time she'd been dreading was finally here. Tristan leaned forwards in his chair, distracting her thoughts.

He looked at her curiously and said, "I thought about you often over the years."

Aya shifted in the armchair awkwardly, not liking the spark in the vampire's eyes. She didn't want to admit it, but she needed the knight's help. He knew Regulus' comings and goings—his residences, his people. And he would know how to help her track down Victoria's lineage. If Aya's suspicions were true, he might have even known her before she was turned.

"I have something I need to find," she said pointedly, and he fell backwards in his chair. She knew he realised he'd been dismissed.

"And you need my help?"

"Yes."

Tristan nodded in understanding. He would know that her abruptness meant he had no choice in the matter. He could assist her of his free will or she would compel him. Simple as that.

"You know I'll help you, no matter what," he told her.

She nodded, slumping back in her chair. "Then we need to leave as soon as possible."

"And your boyfriend?"

Aya couldn't say it, so she just shook her head.

"Do what you want to," he replied, "but I'm goin' with you. With or without your live wire of a boyfriend."

CHAPTER 4

The more Aya thought about it, the more she realised it was the lesser of two evils.

She decided to leave Zac behind. She had to do it. There was no other way.

If she took him with her, there was a chance he'd be used against her, or worst case, he'd suffer his true death. If she left him behind, he would be safe. Hurt, but safe.

She knew he would be furious and lash out at her. Despite what he thought, he was still the chivalrous nineteenth-century Army officer. He would take it upon himself to do what he thought was right... and what was right to him was never leaving her side and protecting her at all costs.

To keep him safe, Aya would have to rip out the heart of the man she loved.

But first, there were a few people she had to see.

Walking up the six flights of stairs to Gabby's

apartment, she squashed the uncomfortable feeling that was churning in her stomach. Knocking sharply on the door, she waited, knowing the witch was at home. When the door opened and Gabby's face appeared, Aya was suddenly unsure about what she was about to do.

The young witch seemed surprised to see her. "Aya?"

"May I come in?"

She frowned for a moment and stood back, allowing Aya to walk inside. "Is something the matter?"

Aya crossed the room and sat on the sofa beside the window and wrung her hands. They'd become close over the past few months as she helped her with her power and now, she was anxious. For all her prowess, Gabby's opinion mattered to her. The witch was the closest thing she'd had to a friend since Tristan, and she hadn't let him get that close to her in the first place.

It broke her heart to smash this life she'd unconsciously built for herself.

Gabby spoke, interrupting her thoughts, "Does this have something to do with that new vampire I've been hearing about?"

"Tristan?" Aya was surprised Gabby knew about him already.

"I guess. Sam said he met him in the street today. And he relayed Zac's colourful opinion."

"Yes, well, Zac didn't take well to him."

"What's the deal with you two? Were you with this Tristan guy?"

"No." Aya shook her head, annoyed. "We spent some time together, but it was never like that."

"So why's he here all of a sudden?"

Aya sighed at the barrage of questions. "Tristan brought a warning. Regulus is looking for me and a lot sooner than I expected."

Gabby sat heavily on the armchair opposite her and groaned, "I thought we might have more time."

"So did I, but apparently, we do not."

"Do you want me to do something? Is that why you're here?"

"No. Nothing like that. I want to keep you out of it." She was trying to build up to saying it. "You've been through a lot and you've only just begun using your power again."

"What do you mean?"

"I have to leave, Gabby," she murmured. "On my own."

She seemed to get it and scowled. "Is this some kind of twisted courtesy call? What about Zac?"

Aya knew she'd ask about him. "It's best if he doesn't come."

"He won't let you leave."

"He will," she said, an ominous look clouding her features.

"So, you're just going to lie? What will you tell him? That you used him? That you don't want him? Or will you just compel yourself away like you never existed? You shouldn't underestimate him, Aya."

"I need to keep him safe," she said almost desperately.

"This will break him, you know that, right?"

"It's for his own good." Aya was unwilling to back down. Her mind was already made up.

"Do you really think so?" Gabby raised her eyebrows. "Just because you've had two thousand years on this Earth, doesn't mean you know what's best for him."

"Do not lecture me on right and wrong," she said sharply, but Gabby was undaunted by her warning.

"You might think you're doing the right thing, Aya, but he'll do the exact opposite of what you expect. Every. Single. Time."

"This is much bigger than all of you. It's my task. I have to finish this."

"You didn't see him when he thought you were dead. That was bad. This will be *worse*."

"I can't help that."

Gabby shook her head. "It's a miracle, but he loves you."

"And that's why I have to leave him," Aya hissed in frustration. "If something happens to him because of me... It's best he stays out of it."

Gabby assessed her for a long moment and shook her head. "I know you think you're doing a noble thing, but this will blow up in your face."

"Perhaps. Perhaps not." She abruptly stood and walked towards the door.

"So, that's it?" Gabby spat after her. "You're just going to disappear?"

Aya turned slightly but didn't look at the witch. "Yes."

Before Gabby could retort, the door slammed shut behind her and Aya was gone.

Aya's next stop was the coffee house. She felt like she was completing some twisted to-do list. Let everyone know she was leaving, cover her tracks, and compel away memories—check, check, check. She'd done it so many times before but had never felt as heartbroken as she did right now. Deep down, she knew she'd hoped to make this place her home—the first one she'd had in almost two thousand years.

Pushing through the door to Mrs. Greene's café, she spotted the blonde vampire instantly.

Liz was behind the counter making coffee for a customer standing to the side, who she was chatting to cheerily. Once the human had paid and gone, Aya walked over and waited for the vampire to notice her.

Sensing her presence, Liz looked up from the counter and caught her eye. "Aya?" She seemed surprised to see her. Not once had she sought out the newborn on her own.

Aya sighed, unsure how to start. They'd never really gotten along. Liz was the complete opposite of her. The vampire took compassion to a whole new level and shied away from confrontation like the plague.

Remembering the night when they'd confronted Arturius, Aya shook her head. Liz's spine had grown a great deal over the past year.

"Is something wrong?" she asked when Aya was silent for a moment too long.

"Have you got a minute?" she asked, glancing around the cafe.

Liz wiped her hands on a towel and nodded. "I'm due for a break." Walking around the counter, she called out to another girl who was manning the sandwich bar. "Luce, I'm just taking five, okay?" When the girl nodded, Liz led Aya across to an empty table in the far corner. "What's up?" she asked, sliding into a chair.

Aya gazed out of the window, watching the outside world go by. "This is difficult for me," she said after a moment.

"I know things aren't too good between you and Zac lately," Liz said. "He's worried about you, Aya."

"I know."

"What's going on? You know you can tell me, right?"

Aya turned her gaze onto the young vampire and suppressed a snort. One of the new things she'd learned about the modern world was that humans liked to go to therapists to talk through their problems. Liz would not be hers, not by a long shot.

"I care for him, you know," she continued, warily. "I don't like to see him hurt."

Aya didn't compel Gabby, but that was because she couldn't. Not effectively anyway. But Liz? Liz she could. She knew she was fiercely protective of Zac, after all. He'd once loved her and now she looked up to him like a big brother. She wouldn't let her do this without a fight, and Aya didn't have it in her to argue.

Leaning forwards, she stared into Liz's eyes and said as evenly as she could, "I'm leaving and probably won't come back anytime soon. All you will remember about me is that I'm a vampire and I helped save Zac. You will forget about my little resurrection trick and what I really am. You will only remember when I say you can." Liz nodded as the compulsion took hold. "Oh, and my blood is poison to vampires. Remember that part, it's important."

"Is Zac going with you?" the young vampire asked in a monotone voice.

"No. It's safest for him here."

"Okay."

Aya stood, pushing her chair back under the table as Liz shook her head, a bewildered expression on her face. "Gotta go, Liz."

"Aya? When did you get here?"

"Just now," she replied. "But I forgot something. I'll see you later."

"Oh, all right." She lifted a hand in an absent wave. "See you later, then."

But Aya didn't hear her—she was already out the door and looking across the street at the gardens.

She'd sat here and listened to the world around her the day after she'd woken. One hundred and fifty years had passed, and everything had changed beyond recognition. It wasn't the same Ashburton she had known in the 1800s, not on the surface, anyway.

The gardens held many memories, not all of them good. Here was where she first met Alex, the human gardener, best friend to Liz, Gabby, and Sam.

In the beginning, he had no idea that he was friends with vampires and a witch. Not until the night Aya and Sam saved him from a vampire in Katrin's employ. As it always seemed to pass in these situations, he found out in the worst way possible. With time, and full disclosure, he came around and he was Aya's greatest champion.

She crossed the street with a sigh. All she had left to do was to see Alex. He was one of the good ones, which made all this that more difficult. Humans had been a means to an end for her. On one hand, they were food. On the other, they were easily manipulated. The more she had gotten to know Alex, the more she saw how selfish she'd been all these years. There had been many humans she'd known and respected, but she'd considered none of them worthy of knowing her secrets. She had never truly called any of them a friend.

Not until Alex.

She found him up a ladder pruning some unruly ivy that'd grown up the trunk of an old willow. It was slowly suffocating the life from the tree and the irony didn't escape her.

She watched him wrestle with the hedge clippers for a moment, debating how she would go about telling him.

"Hey," he said when he finally noticed her.

"Hey."

"Is everything okay?" he asked, dropping the hedge clippers into the turf and climbing down the ladder.

She looked away, not knowing how to begin.

"Things aren't too great with you and Zac, are they?"

"No," she said. "Alex, I have to leave."

"Yeah." He sighed, not surprised at her sudden outburst. "I guessed you would at some point. I just didn't think it would be so soon. Is Zac going with you?"

She knew he'd ask that question. "No. I haven't told him yet."

"Well," Alex sighed, "if you think you're doing the right thing... Truthfully, I thought you'd take him with you."

"I didn't know what was going to happen when I decided to stay," she began.

"Regulus has reared his ugly head, hasn't he?" Alex smiled wryly when she looked at him, her eyes wide with surprise. "That's what that Tristan guy came to tell you, wasn't it?"

"People don't give you enough credit, Alex. You know more than you let on."

"Uh, thanks, I guess."

"I have to lead Regulus away from here. Away from all of you. As long as I'm here, I'm putting you all in danger."

Alex sat on the grass, resting his chin on his knees. Aya sat next to him, trying to figure out what he was thinking. His emotions were changing faster than she could keep up with.

"It must be hard," he said, playing with a clump of grass, "dealing with the bad guys all the time. I mean, it doesn't give you much time to stop and smell the roses, huh?"

"No."

After another minute's thought, he said, "You two belong together."

Aya sighed, fighting the annoying churning in her stomach. "You have a romantic view of life, Alex."

"Well, I have to with all the shit that's gone down recently." He gave her a look. "And so should you."

"I can't do that. Not until Regulus is gone."

"And how long will that take?"

She couldn't lie to him, not about this. Not if it meant she mightn't return in his lifetime. "I don't know. It could take another thousand years."

"So, I might never see you again?"

She shook her head, looking away across the gardens, back towards the main street.

"Do you think he'll come here anyway?"

"He's wanted me dead from the first day I was turned. Where I go, he'll follow."

"If you compel me to forget, then I won't be able to tell him anything. If he comes looking, that is."

Aya's gaze snapped back to Alex, a little surprised that he'd offer. "You would let me do that?"

"Yeah. But just don't take away the memory of you. I want to remember you as the vampire who saved me from the bad guys. You can take all the other stuff away. I just... I just don't want to forget you."

Aya felt the tug at her heart and leaned over and kissed him on the cheek. She felt his embarrassment and smiled. "You're a rare human, Alex. I'm glad to have called you a friend."

As she worked her compulsion on him, a tear slipped from the corner of her eye. It was probably the first genuine tear of sadness she'd shed since the day her family had died all those long years ago.

"Goodbye, Aya." He sighed, wiping the tear from her cheek.

Giving him one last smile, she stood and walked away, not daring to look back.

Reluctantly turning her thoughts to Zac, she sent out her mind and heard the familiar music of his blood. He was at the manor. They'd fought bitterly the night before and she hadn't seen him since.

And now she would have to rip his heart out.

———

Zac hadn't laid eyes on Aya since they'd fought outside the bar the night before. He knew she would be with Tristan, and he didn't want to know what they were doing. Whenever he thought about the knight, his vision turned red.

Sitting on the tall brick fence that separated the garden from the main drive, his heart lurched in his chest as he sensed her coming. He had no idea what to say and truthfully, he wasn't ready to see her just yet. Jumping off the fence, he landed with his back to her and waited.

"Zac," she said, her voice oddly empty.

Turning, he saw she was looking at her feet. When did she get so... submissive?

When he didn't reply, she said, "I have to talk to you."

He swallowed hard, not liking where this was going. They'd fought, but everyone did once in a while. It was normal. They'd work it out given time... wouldn't they?

"Zac... I," she faltered.

"What is it?" he asked, turning to face her fully.

"I can't do this anymore," she whispered, bringing her gaze up to meet his.

His heart almost sputtered and died, and he knew she'd heard it. "What do you mean?"

"You said it yourself... This isn't working."

"Aya, we fought. People fight. We'll work it out."

She shook her head, taking a step away. "Not this time."

She was leaving him? Where the hell had this come from? "Does Tristan have something to do with this?" he asked, not able to keep the anger out of his voice.

"No. Tristan has nothing to do with this."

He snorted, clenching his jaw. "It's a little coincidental, don't you think?"

"I have to go. This was wrong."

"Aya, please," he whispered, caressing a hand down her face. "I need you. You are my life."

"That's the problem," she whispered.

Zac's eyes widened in disbelief. "You can't mean that."

"It was an empty dream, Zac. Deep down, you knew I would have to leave one day." Looking away, he snorted., "Then perhaps I wasn't deep enough."

"I'm sorry. I didn't mean for it to turn out this way."

"I bet you didn't."

"I didn't want to get too attached," she murmured. "That's why..."

He threw his hands in the air in frustration. "Get me attached enough to do your dirty work, but not so attached that you couldn't leave afterwards. Am I meant to be grateful for that?"

She didn't respond, only stared at him with those icy blue eyes of hers. He couldn't understand the look that was plastered on her face. The look that said her heart was breaking. How could she have the audacity to hurt when she was telling him she had used and betrayed him?

"I get it, Aya. You used me. You used us." His glare cut right through her. "Two Romans and a founding witch. I bet you couldn't believe your luck."

"Zac, it wasn't like that," Aya pleaded.

"It was exactly like that." He turned away and stalked back towards the house, his expression complete darkness.

"Zac..." she began.

Abruptly swinging back to face her, he snarled, "What are you still doing here? Your welcome expired thirty seconds ago."

She took several steps back, but he didn't stay to watch her go. The front door slammed closed behind him and it was a miracle the door jamb didn't splinter with the impact. As he stormed past the parlour, Sam came out into the hallway and went to place a hand on his shoulder.

"I don't want to hear it, Sam." His voice was tight

with his restrained anger and hurt as he dodged his brother's hand. He knew Sam had heard everything.

His little brother frowned. "I wasn't going to say anything."

Stopping, he swung around and sneered, "Perhaps I should be the one who's saying I told you so."

"Zac—"

He raised his hand to stop him from continuing and grimaced. "Don't. Just don't."

She'd left him again, but this time, it was of her own choice. He could just let go. Let his humanity go and forget all the pain he would no doubt be feeling for a long time to come. But it meant he'd surrender to the monster he was so desperately trying to escape. There was a catch twenty-two if ever he saw one.

Pinching the bridge of his nose, he sighed sharply and made a beeline for the liquor cabinet. Sometimes his dependency on alcohol worried him. Right now, he needed it to avoid taking his anger out on something or someone.

"Gabby called," Sam said, watching Zac carefully as he rattled through the mostly empty bottles.

"And?"

"She compelled Liz and Alex to forget everything about her past," Sam said, "before she came here."

"And Gabby?"

"I doubt she could compel Gabby now, even if she wanted to."

"Yeah, well, doesn't matter much. We're still bound

by the curse. If it even exists." Zac rolled his eyes. Like he cared, anyway. Let the hellfire consume him.

"What could we do with it anyway? Regulus would want retribution on us, regardless. We were accessories to his brothers' murders and the witch who made him."

Zac grunted. "So, at least we're number two on the most-wanted list? Is that meant to be reassuring? Because I couldn't care less."

"Zac," Sam said sharply. It didn't take much for the asshole to come back to the surface, did it?

"Sam," he echoed, looking back over his shoulder. "I know that look and I don't like it."

Sam clamped his mouth shut, but Zac could tell he wanted to tell him off. When did the roles reverse? When did his little brother turn into his parent? *Almost a hundred and fifty years ago,* a small voice whispered to him.

"Aren't you pissed that she used you?" he asked. "Aren't you pissed she compelled your girlfriend?"

"Stop it, Zac."

"The cruelest blow was not compelling either of us. *It was too much effort.*"

"*Stop.*"

"I have to get out of here," he blurted, grabbing a bottle of scotch from the back of the cabinet.

"Don't," Sam said. "Stay here. Don't—"

"Don't worry, Samuel," he said, picking up on his brother's fear. "I'm coming back."

CHAPTER 5

Zac stepped through the front door of the manor and began walking, the bottle of scotch clutched in his hand.

Perhaps he needed to go off on his own for a while. He'd done it before, but those times there'd been wars to fight. World War I, World War II, Vietnam. It would be pathetic if he went off sulking because of a woman, even if she was the love of his unhinged immortality. Even as he thought it, he understood that he needed time to wallow before he could think about what to do next.

He'd been walking for a long time before he realised he was at the cemetery. When he'd come here in the past, it was at a run and when vampires ran, it didn't take very long at all. At the pace of a regular human walk, it took a hell of a lot longer. Somewhere along the way, night had fallen, which made him feel more alone than ever.

Coming to a halt before a headstone that read *Degaud* across the base, he noted the irony of the situation. Death followed him wherever he went.

The stone was dulled by age, the elements, and a healthy dose of neglect. The inscription was covered in splotchy yellow lichen.

"Mother, *Father*." He inclined the bottle towards the headstone. "Glad I lived up to your expectations. I'm still the murderous, selfish bastard you always hoped I'd become."

Kneeling, he scraped the moss and lichen aside, revealing the simple etching. He never knew who'd made it as he and Sam were meant to be as dead as they were. Their father was an only child—the first Degaud to be born in America after his parents had immigrated from France. Their mother's story was much the same. Both of their families had come to the new world to take advantage of rich new lands. Any family they'd had left was in France and unknown to them.

The inscription now free, he read what'd been put there in proxy. *Louis Henri Degaud 1817-1865* and below was *Marie Degaud 1820-1865*. That was all.

"There was no light," he scoffed, perching on the side of the headstone. "But you'd know that, wouldn't you?"

In all the time he and Sam wandered, they'd never come home. Not until the previous winter. This was the first time he'd seen his parents' grave, even though it'd been the site of various incidents a few months prior.

They'd summoned Aya with Gabby's help. He'd almost died his true death here when they had confronted Katrin, one of the five founding witches. Katrin the Betrayer.

Despite the connections with Aya, it was the perfect place for him among the bones of the dead. He was dead as well.

Groaning, Zac ran a hand through his messy hair. Tristan was right. That old, musty, Irish bastard was right. She was manipulative.

"Seems she just wanted a recharge before moving on." He rolled his eyes and sighed, talking to himself as much as his dead parents. "And to think I loved her." Even he wasn't fooling himself. "A fool in life and death."

He cast the empty bottle aside and it shattered on a smaller headstone beside his parents. It was another Degaud plot, and he read it more out of courtesy than curiosity.

"Oh, that's just great." He threw his hands in the air, exasperated.

Cpt. Z. Degaud
4th Louisiana Inf.
Feb 16 1842
Apr 6 1865
Beloved son and brother

They'd buried their son in an empty grave. Of

course, they had. Sam's grave would be around here as well, just as empty. But this was their curse, wasn't it? To live on while everyone aged and died?

He lay on top of his grave, the top of his head resting against the headstone, hands on his stomach and feet crossed at the ankles. Millions of tiny little stars twinkled above him through the trees, and he wondered if this was what it was like being in a grave. What was he, stupid? He wouldn't know, he'd be dead.

The last time he looked up at the night sky as a human, he had been dying. For most vampires, their human lives faded after a hundred or so years, but Zac was sure he'd never forget his. Closing his eyes, he let his mind wander.

And there he was, lying on that mound of corpses again, his own life choking him to death as it pooled in the back of his throat. He willed himself to die, but nothing happened. His heart still beat in his chest, his lungs still drew in air. He was dead, but his body seemed to refuse the notion. Food did nothing. It was blood that kept him alive. Ironically, it had been his own blood that was going to kill him first, not the gunshot wound. He would've choked on the one thing that now kept him alive.

His entire life was one long joke.

When the sound of something rustling in the undergrowth caught his attention, he sat up sharply. He hissed when he made out Gabby walking through the cemetery, picking her way through the headstones to where he sat. She was wearing a black jacket that made her blend into the darkness, but he saw her clear as day.

"Gabby." He sighed, rolling his eyes. What the hell was she doing out here in the middle of the night?

"Hey," she murmured, hovering by his grave. She peered at it for a moment, reading the inscription, and frowned.

"Never sneak up on a vampire," he snapped. "Especially one with a death wish."

"I knew this was how you would react." She shook her head, sitting beside him. She wasn't worried in the slightest, and Zac knew that she could probably bring him to his knees and make him beg for the life he didn't want if she even felt the tiniest bit threatened by him.

"You spoke to her?" Despite himself, his heart skipped a beat.

"Right before she came to see you, it seems."

"Whatever." He wished he still had some scotch left.

"I told her it would be an awful idea."

"Obviously." He didn't want to know what she'd said to her, it would only infuriate him further. "What do you want?"

"To see if you're okay."

"Well, I'm not. Why do you care all of a sudden? It's not like we're besties, Tabitha."

She let out a laugh. "It's nice to hear you call me that again. It's been a while."

"It's also been a while since I was an ass, but things change."

"That they do."

Zac snorted. "What are you doing out here?"

"I was trying to get back into the swing of things. You know it's better at night with the stars and all, especially for me."

"Screw the stars," Zac hissed, falling back onto the grave again, flinging an arm across his eyes. He didn't want to look at her or the sky.

He felt the air shift as she lay back beside him. "You're all right, you know that?"

"Are you feeling okay?" He knew she'd probably been watching him from the moment he stumbled into the cemetery.

"Yes." She laughed before letting out a lengthy sigh. "Who do you want to be? That's what it's about, isn't it? What it's always been about?"

"Gabby, don't," he said, a note of warning in his voice.

"You have to ask yourself the question eventually."

"I know," he said with a finality meant to dissuade her from continuing.

He'd always had a tentative alliance with Gabby. It was Liz and Sam she was really friends with. They'd always fought tooth and nail over everything. Even the day he'd asked—no, told—her to help him when he'd pissed off Katrin, the two thousand year old witch who had it in for him. Everyone else was just guilty by association. Then Aya had come along.

Now that he was here with Gabby in the middle of the night, lying on his grave, she didn't seem all that bad. He might even like her a little, even though she was a witch.

Zac realised he'd let the whole witch versus vampire thing drop the moment Arturius had kidnapped her. He hadn't even realised. He wondered when she'd gotten over it.

He didn't even realise they'd been lying there in silence for at least ten minutes until Gabby asked, "Did you really love her?"

Her question stabbed him right through the chest and it felt as sharp and vividly painful as the bullet that'd ended him. "What a stupid question," he hissed.

"It's not," she said, and he felt her gaze on him. "Even vampires can love."

"I thought so," he whispered, letting his arm fall back to his side. "But now I'm not so sure." Turning his face towards hers, he saw her struggle with what she wanted to tell him. He knew Aya had said something to her about him and he couldn't help it. "What did she say?"

"I think she's just doing it to protect you."

"What makes you say that?"

She looked away. "It seemed difficult for her."

He snorted, not really believing her. Nothing was

ever difficult for Aya. There was no doubt in his mind that she had left with that annoying knight Tristan. He knew something that Zac didn't and now he was disposable. She'd recharged her batteries and found a fresh lead on Regulus, the last Roman. He wasn't needed anymore.

"Nothing's difficult for her," he said out loud.

"Nobody's that heartless, not even a vampire."

That annoyed him and he struggled to keep his anger in check. "Why are you defending her?"

"I'm not, I—"

"I get it, Gabby. Witches and Celestines walk hand in hand. You're all buddy-buddy with your secret witch business."

She sighed but remained silent.

"Listen, Zac," she said after a minute. "Perhaps this was just the lesser of two evils. Perhaps leaving was the kindest thing she could do."

"What's done is done, Gabby," he huffed. "No use playing detective. I don't really want to hear it."

"Give it some time, Zac."

He jerked his hand away when he felt her warm fingers curl around his. "Time is all I've got."

"Don't forget the two vampires, a witch, and a human, too."

Damn it. Gabby was right. Why did she always have to be right? He let out a strangled laugh, turning his face away from her. "I never thought I'd hear myself say this, but I'm glad you were here." A witch and a vampire as best friends? At least miracles happened sometimes, and this was a Christmas miracle.

"Are you in control of your senses?" she joked.

"Unfortunately."

"Well, right place, right time, I guess."

He tensed. Someone else had said those words to him when he had been in the same position. Except this was a grave he was lying on and not a ditch. Morgan had picked him up and brought him back from insanity and now she was dead, all because she'd tried to help him again. All because she'd loved him. Now, Aya had thrown him away and what was love but a way to hurt him and everyone else beyond repair.

"Gabby?" he whispered.

"Yeah?"

"I have a bad feeling that this is it."

"What do you mean?" Her voice had a note of worry that annoyed him, but he let it slide.

"That I've been who I was meant to be all along."

CHAPTER 6

Zac was so lost, the only place he could find was the bar. For obvious reasons, but it was the only place that didn't remind him of her.

The bar was full of college students, locals who'd come back to Ashburton for fall break. Many of the girls approached him, but he rebuffed them all and after a while, they got the hint. He would not be one of their hormone-fuelled projects. Not unless the police wanted to find their bloated bodies in the river next week.

When a vampire sat next to him at the bar, he rolled his eyes. This was a very familiar scene, wasn't it? This was how their trouble had begun all those months ago. He bet that whoever it was, wasn't just here for the delectable college girls.

Glancing out the corner of his eye, he took in the vampire who was staring at him, waiting for a response.

The man was heavily built, broad-shouldered, and imposing. His black curly hair was cropped short and his wide-set eyes were such a dark brown, they could easily be mistaken as black. As he reached out and took the glass the bartender placed in front of him, Zac noticed his forearms were densely muscled, which meant he was either a soldier or a labourer when he was human, used to bearing heavy loads. On second glance, he had a hard face that couldn't easily be read.

Zac glared up at the vampire, cocking his head. "And who the hell are you?"

The vampire smirked at the icy reception and proclaimed smoothly, "Marcellus Caelius Regulus." As Zac's expression changed into one of surprise, Regulus laughed. "I see my reputation has preceded me. But you've heard the stories. Aeriaya would have told you much, I presume."

Zac sighed loudly and took a large mouthful of scotch, irritated at the Roman's fishing. "She's not here."

"I know," he said smoothly.

"Then what the fuck do you want?"

"I'm looking for Zachary Degaud," he replied.

"Well, you've found him. I'll ask again, what the hell do you want?"

"Ah, so you're Victoria's pet. I thought as much," he said knowingly, assessing the young vampire. "She had a romantic view of immortality. So much so, she neglected to ponder on the cost. If you follow."

"I gather you're the asshole who changed her and let her ruin my life," Zac sneered at the founder, not caring if he pissed him off or not.

Regulus laughed and nodded. Well, that was just fantastic. There were two degrees of separation between him and the biggest ass of all time.

The Roman leaned forwards in his chair and looked him square in the eye. "She sent me word of you before her head was ripped off. I heard your bloodlust was legendary."

Zac snorted, scowling at the memories his words dragged up to the surface and turned back to his drink.

"She was quite annoying, you know. Had it in her that she was in love with me," Regulus scoffed. "Absurd, really, since I was using her, but you know how women are..."

Zac shook his head and looked away. That was another familiar story.

"You know she was a witch before I turned her." When Zac's expression fell, he added, "I see Aeriaya neglected to let you in on that little tidbit. I wonder what else she forgot to tell you?"

"If you're here to gloat, Regulus, don't bother."

"I don't need to gloat, Zachary. My being here is a means to an end. That end is none of your business. The end that I do want to know about is the one you helped Aeriaya give to my brother. Both of them."

"Caius was an amateur, and Arturius was a brute who hid behind the skirts of his brainwashed witches. He was as idiotic as they come. He deserved to die."

"If we're talking about people who deserve things, then perhaps you deserve to die for murdering your maker. Or all those poor helpless humans you drained so you could go on living."

Zac clutched the edge of the bar, his fingers denting the wood as he tried to control his temper. "Then you deserve to die just as much as I."

"Funny thing about life..." Regulus tilted his head, eyes twinkling. "Sometimes people just never get what they deserve."

Zac clenched his jaw and remained silent.

"I can see why everyone around here is so concerned about you." The Roman reached over and pulled his hand from the bar. "Such a temper."

Desperate for a subject change, he asked, "Why wasn't Victoria linked to Katrin?" He knew that Aya probably neglected to tell him that part as well.

"She was one of mine. Alistair was one of hers." He glanced at Zac then said, "You don't remember him, do you? Alistair."

"I remember plunging a stake into his heart. That's pretty vivid."

"He was helping Victoria. As I understand it, he knew a lot about you."

It was that moment when Zac finally got it. The night Victoria killed his family, a vampire visited her. A vampire named Alistair. He'd known exactly who Zac was the day he'd walked into *Max's*. Aya was his target, but he found a bigger prize. Zac had killed Victoria and he wanted payback. That was why he felt it necessary to make his life hell.

"I see you understand it now." Regulus thumped him on the shoulder. "Alistair had a thing for Victoria, so you can understand why he wanted revenge."

"Is there a reason you're goading me on, Regulus, or is there something you wanted?" Zac asked loudly, fed up with whatever game it was the Roman was playing.

"I have a proposal for you."

"And?"

"What I'm proposing is that you come and work for me."

Zac snorted. "You're kidding, right?"

"I see a lot of myself in you, Zachary. I came from very humble beginnings. I was good as dead until the Legion changed my life and look at me now." He stared at Zac, measuring his reaction. "The downtrodden have the fiercest fire inside of them. Those are the people I want to fight beside me. You most of all. The pain you have been through only fuels the fire within."

Zac glared at the Roman, wishing he could just rip his head off and be done with him. "If my entire life is such common knowledge, then you already know that my answer is a huge go screw yourself."

Regulus laughed. "Don't be so hasty, Zachary. You may have had a hand in killing my brothers, and on a good day that would've earned you a painful death, but today I'm offering you a purpose. One that you're severely lacking. Have a think about it. I'll be around."

"Don't bother. My answer will still be no."

"You know I could just compel you." He leaned back on the stool, surveying his response.

"Then why don't you?"

"Now, Zachary, where would be the fun in that?"

He sighed, rolling his eyes, refusing to reply.

"You know, you're very disappointing. I was expecting a lot more bite from you."

"If I'm so disappointing, why don't you just piss off and leave me alone?"

Regulus chuckled and threw a few bills onto the bar. Standing, he gave Zac one last look. "I wouldn't count on that."

It was late when Zac finally left the bar. Most of the humans had gone already, so the street was empty save for a passing car or two. Enough time had passed since his encounter with Regulus that he hoped the Roman had disappeared for now.

As he turned down the street to begin the familiar walk home, he stopped. Tilting his head to the side, he listened. Something wasn't right.

He glanced down the street to his left, which was shrouded in darkness. Every so often a streetlamp broke up the murkiness, muted orange light illuminating the pavement. It was then the wind shifted and blew in his direction, bringing with it the unmistakable scent of blood.

Annoyingly, his teeth ached, and he shook his head to clear his thoughts. Regulus probably cornered a few college girls from the bar and if that was the case, Zac didn't want to stick around to find out. From the pungent smell coming from down the street, it was too late to do anything about it anyway.

But before he could move, the Roman sauntered out of the darkness, blood staining his mouth.

"Zachary, just in time," he said with a grin.

"Lucky me," he said sarcastically, turning to walk away, but he was cut off before he could take a step.

Regulus stood in front of him. "I've saved one for you."

"If it's all the same to you, I think I'll pass." He glared at him, his eyes cold.

"Oh, but I *insist*."

Regulus grasped Zac around the scruff of his neck and pulled him down the street into the shadows. Letting him go, the Roman gestured to a young girl who looked about twenty years old. She cowered against the fence of the adjoining property but had no choice but to obey. Compelled and silent, tears rolled down her cheeks, betraying her terror.

"I'm sure you're starving," Regulus drawled,

gesturing to two bodies that lay slumped beside the woman. "As you can see, I've already eaten."

Zac's jaw tensed as he tried to fight the burning that'd begun in his throat. This was the very thing he'd been trying to fight for decades. Thinking about his relapse months before, he felt sick to the stomach.

"No," he said, taking a few steps back.

"Take her, Zachary. I know you want to."

He backed away even farther.

"I can see it in your eyes," Regulus taunted. "You want her. Her friends were so delicious."

When Zac still didn't move, Regulus roared in annoyance and he watched in horror as the Roman grabbed the woman and sunk his fangs into her neck, severing an artery. Pulling back, he let her blood flow freely and it soon soaked her blouse.

"Can you smell it?" the Roman asked, pushing the woman towards Zac. "Isn't it intoxicating?"

He stumbled backwards as she fell to the ground, sobbing uncontrollably, unable to scream or run to save herself.

The Roman shoved him. "Stop fighting it, Zachary. You know you want to."

"Stop it!" he roared, tearing at his hair, fighting the overpowering scent of her blood. His throat burned.

Zac pushed past Regulus, desperate to get away, but the founder pulled him back, pushing him onto the woman. Her sticky blood soaked his shirt and coated his hands. He couldn't stop himself from lifting his shaking fingers to his nose and inhaling the rich coppery scent. Groaning as his fangs grew, he knew it was too late.

"*Yes*," Regulus hissed. "*Take her.*"

Zac's eyes rolled back into his head and he was over her, his fangs tearing into the open wound of her neck like an animal. He was pulling her body up off the ground so he could bite deeper, drawing her blood in heaving gulps like he couldn't get enough.

Groaning deep in his chest as his mouth filled with her sweet blood, he sucked the life from her, whatever she was pleading falling on deaf ears. To his horror, he felt disappointed when her heart stop beating, her body becoming limp in his hands.

Disgusted, Zac dropped her and fell backwards onto the pavement.

What had he done?

Regulus had pushed him into this so easily and he'd killed the woman like she was nothing. Even when he disappeared after his last fight with Sam less than a year ago, he hadn't killed anyone. None of those women had died, they'd just been traumatised. Aya had brought him back that time, his lifeline. Now she was gone. He was alone.

"*Magnificent.*" Regulus shook his head. "Imagine what you could do when your heart's in it."

"Bastard," he spat, trying to wipe the blood away.

Regulus grinned. "Yes... I suppose I am."

Zac burst through the front door of the manor, the wall splintering where the heavy oak door collided with it. He ignored Sam's concerned voice and flew up the stairs into the bathroom. He would have smelled the blood.

Groaning as he tried to fight for some semblance of control, he slammed the door behind him, shutting out his brother's incessant pleading.

He was covered in the woman's blood. It was everywhere. Staining his face, arms, and hands, it felt like acid. His shirt was stiff with it and it stuck to his skin. He writhed like he was burning, pulling his shirt off, kicking his boots aside. The stench of it was unbearable.

Zac could hear his little brother pound on the door, but he ignored him. Catching his reflection in the mirror, he froze.

Monster.

Roaring in agony, he punched the mirror with all his strength, shattering it into a million tiny pieces.

Sam burst into the bathroom when he heard the mirror splinter, holding his brother's arms behind his back.

"*Zac,*" he yelled into his ear. "Calm down. Whose blood is this?"

He twisted out of Sam's grasp and pushed him out of

the room. Turning on the faucet in the shower as far as it could go, the room filled with steam. He stood under the stinging cascade of water, not bothering to take off the rest of his clothes, and they soon soaked through. Desperately, he tried to scrub the dried blood from his skin as the grey tiles swam with red water. He had to get rid of the smell.

Sam was back in the bathroom. "Zac, what happened?"

He was still scrubbing his arms, refusing to look at him. "Get rid of it." But Sam didn't move, he just stared at him with a pained expression that looked a lot like horror. "Get rid of it!" he yelled again, blinking furiously through the stream of water.

Sam seemed to understand this time and gathered up his discarded clothing and disappeared. When he came back, Zac had curled up in the bottom of the shower, his head between his knees, the water still running.

***

Sam didn't dare touch Zac until he'd cleared the bathroom and any traces of blood he found in the house. Whatever his brother had done, this reaction was new and it scared the hell out of him.

He eased his arm into the shower and turned the faucet off, his brother's shoulders heaving with the mere effort of breathing.

"He made me," he rasped, the sound of his voice muffled.

"Who made you?"

"Regulus."

Sam drew a sharp breath. They'd expected his arrival, but not so soon. Truthfully, he had hoped they'd avoided the Roman from ever coming to Ashburton once Aya had left. What had he coerced Zac into doing?

He didn't push Zac for more answers. Instead, he coaxed Zac to stand, throwing a towel around his shoulders. "Dry off, brother. It's all gone. I'll get you something to drink."

Zac nodded numbly and shuffled into his bedroom, trailing pools of water. By the time Sam came back with a bottle of whiskey and two glasses, he was in dry clothes, sitting in the middle of the floor, staring vacantly into space.

Sam knew this was his way of coping, to keep himself from going AWOL. Shutting down was probably the best thing for a vampire to do in this situation.

Zac took the glass he was offered in a shaking hand and downed it. When Sam refilled it, he drank that as well before casting the glass aside.

"I killed her," he whispered, his hands in his hair. "*I killed her.*"

"Who?"

"I don't know."

"Did he compel you?"

"He..."

Sam waited. Zac had killed before—he would be a fool to deny it—but the last time was forty years ago, just after he had deserted in Vietnam. His brother had run off and joined the US Army and whatever had happened to him there had finally driven him to make the choice to try to be better, to be something else.

"Zac? Did Regulus force you?"

His brother grimaced and shook his head. "He didn't have to."

The cold, hard light of day woke Zac earlier than he would've liked.

Groaning, he ran his hands over his face. Memories of the previous night came flooding back and he rolled onto his side, almost throwing up. His humanity was eating through his stomach like acid. How much more could he take before he snapped again, he had no idea.

When he finally dragged himself from bed, he glanced into the bathroom. The floor was still covered with broken shards of mirror. It sparkled in the sunlight flowing through the open windows. The water had dried, but there was a wet stain on the carpet where he'd flung his damp jeans the night before.

What a mess. Literally.

Regulus. What was he going to do? Regulus had asked him to join his sordid little network, to work with him. And do what? More killing?

Pushing him onto that young woman last night had

been the beginning of either forcing him into the decision the Roman wanted or making him realise the truth. And the truth was…

Regulus was right, but there was another thing he didn't factor into the arrangement he had offered.

Revenge.

The Romans had ruined his life from day one. That day in the woods in Virginia, where he was shot, that was the moment their demise became his problem. He just didn't know it until he'd met Aya. Just because she'd thrown him away didn't mean he should disregard his revenge. Maybe going with Regulus was the only way to end this for good. To end everything.

But now the Roman was here in front of him. Regulus had only shown Zac that fighting his urges was useless. He was born into vampirism as a cold-hearted predator. Sam wasn't. Pure, sweet Liz wasn't. They were the good things about being vampires, which was why he had to leave them behind to go with his greatest enemy.

He could never kill Regulus, not on his own. *She* was the only way. And Zac was sure that wherever she'd gone, she'd be looking for an opportunity to do just that. If she turned up, he would help her, but he didn't want to lay eyes on her again. Just like he had been to her, she was just a means to an end. Until then, he would align himself with his own kind and stop fighting his nature. He didn't have the strength to resist anymore.

He would go with Regulus. It was his only option if he wanted to come back.

Pulling on a pair of dark jeans and T-shirt, he thumped downstairs and shuffled into the parlour. He caught Sam's eye as he turned around on the sofa. How was he going to tell him?

"Are you feeling better?" Sam asked.

"Somewhat." He shrugged, sitting across from his little brother.

"What's happened?" Sam could tell he'd decided something and from the tone of his voice, he knew he wasn't going to like it.

Zac had never given his brother a reason to like anything he did. His decisions had always landed both of them in hot water, but not this time. This time Sam would stay out of it.

"Sam..." After everything, he had trouble saying it.

"You're going again, aren't you?" The look in his little brother's eyes was one of disappointment and he almost caved.

"Yes."

"Why? Because of Aya? Because of what Regulus made you do? You can't go off again, Zac. Not this time."

"This time is different, Sam." He heard himself plead and it didn't sit well.

"Why?"

"This is it. This is my last chance. If I can't control myself this time, then it has to end."

"Brother..."

"Sam, please," he pleaded, knowing his brother would fight him to the end. He had to convince him. If he couldn't find who he was this time and find the balance between his humanity and vampirism... then it had to end. He had to die.

"I won't let you." Sam's hand was on his arm. "I won't let you go."

"Sam, you have to."

"Zac, no. This isn't the way. Let me help you. We can leave and go somewhere else. Somewhere where Regulus won't be able to find us."

"And what about Liz?" he snapped. "What about her?"

Sam hissed and sat back, rubbing his temples. "She'll understand."

"No," he snapped. "She won't understand at all. She loves you, and you deserve to be with her. *Always.*"

"I—"

Zac held up a hand to stop him, determined. "You deserve a better life, Sam. You've always wondered when I'll go off the deep end. Following me around for decades to make sure I'm doing alright, to pull me back. That's not what I wanted for you." He sighed, running his hands over his face. "I never wanted this for you."

When Sam grimaced, Zac knew that he understood what he meant. The fact that he was a vampire. That it was his fault that his little brother had become this... this *thing.*

"I know, brother, but it is what it is."

But Zac wasn't listening. "You have Liz now. You need to be with her. She needs you. Go to LA with her, go back to college if that's what you want to do, but just live the life you want."

"Zac," Sam began, his face flooded with concern.

"Sam, please do this for me. I'll be okay." His little brother stood and embraced him without a word, finally understanding. "When this is all over, when I've found whatever it is I'm looking for... I'll come find you. I promise."

Gabby walked down the busy street that was clogged to the brim with tourists, bumping shoulders as she went. People milled about shops devoted to dark magic and voodoo, *oohing* and *ahhing* at the strange items for sale.

None of it worked. It was all junk designed to line shopkeepers' pockets. Gabby could tell without even looking.

Bourbon Street, New Orleans, had always been the home of many types of power. These days, one had to know exactly where to go to find it or they would only come away with rubbish. Luckily, she knew what she wanted and was determined to get it.

She walked into a small, unassuming café named

Devil's Kitchen, known for its selection of specialty cakes to the outside world. To those who knew things, it was so much more. All kinds of supernaturals congregated here to trade, inform, threaten, and 'hang out'.

Scanning the busy café, she laid eyes on an imposing figure. From the reverberations in the air, she knew this was the person who'd summoned her here.

Gabby knew it wasn't good news when a witch had contacted her during her meditation the previous evening. There were only a few people alive who knew the truth of who and what she was, and not all of them were good. Despite this, she knew it was in her best interest, along with everyone else's, that she came here today. There was no fear or worry in her heart, only a morbid sense of curiosity. What could he possibly want from her?

Sighing, she crossed the room and sat across from the dark figure. Raising an eyebrow, she said, "This better be worth my time."

Regulus smirked at the young witch. "Ismena was always quite talented. Good to see she passed it on."

"If anyone finds out I came to meet you..." she began, an unmistakable note of warning in her voice.

He disregarded her warning with a flick of his hand. "But, dear Gabrielle, they won't. Not anyone that matters, anyway."

A waitress stopped by the table then, but Gabby waved her away. She didn't want to stay here a moment longer than she had to. "What do you want, Regulus? I have better things to do, you know."

The Roman leaned back and surveyed her with a glint in his eye that should've unsettled her, but she only glared at him.

His lip curled up into a sneer and he said, "Don't think for a second that I don't know what you've been poking around for."

"And what might that be?" she asked.

"Want to make your own army, Gabrielle?"

His fingers were in a lot more pies than she'd thought. Since she'd gotten wind of his arrival, she'd been trying to track down the spell that'd created the founders, hoping she could undo it. So far, she'd come up with nothing but hearsay.

She raised her eyebrows. "Who needs an army when all I have to do is to will my enemies to their knees?"

"Now I see why Arturius liked you. You have some mouth, Gabrielle," he said suggestively, wiping his bottom lip with a thumb.

"In your dreams." She rolled her eyes. "I know you've been poking about Ashburton and I suggest you leave him alone."

"Now why would I do that?"

"That town and everyone and everything in it is under my protection." Her eyes narrowed in warning. "Leave him alone. He's been through enough without you trying to destroy him as well."

Regulus slammed a fist down on the tabletop, making her jump. "Zachary is mine," he spat. "He's already agreed to come along, so save your threats for someone who wants to be saved."

"No..." Why would he do such a thing when she was there to help him?

"*Yes*," Regulus said. "Now, if you don't mind, *witch*, I have some business to discuss with you."

He pushed a vial of blood across the table and she scooped it into her bag, glancing about the café to see if anyone had noticed. "What the hell are you doing?"

The Roman laughed. "Do you think any of the people in here are a match for me? I've been around a long time, dear. If I desired it, everyone in this café would be dead before they reached the door."

"What do you want me to do with this?" she asked through gritted teeth.

"You will link me to Zachary."

"Why?"

"Insurance, dear."

"Insurance from what?" Even as she asked, she understood the answer. If Zac died, the link would let Regulus know. Or if Zac attempted to kill him, then the magic would end him instead. It was exactly what Katrin had done to the Romans and every other vampire who'd served her.

He ignored her question. "I know where your parents live and that darling witch Sophia. She's a live wire, that one, considering her age."

"Don't you dare threaten me, Regulus, or I'll—"

"Or you'll what?" He leaned over the table, his eyes becoming dark.

Gabby sat back as far as she could in the booth, knowing her threat was empty where Regulus was concerned. When he'd said the word 'discuss' earlier? What he really meant was 'order'. There was no choice if she wanted her friends to remain safe.

Could she use her power on him? There was a high chance he was also protected from her spells like Arturius had been. After she'd detained Caius all that time ago at the silo, they'd learned how to counter her abilities.

"Do what I ask, and nothing need happen to them." The Roman smiled, leaning back, knowing he had her in the palm of his hand. "Oh, and what I continue to ask you to do."

"Asshole," she spat, much to his amusement.

"I've been called much worse." As she stood to leave, he added, "And I will know if you haven't done it. So, I suggest you do what I ask the moment you get home. I intend to leave as soon as possible."

He didn't have to threaten her. She knew exactly what would happen if she defied him. Glaring, she stalked towards the exit of the café, her skin crawling.

"*Adiós, preciosa,*" he called out after her.

CHAPTER 8

L ondon had completely transformed in the last one hundred and ninety years since Aya had last been here.

She marvelled at all the advances so much that she almost forgot the depression she'd sunk herself into. Not even the airplane she and Tristan had taken to get here had pulled her out of it. Usually, she would've taken in everything about that. He'd arranged a counterfeit passport for her, which was much more effective than compulsion. Airport security and all the rules and forms that had to be filled out and followed puzzled her. Humans had become more suspicious of one another to a point where it almost seemed absurd.

Apparently Tristan liked the finer things in life and had bought first-class tickets and a rather fine room at The Ritz, one of the best hotels in the city. Not that she complained. He said he had a black credit card that let people know he was stinking rich. Aya had no need for finances. She had always taken what she had needed from people who had too much of it to care.

The first few days, Aya walked the city that was so eerily familiar. Cars, trucks, busses, and taxis clogged the streets where there once were horses and carts, electric lights replaced gas lamps, and tourists flocked to the museums and landmarks like locusts.

She strolled through streets that used to be the slums of Cheapside, past the gates of palaces that'd housed some of the most terrifying and powerful monarchs of the Middle Ages.

There, where people picnicked and took their morning jog, she remembered the gallows of Marble Arch, where humans had died in the thousands.

But the explosion of art and culture that'd overcome London was something else. Aya almost felt sorry that she'd missed it all. She would have, but what she'd done to Zac haunted her steps. He'd walked away from her believing she'd betrayed his trust. Used him. Tricked him.

But for all her agony, she couldn't help the relief that came with knowing she only had to look out for herself again. Tristan was smart—they'd worked together for over a hundred years. He knew she was a solitary being and didn't feel the need to latch onto her. She didn't need to protect him.

Love was an unnatural feeling for her. She would do anything for Zac, even if it meant leaving to protect him. He'd said it himself, their love was driving him mad. Perhaps if they'd met under other circumstances, it would be different.

Aya couldn't love him the way he wanted, the way he needed. Not right now, not until she found Victoria's secret and Regulus was a pile of ash. When the threat was eliminated, she would find him again and hope it wasn't too late. She needed his love as much as he needed hers.

Hope was a strange thing...

"You need to forget him." Tristan's voice broke through her melancholy. "Wallowin' is not productive, Arrow."

"How do you know what I'm thinking?" she hissed.

"It's written all over your face," he replied. "Regulus will keep. I know, for a fact, he's not in London right now. He will come back, but we should use this time to find out about Victoria."

"Yes, of course."

"That is, after all, one reason we came here."

"Where do you suggest we begin?" she asked, having no idea how to go about it in this day and age.

"The British Library," he told her. "It holds a great deal of records. Births, deaths, that kind of thing. If we're lucky, it will hold records of her ancestors."

"I don't like our chances," she said. "I have a feeling any trace of her might have been erased, especially after Regulus turned her."

Tristan winked. "You forget, Arrow. I was in

Regulus' back pocket for two hundred years, and I have an excellent memory."

She sat up sharply. "What do you know, Tristan?"

"I know her true name. I'm hopin' that we will find what we need with that. There is a high chance that everythin' is there—"

Aya sighed, cutting him off, "Maybe, but don't get your hopes up. Witches are annoying when they want to hide something."

"That they are, but I don't know where else to start."

Truth was, neither did Aya. She'd known little about Victoria other than the glaringly obvious. She'd been a witch and foolishly, she'd fallen in love with Regulus. From what Zac had told her, she had dropped out of favour with the Roman and had followed Aya to America, where she'd already gone to ground before she could catch up.

"Then," she said, "let's go to the library."

The British Library stood near Kings Cross and St. Pancras station. The buildings had been modernised somewhat, but they still bore a striking resemblance to what they had once been and still were—train stations.

Here, Tristan told Aya, "You could get a train to Paris in under three hours through a tunnel that'd been built under the English Channel."

Watching the flow of humans, Aya shook her head. She couldn't seem to get over the amount of people going back and forth, into the station and the underground, onto busses and on foot. London had always been busy, but it had multiplied by thousands... perhaps even millions.

To her annoyance, Tristan pulled her down the street and into the main foyer of the library, where the clerk sitting at the cloakroom eyed them suspiciously. They really were a pair. Tristan, with his tall stature and broad shoulders and shock of curly hair and her, in her dark clothing and long hair, which he had told her made her look like a punk... whatever that was. To human eyes, they didn't fit together at all.

Aya glared at the clerk, who looked away quickly, and she followed Tristan towards the stairs, taking them two at a time.

Emerging into a modern reading room, with books lining every available space, she asked, "So, what's Victoria's real name?"

"Dowling was her family name. She came from Wiltshire to the west. That's all I know."

"Surely she would've been intelligent enough to use a different family name." Aya rolled her eyes as they came to the enquiries desk.

"Perhaps, but we have nothin' else to go on." Tristan turned to the woman who sat there and said, "Hello."

The librarian looked up from the desk and smiled.

She seemed rather young to be stuck in the library all day. Late twenties, perhaps, long red hair and pale skin that was dusted with freckles. She pushed her glasses up onto the bridge of her nose and asked, "How may I help you?"

Tristan leaned forwards on the desk and winked at her. "If you don't mind, could you find everythin' you can on one Victoria Dowling, born in Wiltshire in the mid- to late- 1700s. She died around 1788."

The librarian frowned and shook her head. Finally, she smiled brightly at the vampire and nodded. "Of course. I might be some time, sir. Do you want to wait or come back?"

Aya gave him a look.

"We'll wait," he told her, and she hurried off into some dark recess of the library to do their compelled bidding.

"What are you really hopin' to find, Arrow?"

"Victoria was a witch. It has to be something to do with it, I know it. Perhaps we can find a living relative, a name that I remember, a story, a picture, a gravesite. Anything. Witches are secretive, but that doesn't mean I can't find what they're hiding."

Tristan sat in one of the chairs at a free table and kicked his feet up, much to the annoyance of a woman sitting across the way. "And what do you think she has to do with your boyfriend's blood? It wasn't like she was anythin' special."

"I have a feeling, Tristan," she whispered, sitting

beside him. "Zac's blood is potent to me, to my abilities. It has something to do with those parts of me, I know it."

"You never told me where you came from," he said carefully. "I know you're a hybrid, Arrow. But with what? Sometimes you scare the hell out of me."

"I'm not at liberty to discuss such things," she said absently.

"But Zac knows all of it, doesn't he?"

"That was a matter of consequence. He is bound to secrecy as much as I."

"You gave him your blood." Tristan shook his head.

"It seems I don't give you enough credit, Tristan. You've become more observant in the past six hundred years. Congratulations."

"Of course," he said with a shrug. "Hangin' out with the bad guys makes observation a necessity."

Sighing, Aya didn't bother answering. She didn't have the patience to argue with him, especially since he was in such a cocky mood. Instead, she let her gaze wander the reading room, taking in the stacks, where shelves upon shelves of books stretched up three floors, the edges of each lined with thick glass.

Watching the humans who sat at the surrounding tables, she regarded what each were reading. Most seemed to be students—some had piles of medical texts, while others had old-looking books on ancient cultures.

One man caught her attention, though. He didn't

seem to be doing anything. Taking in his rumpled appearance, she frowned. He looked like he hadn't slept in days, his messy brown hair looked greasy, there was several days' worth of stubble on his chin, and his eyes were dull. Looking at the books he was studying, she tilted her head to the side to read the titles more clearly. *Witchcraft in the Middle Ages, Celtic Myth*, and one that made her eyes narrow, *Wales and Witchcraft 1542.*

1542 was the year she assisted a woman in northern Wales who had been harassed by a witch who'd given herself to evil. That woman—the witch who'd been pure—was one of Gabby's ancestors, and the witch that'd written the summoning spell that'd woken her all those years later in Ashburton. The spell Gabby and Zac had cast. She wondered what the book was about and what exactly it said about that time... and if any of it was accurate.

Aya caught the gaze of the man, who automatically glanced back to his work. Looking him over curiously, she detected nothing out of the ordinary. If he knew who they were, he would've taken the first opportunity to leave. Most people would. He was still there fifteen minutes later, working, and it was obvious he was in for the long haul.

Tristan raised an eyebrow at her and she shrugged, disregarding the man. His research could mean anything, and they'd been in London for only three days. In that time, Aya was positive they hadn't been seen or followed. And when she was positive about something, it meant she was always right.

When the librarian finally came back, Aya had well and truly had enough. Tristan reached the desk before she did, and she stifled a sigh.

"I've found something, but it's not much," the librarian said, pushing a piece of paper across the desktop.

Aya snatched it before Tristan could get his hands on it. "A grave site?" she exclaimed, her eyes scanning the paper.

"Yes, it's the same name and it matches the dates you gave, give or take a few months. It's all I could find, I'm afraid. I'm sorry I couldn't be of more help. Records are rather patchy from that time."

"No," Tristan said, taking the paper from Aya. "You've been a grand help. Thank you."

Aya glared at him and turned back towards the librarian. Leaning forward, she said, "Now forget we were ever here."

The librarian looked confused for a moment, her gaze piercing through the two vampires like they weren't even there. When she turned away, Aya snatched the paper back from Tristan and strode across the room towards the exit.

"Where are you goin' in such a hurry?" He had to run to catch up with her.

"Where do you think?" she rolled her eyes, shaking the piece of paper in his face. "Salisbury."

Aya leaned her forehead against the double-glazed windows of the train, watching the countryside flash past, and thought back to a time long past. She'd always had a soft spot for this country, but perhaps it was merely because she was born here. Not this place exactly. Her home had been farther north in a place that was now called the Lake District. A tiny village—that the humans called Grasmere—that'd sprouted up there in later centuries was eerily close to her forest. She hadn't been back to that place since she'd found what was left of her family.

Remembering when she'd first met her unlikely friends in Ashburton, Aya had told them she was from there. Snorting at the thought, she conceded she should probably amend that to 'friends who were unlikely to welcome her home'. *Home*... How she had wanted to make that place her home.

Tristan shifted in his seat opposite and her gaze flickered to his. She scowled when she saw his puzzled expression. He was trying to figure out what she was thinking. Pointedly ignoring him, she looked back out the window and filtered him out.

The countryside of England, or the United Kingdom as it was now called, was even greener than she had remembered. The sky was grey and heavy with clouds that constantly threatened rain, and the air was heavy with moisture. She already noticed the nights becoming colder, even though it was still only the first week of October. Winter wouldn't officially start until December, but it seemed autumn was going to be skipped entirely this year. Snow would come early, and it would hit hard.

Finally, she felt Tristan's gaze turn away. Peering out the corner of her eye, she regarded the knight as he looked out the window and wondered when she'd decided to trust him. It hadn't been a conscious decision, it'd just happened. Why the hell could she trust Tristan of all people and not Zac? But what was trust when she couldn't share her true self, even with the knight. She had to keep a part of herself from everyone she met, it was just the way it was.

But not with Zac. She still didn't know why she couldn't tell him her fears over what her power had done when she'd taken Arturius. It was like she'd had her heart ripped out again. As she sat there on the train, she knew that nothing had happened. She was as she always was and that was a hard truth to swallow. Had she pushed him away for nothing?

Shifting her thoughts back to the gravesite, she read the piece of paper again. What was done was done, and she had a task to follow. The fact that they had found a record of a gravesite was a warning. Someone either wanted to be found or wanted to trap whoever came looking. It'd been way too easy finding it in the first place. When she laid eyes on the grave, then she would know.

It was only an hour and a half after they had left Waterloo Station when the train pulled up at Salisbury. As the doors swished open and Tristan led her out onto the platform, she breathed in deeply, the sweet country air filling her lungs. This was much better than the putrid stench of the city. The knight grinned at her and she pushed past him, walking towards the ticket kiosk where a map of the area was posted under a sign that read, 'Tourist Information'.

"What is the name of the church?" she asked as Tristan came to stand beside her.

"St. Andrews," he replied. "But it's now called St. Johns. A newer church was built there around a hundred years ago."

"Then I hope the grave is still there."

"It should be. The English have always been into preservation. The old church still stands there, or so I have read." He pointed to a spot on the map, not too far away from where they stood.

"Then let's go see it for ourselves."

Coming out of the station, Aya stopped a moment to survey the skyline. Salisbury was a typical English village, despite the modern fixtures that'd been integrated with the old. Many original buildings still stood, and in the distance, she could see the spires of the cathedral she knew to be around a thousand years old. It had that Dark Ages look about it—the dominance of religion over the countryside.

"You know that's where they keep the Magna Carta

these days." Tristan inclined his head toward the spires in the distance.

"Too bad you never got to live to see it," she huffed, drawing her leather jacket closer around herself.

"*Ouch.*" He feigned offence. "1215, wasn't it? I scarcely remember those days."

Tristan had been away on the Crusades then, and somewhere around the same time had been taken by vampires in the putrid depths of Constantinople. He'd never told her the full story, but she knew enough of what some vampires had become to fill in the blanks. A lot of what they'd stood for in life often carried over into death—one of those being their stout hatred of people who worshipped gods other than their own. The things humans did in the name of religion baffled her.

"This way," the knight said, drawing her attention in the opposite direction of the cathedral. "It's not far up this road."

As the church grounds came into view, Aya saw that Tristan had been right. The older church still stood, but a larger, more pristine building stood a little farther down the street. This seemed to be where they held services now. There was a sign that said as much.

"I'll start at the opposite end," Tristan said, walking off across the yard as she scanned the headstones.

The information the librarian had handed them hadn't given them much detail. Only that Victoria had apparently been buried in these church grounds somewhere around the time she'd died—and what that really meant was the time she'd been turned. The grave would be empty, but it was the inscription that interested her more. She hoped it would show them the way forwards.

A lot of the headstones she passed were either so worn they were illegible or were cracked with pieces missing. Some were in better shape, but not one had the name they were looking for. A chilly wind whipped around her and she tugged her hair out of her eyes and continued her search across the yard where she halted.

This was it.

"Tristan," she called and a moment later, he was beside her, staring down at the headstone that bore a lengthy inscription.

Victoria Dowling

1767-1788

What beck'ning star, in the moonlight shade
Shines so bright, and points to yonder glade?
Is it a crime bear too tender or too firm a heart,
To feel a lover's or a Roman's part?
Deep below, sleeps a vicious sword,
Beware ye who breaks the sleeping ward.

"Tristan." Aya reached out and grasped his wrist. "Something's not right."

"What do you mean?"

"This inscription..." She read it again just to make sure. "It's a message."

"A message for who?"

"For me."

It was then she felt a tingling on the back of her neck and her gaze flew up, scanning the surrounding yard. Someone was watching them and trying to go unnoticed, she was sure of it. And there, at the farthest corner of the old church, a figure hovered just out of eyesight. A human man ducked his head around the old stonework, watching what they were doing. From the look of him, she concluded he was a priest. He had the collar and everything, so it was a dead giveaway.

When their eyes locked, he knew he'd been made, so he walked towards them, his stride reluctant.

"He's been watching us," Aya said quietly enough that the priest wouldn't hear.

Tristan nodded his acknowledgement, but said nothing.

"Hello," the priest called out as he neared. "I am Maximus, a priest here at St. Johns."

"Pleased to meet you," Tristan said, turning on the charm as Aya wondered about his name. "We've come to find a particular grave site. This one, in fact." He pointed to Victoria's grave and Aya noticed the priest's face pale slightly.

"Oh," he said. "I would be more than happy to assist you. I've spent considerable time researching the history of the church here. What would you like to know?"

"Anythin' you may know about this particular family. We are doing some of our own research and are tryin' to piece together a family tree. This one was a bit of a long shot for us. We're not even sure we have the right Victoria Dowling, so we would be ever grateful if you could tell us anything you may have on her?"

Aya had to give it to Tristan, he had a way with words without ever needing to use compulsion to get what he wanted. Maximus looked down at the headstone as if he were trying to keep clear of their scrutiny. She felt a prickling sensation that he suspected what they really were, and he was trying to avoid being compelled.

"This particular grave..." he said slowly. "We don't have any record of. All we know is that she was a young woman who lived in the area for a time, went away, and then came back. The church records at this time were better than most, but the priest that took care of the parish wasn't known for his penmanship or organisation."

This man was lying through his teeth. "That's all you know?" Aya asked, narrowing her eyes as he looked up at her, trying to will him to tell them the truth.

"Yes," Maximus replied, looking sheepish. "Unfortunately, our records are incomplete. I, along with several local historians, have tried for many years to piece together more information and fill the gaps, so to speak, but at this stage, it looks like that is the breadth of it. There are many things we will never know about those who were buried here."

Aya gave the knight a look and he shrugged, signalling that he understood. Her attempt at compulsion didn't work. They needed to retreat and keep both eyes peeled for trouble. She wondered who exactly this priest Maximus would inform about his unlikely visitors.

Aya sighed. "Well, thanks anyway."

Maximus inclined his head and retreated across the grass, disappearing around the corner of the old church.

Aya peered after him, her suspicions aroused. "He knows something. Why else would he be immune to compulsion? Especially mine?"

"I don't know," he said, looking back down at the grave. "It was bloody creepy." He shivered, pulling his coat tighter around himself before glancing about. "I think we'd better be goin'."

Without acknowledging him, Aya stalked across the yard and began backtracking the way they'd come. As they walked into the main part of Salisbury, as the murky daylight quickly faded into night, Aya pondered what'd happened at the church. Questions answered with questions.

"Do you want to find somewhere to stay, Arrow?" Tristan asked, his voice cutting through her reverie.

Nodding, she asked, "Guesthouse, pub, hotel?"

"Doesn't matter," he told her. "Most humans live in them in these small villages."

"So?" she asked, knowing full well why he'd mentioned it.

"I know you don't have any problems gettin' inside, but I might."

"Whatever." Noticing a pub, she walked towards it. A drink sounded good right about now.

"Hey, wait up," Tristan called after her and tried the door before she could get to it. When he could step into the pub, she followed.

They walked into the warmth, and into Wednesday night's football game. Every available space was crammed with people, the noise drowning out almost everything. In the centre of the room was the bar—which was lined with every type of hard liquor a person could want—refrigerators stacked with imported bottled beers, and along the mahogany bar were more beers and ciders on tap.

At the far end of the pub was a flat screen television, where most of the punters that'd crammed into the place huddled around, yelling out profanities when their team missed a shot or the opposing side took the ball.

When a booth along the side wall was suddenly vacated, Tristan slipped into it, pulling her along. A human man slid in opposite them with a jug of beer and three pint glasses only a minute later. He carefully poured them out a glass and pushed a full pint across the table to each of them.

Aya raised an eyebrow at him and when he looked

at her, she had to hold back a snarl of anger. She'd seen this man before. He was just as rumpled and tired looking as he was that morning. Greasy brown hair, dull eyes. This human looked like he hadn't slept in days.

"Long way from London, aren't we?" she hissed at him, much to Tristan's surprise. He hadn't noticed him in the library that morning at all.

"I have been sent by Maximus," the man murmured, taking a sip of beer.

Aya stared at him, waiting for further explanation.

"He couldn't speak to you so openly this afternoon. There are eyes watching... if you know what I mean."

"Who's eyes?" Aya asked, glaring at him across the table.

"I can't talk about it here, you must understand. If they know I'm here, then I'm good as dead."

"Lucky you." She rolled her eyes. "What do you have to say? Make it quick, or you can add another person to that list of who wants to do you in."

"I've heard the stories about you," the man said. Tristan leaned forwards to grab him, but Aya kicked him sharply in the shin.

"I'm sure you have, so you understand that I'm deadly serious. Whatever you have to say, *spit it out.*"

"It was pure chance I saw you at the library this morning," he began. "Then when you turned up here... We've been waiting for you for a long time, Hunter."

Her eyes narrowed when she heard the use of the name that came with her deadly reputation. "Who?"

"I cannot tell you everything, but if you want to know more, I will arrange a meeting between you and our informant."

"Stop speaking in riddles, human," she hissed, leaning forwards and slamming her fist on the tabletop. To her annoyance, the man didn't flinch.

"Go to the British Museum in London two days from now. There, you will find the Medieval Britain gallery is closed for renovation. Inside, you will find your answers. Midday." Before they could enquire further, the man slipped out of the booth and disappeared into the busy pub. Aya tried to find a trace of his mind amongst the rowdy locals, but he was gone. It stunk of witchcraft.

"What the hell?" Tristan cursed. "What a whack job."

"Yes," Aya scowled, "and I couldn't compel him, either."

Tristan snorted, but didn't offer any comeback. Instead, he inspected the jug of beer, dipping in a finger then testing it against his tongue. Satisfied, he drained his pint.

Aya watched him with annoyance, then said, "Something big is going on here, and I bet it has something to do with whatever Arturius and Regulus were trying to find. Something Victoria was messed up in."

"Somethin' with her blood? Whatever that is, it sounds like bad news."

"Whatever it was, she passed it along to Zac and his brother. If this gets out, they could be in serious danger."

"We don't even know why yet, Arrow."

"No, but that's why we need to meet this mysterious informant."

"Arrow," Tristan exclaimed. "You're not serious? You said it yourself, this stinks of witchcraft and that guy knew who you were. This is a trap."

"There hasn't been a trap yet that I haven't been able to get out of," she said offended.

"There's always a first."

"I'm doing this, Tristan. You can come along if you wish, but I am more than capable to do it on my own."

Tristan groaned as his head fell into his hands. "You're trouble, you know that Arrow?"

She smiled slyly at the knight. "Big trouble."

"Yeah, well, I hope we get out of it alive."

Aya knew she would get what she wanted from this informant. She tried not to think about who was lying in wait for them. It could be any number humans, witches, or vampires. That one she would leave as a surprise, but her money was on witches. Lots of them.

And she tried not to think about her suspicions about who Victoria had really been. That she had something to do with the Celestines. The inscription on her grave had been glaringly obvious that was the case, but that couldn't be true... They'd died thousands of years ago and she'd been the last. Victoria wasn't born until seventeen hundred years later. Any link between the witch and her kind was only in the gift—blood had nothing to do with it.

The part that worried her most was, *Deep below, sleeps a vicious sword, Beware ye who breaks the sleeping ward.* Did it have something to do with what the Romans were looking for? She hoped not, because that was a warning that should be heeded. Someone had gone to a lot of trouble to leave that message for her, and she intended to find the reason why.

They were no closer to finding out the truth than before. What the hell was Victoria? Whoever this informant was, Aya would get the truth out of them, even if she had to take it by force.

CHAPTER 9

London.

It was a different London than Zac had remembered. The first time he'd left Sam and wandered the world on his own, he found himself here and had enlisted in the British Army. What felt like the entire world was at war over some guy getting shot, but he didn't care for the reasons.

He found himself amongst the rain, mud, and stench of blood on the Western Front late in 1914. Blood that stained the battlefields and the men about him. So much blood that it drove him mad, but it didn't matter how many men he killed as long as they were the enemy—Turks, Germans, they all came under the one banner.

It was a different kind of war than Zac had fought fifty years prior. He'd served in the Confederate trenches at Petersburg, which were bad enough, but this was a fresh kind of horror. There were many new, sadistic ways to kill a man—bombs, machine guns, land mines. Air raids and dogfights were commonplace, and submarines consistently sunk the massive destroyers and battleships of the Navy.

For Zac, it was much more effective to take a man down with his knife. Most times, they didn't even see him coming. He was too fast in the confusion of no-man's-land. When he couldn't take the stench of stale blood any longer, he compelled his way to the Dardanelles, but was too late to help the Allies at Gallipoli. Bodies littered the beaches in the thousands and the retreat had long sounded.

Once the war was over, he eventually found Sam again, having learned nothing new about himself. The dead had piled up around him and he didn't care. He was still the monster he always was and always would be.

It took him almost sixty years, and several more wars, before he thought about it. That horror was called napalm. *That* was torture and suffering. At least he had the decency in all his violence to make death quick.

When he'd seen the true face of chemical warfare, Zac had thrown down his rifle and simply walked away, not bothering to compel anyone. He'd been branded a deserter, an enemy of the United States, but he didn't care one iota. War was terrible and brutal, and finally, he'd realised he had to search for something else. It would be a long time being immortal if he didn't.

Obviously, he was still running around in circles, beating his head against an impenetrable brick wall. He'd given his life to Aya, tried to become something better, but she'd thrown it back at him. Even she didn't want him. Was he too far gone to ever come back?

"Zachary." Regulus' haughty voice interrupted his trip down memory lane.

He knew he had to follow Regulus' orders down to the letter if he wanted to continue living. What he was living for, he wasn't entirely sure yet. He just knew that he didn't want to die any time soon.

"Hungry?" The Roman grinned at his new protégé.

Zac glanced disinterested down the lane that Regulus had inched him towards. A woman was walking down the cobbled stretch between the lightened populated roads, her stiletto heels tapping as she went. She was coming straight at them. He could smell her.

Regulus was almost frothing at the mouth, but he elbowed Zac in her direction instead of taking her for himself.

"Show me," the Roman commanded.

The cold snap had brought down a heavy mist that hung about them, shadowing their forms into the night. The woman, however, was like a beacon in the darkness, her breath vaporising about her as she walked towards them, oblivious. Regulus wanted him to feed on her, but not just that—he wanted him to hunt.

Taking a deep breath, Zac felt the air shift as Regulus disappeared. He felt the Roman's gaze on him, which meant he hadn't gone far.

The tap of the woman's heels grew louder as she neared, and he couldn't help but turn and watch her approach. He'd played this game many times before. It was one of Victoria's favourites and it'd soon become one of his in the early days.

As the woman rounded the corner, he stepped into her, as if he was hurrying the other way, their shoulders colliding. He saw her fall and reached out a hand to steady her, but deliberately missed.

Zac smelt her blood the moment her knees scraped on the footpath. He was suddenly starving.

Before he understood what he was doing, the predator took over.

"Are you okay?" he heard himself ask.

Reaching out, he grasped the woman's arm, helping her to stand, one of her shoes coming loose. Blonde hair tumbled around her shoulders and her red woollen scarf had fallen off. He bent down to pick it up, catching the scent of her blood on the crisp air.

"*Shit*," she cursed, hissing as she surveyed the scrapes that now adorned each knee. "Thank you."

"My pleasure." He smiled lopsidedly at her, handing her back her scarf. She was quite pretty, but she hadn't bothered to look at him yet. "Sorry I ran into you, and all."

"Oh, that's okay. Shit happens, I guess." She waved a hand, barely looking at him. Her accent was thick, and he had trouble making out some of the words. She jumped on one heel for a moment, pulling her dislodged shoe back on.

"Where are you going? Do you need a hand?" he asked, letting concern flood into his voice.

"Oh," she said, looking down the high street, then back to him, their eyes meeting for the first time. "I'm going to the pub down there a ways." She waved off into the distance vaguely, seemingly more interested in him once she'd gotten an eyeful.

"May I walk you?" He smiled again and gestured to her scraped knees. "Just in case…"

"Sure."

They walked in silence for a block before she asked, "What's your name? I'm Cassy."

He let a smile play at his lips before he said, "Zac."

"Nice to meet you."

"And you." He let his arm brush against hers, pretending not to notice.

"Where are you from? Are you American?"

"Yes, I'm American," he said. "Louisiana."

"That would explain the accent." She laughed, stopping by a building before a pub, which he assumed was the one she was going to. The street was empty outside, probably because of the weather, and the sounds of voices and music drifted out on to the street as the door around the corner opened and closed.

"Southern through and through. And you?" he asked as he leaned against the wall, as close as he could without tearing out her throat right there and then.

"Manchester." She laughed as if it were a joke he should get.

Reaching out, he tucked a piece of blonde hair behind her ear, letting his gaze flicker to her mouth, then back to her eyes. "Do you want to go get a drink someplace quiet?"

That was all it took. She nodded, hardly believing her luck. Zac could never get over how easy it was. He hadn't needed compulsion at all. He led her down the high street, walking close enough that his arm continuously brushed hers.

"It's one of those hidden lane way places," he said. "You wouldn't know it was here unless someone told you about it."

"Then how do you know?" she asked with a giggle. Oh, how he loathed women who *giggled*.

He winked. "I know one of the bartenders."

When they approached a lane that looked deserted enough, he took her arm and guided her down into the darkness. The sound of her heart pumping blood around her body was driving him mad.

"Are you sure this is the right way?" She sounded wary. "It looks too dark."

Zac stopped and looked back towards the high street, wondering if this had gone far enough. If he'd played with her enough to please Regulus. He almost felt sorry she had to die. She took a step backwards then, as if she sensed the imminent danger. But he had her far enough in the darkness that it didn't matter what she did next.

"I confess," he told her. "I just wanted to get away from the crowd."

"Why?"

Fed up with the chase, he pushed her roughly against the wall and for added flair, kissed her. He didn't know if it was surprise, but she opened her mouth to him and kissed him back, slipping her tongue into his mouth.

It wasn't a nice kiss, not compared to *her*, but it did the trick. As he felt his fangs elongate and pierce the soft flesh of her tongue, he groaned. Her blood trickled into his mouth and smeared as their lips pressed together.

She sobbed and squirmed in his grasp as she felt him bite deeper, trying to scream, fists beating uselessly against his chest.

A memory flashed through him then. This was the point where Aya had stopped him. He'd disappeared and she came to pull him away from his binge, but he was a long way from home and Regulus would never call a halt to this.

Zac drew back, tucked a strand of hair behind the woman's ear, and placed a hand over her bloodied mouth. Her eyes widened as she beheld the blackness that his had transformed into.

"*Shh*," he whispered. "Don't scream. You'll only make it worse."

As the compulsion took hold, he took his hand from her mouth, her lips quivering as she sobbed silently. Pulling her hair from her neck, he tore away her scarf, letting it fall to the ground.

"Please," she cried. "I don't want to die."

"We all have to die at some point," he murmured against her ear, his lips brushing her soft skin.

"I don't want to die. I don't want to die."

He couldn't stand her incessant pleading. Covering her mouth with one hand, he sunk his fangs into her neck, pressing himself hard into her small body.

As the warm, coppery blood ran down his throat, he purred deep in his chest. He'd forgotten how amazing it felt to drink a human to the point of death. He felt the blood coursing through his veins, awakening a strength he hadn't felt in years. Her struggling became weaker, hands that'd beaten furiously, now dropped limply to her sides. As he felt the life leave her, he let go, gasping for breath, her body sliding to the ground.

"Bravo!" The slow clap that signalled Regulus'

approval echoed down the narrow lane. "That was quite something, you know. I'd rate it a four out of five."

Zac let the blood drip down his face as he sunk to his knees. He didn't want to do this anymore, but it felt so good. No mercy where his enemies we concerned—those he would tear apart without a second thought—but this woman was an innocent. He'd hunted her like an animal.

"This is your nature, Zachary," Regulus said, looking down at him. "You're not human anymore. They are to us as cattle are to them. Stop fighting it."

Zac thought he had, but obviously not.

The Roman snorted. "I've got a job for you. Get this right and I'll get you to do something important for me in the morning."

"What?" he hissed, wiping his face clean with the woman's scarf. He'd already forgotten her name.

"This one's just killing," he said. "Tomorrow is more involved."

Pulling himself to his feet, he glared at Regulus. "What do you want me to do?"

"That's the spirit." He clapped Zac on the shoulder, steering him away from the dead woman. "Three blocks from here you'll find a little hole in the wall called *The Ship*. Nice little place full of tasty, tattooed girls and hipsters. Inside, you will find a man who is very much a vampire who is flaunting his Roman-given right to feed on anyone and everything he wants. And he doesn't care who suffers or sees him do it."

"And why do you care?"

Regulus' eyes narrowed. "London is *mine*, and I will not have that little bastard flaunting his insubordination in my face. He has been given far too many free passes and it's time for my threats to be made his reality."

"Who is he?"

"He goes by the name of Vince. Slimy insignificant thing, barely in double figures. Slicked back hair, tattoos. I don't care what you do to him, as long as he'd dead by the end of it."

Zac nodded, the taste of blood still thick on his tongue.

"Hop to it then," the Roman said, walking away. "I'll find you when you're done."

The Ship sat down a lane crammed between a clothes shop and a stinking, dark alleyway. The whole front of the place was taken up by two windows and a door, that was it. Regulus had said it was a little hole in the wall, and he was right. If Zac hadn't been looking for it, he would've walked straight past.

He stood looking at the sign hanging over the door for God knew how long, people passing him on the gloomy street, bundled up against the early onset of winter. Scarves, coats, hats... the humans were bound up so tightly, he barely caught their scent as they hurried past.

Finally, Zac's gaze came down to the door of the pub. Time to get his hands dirty.

He pushed the heavy wooden door open with a sigh and walked into the warmth.

It was busy for a weekday night. Rock music blared from a cheap sound system and young alternative types stood around in groups drinking the cheapest beer they could get their hands on. Windows ran along the side, opening out onto the alley and the bar ran opposite, taking advantage of the length of the space. In the back corner were some vintage pinball machines, but otherwise, it didn't have any furniture other than a couple of barstools and tall tables here and there. It was standing room only.

His assessment of the place was interrupted when a young man bumped into him, spilling the top inch of his beer down Zac's heavy black coat sleeve.

"Oh shit. Man, I'm *sorry*," the man said, drunkenly wiping the beer away with his bare hand. When he realised Zac wasn't moving, he looked up and the smile fell from his face.

Zac glared down at the human with unmasked annoyance, his eyes tinged with black around the edges. The man stumbled back a step, almost dropping his beer entirely. Letting a sneer tug at his lip, he hissed through his teeth and turned away, walking towards the bar, disregarding him.

There were a few people waiting to be served, but he leaned over the top of the bar. Someone standing next to him went to call him out, but got one look at him and thought better of it.

"Hey," Zac called out to the bartender to catch his attention.

"Yeah," the guy said, leaning against the bar. "What you want?"

"I'm looking for a guy named Vince."

The bartender pointed towards the rear of the pub where a pair of grey eyes were staring at him in horror.

He was just as Regulus had described. Slicked back hair, short-sleeved button-up plaid shirt, and arms full of tattoos. And Vince seemed like he was smart enough to know what Zac was and why he was here.

Before he could take a step towards him, Vince was out of his seat and at the rear door, pushing through so hard it slammed against the wall with a deafening crack. Zac was after him a split-second later, pushing people aside. He vaguely heard the bartender call out after him but wasn't about to let the slimy little vampire give him the slip.

As Zac ran after Vince, he held back, watching the younger vampire. He was out of the alley and onto the main street in full view of everyone, but that didn't seem to stop him. Now Zac understood Regulus' annoyance with this one. He ran faster than he was supposed to, pushed people aside with more strength than possible, and still, he ran.

Zac wasn't as stupid as he was. While the humans were looking the other way, he jumped as high as he could manage, his fingers curling around the guttering of the adjoining building. A second later, he'd hauled himself up to the roof and followed where he couldn't be seen. Jumping from building to building, across streets and alleyways, all the time not losing sight of his prey.

Vince was all over the place. It was like he hadn't got a handle on being a vampire at all. He'd disappear around a corner only to run into a dumpster or bash his shoulder against a tree. He'd stumble and fall to his knees, looking over his shoulder with blind fear. *What an idiot.*

When he disappeared into a private garden in the middle of a square, Zac jumped from the roof of the row of bordering houses, crossed the street, and vaulted over the fence.

Vince stood in the centre, his back pressed against the decorative fountain, his eyes wide and full of panic. Zac stood hidden in the shadows and regarded him for a moment. The Roman had told him the vampire was barely in double digits, but from what he'd witnessed, he had to be newer. He was days or a handful of weeks, not ten years. No one was that stupid.

"I know you're there," Vince called out into the unlit garden, his head turning at the slightest sound.

Rolling his eyes, Zac sauntered out into the middle of the square, in full view of the younger vampire.

Vince jumped back and cried, "Stay away."

"You know I'm not going to do that, Vince," he murmured, his hands stuffed into his coat pockets.

"You haven't given me a chance. It's only been a few days. Just a couple more, that's all I need."

Zac narrowed his eyes, but it wasn't his place to ask what he meant. He was just here to deliver a message.

"You can't kill me," Vince pleaded, holding his hands up in front of him.

"Oh, Vince... of course, I can."

"Wait," his voice betrayed his blind fear. "We can come to an arrangement. Anything you want. *Anything*."

Who was Zac to question Regulus? Unless he wanted to end up dead beside this slimy little weakling of a vampire, he had to. The thought must have translated to his face because Vince's face fell and he moved to run, but Zac was faster. He shoved him to the ground, his knee hard in his stomach, keeping the younger vampire in place.

"Don't make this harder than it needs to, Vince," he said, looking down at him. "It'll be over in a moment."

"*No*," he cried, trying to squirm his way out from under Zac's knee.

Sighing, he looked up, knowing Regulus wasn't far away. He could feel the Roman's beady little eyes on him. Without a second thought, he plunged his hand into Vince's chest cavity and felt his fingers curl around his still beating heart. Before the vampire could let out a blood-curdling scream, he wrenched it free with a sucking sound, spots of blood splattering the pavement.

As Vince's eyes glazed over and his body desiccated, he looked down at the heart in his sticky red hand, then down at the gaping hole from where it came. Shrugging, he stuffed it back in, wiped his hand clean on Vince's ugly plaid shirt, and picked up the body. Standing on the sidewalk outside the garden, he waited.

A dark-coloured sedan screeched to a halt beside him and the trunk popped open. Kicking it open all the way, Zac dumped Vince's desiccated body inside next to the human woman he'd fed on earlier, then slammed it shut. Climbing into the passenger seat, he glanced over at Regulus, who pressed his foot on the gas. As the car shot out onto the street, cutting off a taxi, all he could think about was how weird it felt driving on the opposite side of the road.

Regulus looked at him with a sick sense of triumph and he wondered what the hell he'd ask him to do next.

The Roman's voice cut through the silence. "Ready for your next job?"

Resting his head against the headrest, Zac sighed. "What do you want me to do?"

CHAPTER 10

The sun had risen by the time Regulus pulled the car up in front of an old two-story house in the middle of a long street packed with almost identical structures. To Zac, they all looked the same, and the only distinguishing feature was the numbers on each door.

The Roman looked over at him as the engine stilled and clicked as it cooled down. "There," he said, pointing to a house on the opposite side of the street, "number seventy-eight."

Zac raised an eyebrow at the Roman. "And what's there?"

"Who," Regulus replied, narrowing his eyes at Zac's tone. "A vampire by the name of Garett lives here. He believes no one knows where he lives, but I've had my eyes on him for a long time."

"And he's pissed you off, too?"

"The little shit has been double dealing," he said

with a snort. "It's no secret Arturius and I were less than friendly, so you can imagine how annoyed I was to find out that he'd been feeding information to the both of us. Different information, I might add."

Zac looked up at the house, noting that all the curtains were tightly closed and there were bars across the glass. The place was like a fort. He wondered if a human lived there and what other security was on the place.

"If even one of these worthless little worms gets away with it, then more will follow," Regulus continued. "I do not get played, Zachary. There are severe consequences for those who dare."

"And I'm the one who needs to deliver them," he said.

Regulus' lips pulled into a smirk and he thumped him on the back. "You catch on quick."

When Regulus had said this job was more involved, Zac should've realised that it meant gathering information. The Roman's idea of gathering information was a euphemism for torture.

"Is there a human?" he asked.

"No."

"Anything else?"

"Nothing. This one thinks he's untouchable," Regulus said with a note of annoyance.

"What do you want me to do?"

"Get the truth from the little shit any way you can. Then, you kill him."

Zac opened the car door without another word, the frosty morning air hitting him like a hammer.

"Zachary," the Roman called out after him. "Once you're done, come find me."

A white card flew out of the car, hitting him in the chest before falling to the ground. The car roared into life and shot forwards. Before it went too far, he reached out and slammed the door closed. Once the black sedan disappeared around the bend in the street, Zac looked down at the card on the asphalt. Picking it up, he realised it was an address.

He had his orders and his summons, so he shouldn't be surprised that he was dumped so unceremoniously on the side of the road. Regulus had brought him here to work *for* him, not *with* him, and until he could prove himself, Zac wouldn't be trusted with anything other than satisfying the Roman's amusement. He had to do this and do it spectacularly.

Waking towards the front door, he surveyed the façade for any nasty surprises. But Regulus had been right. This Garrett had an illusion of grandeur. He thought he was going to get away with it. All the windows were blacked out, but otherwise, there was nothing remarkable about the outside.

The front door had no handle, just a deadlock and a bell, so there was only one option available. Ramming into it with a shoulder, the door splintered inwards with a sharp crack and Zac caught it before it could hit the wall. When he didn't hear any movement, he walked into the gloomy house, his gaze taking in every surface and opening along the hall.

The front room was a typical lounge. Heavy curtains were drawn over the windows, blocking out any sunlight that might've lit the room. There were the typical furnishings he'd expected to find—a sofa, old-fashioned fireplace, television, and a large black coffin.

Zac snorted at the irony. The house was a fortress against the light and this guy was encasing himself for good measure. What a walking cliché.

Breathing deeply, he focused on the lid and rolled his eyes. Someone had already gone to bed.

No sound came from within the coffin, so Zac continued down the hall, checking out the adjoining kitchen. The sink was full of dirty glasses and empty beer cans but was otherwise bare. Upstairs held a bathroom and two bedrooms severely lacking in personal items.

Clothes were flung haphazardly over the bed and the closet was ajar, the arm of a coat preventing it from closing properly. There was a laptop on the floor, which he picked up and turned it on. Zac looked through the hard drive but found nothing of interest. At least this guy was smart enough not to keep anything of use in plain sight. Unfortunate for Zac, though.

Looked like it was time to wake Garrett up and see what he had to say.

The vampire still hadn't realised he had a visitor, so

Zac made sure he was wide awake. Walking across to the windows, he swept the curtains open, letting the daylight illuminate the room. Without a second thought, he flung open the coffin and let a smirk cross his face as the vampire within screamed as his skin burned. He flung his smoking body into the shadow of the adjoining kitchen, cursing.

His eyes fell on Zac, who stood in the centre of the room, sneering.

"What the hell," the vampire hissed.

Zac raised an eyebrow. "Sleeping in a coffin, are we?"

"Not all of us have fancy daylight spells, arsehole." The smoke dissipated as his body healed itself in the shadows. "Who the hell are you?"

"It doesn't matter who I am."

"The hell it does. *You're in my house*."

"You've been telling tales, Gerald."

"My name's Garrett." He looked at Zac warily. He knew exactly why he was being paid a visit—he just didn't know which Roman had sent him yet.

Zac snorted. "Which one got the right information?"

"Which who?"

"Don't push it, Gary."

"It's Garrett," he hissed.

"Why don't you come out here where we can talk like civilised people?" Zac said, knowing full well he couldn't.

"You could at least close the bloody curtains." Garrett gestured towards the sunlight streaming into the room. "Can't put together a coherent thought if I'm burning alive, you know."

Sweeping the heavy material over the window, Zac sneered, "What makes you think you'll be leaving here alive, Gerry?"

"*It's Garrett*," he yelled.

Zac was across the room in a second. Grasping the front of Garett's shirt, he dragged him towards the window. Before he could pull the curtains open, the vampire screeched at him.

"Wait!" he yelled, hands in front of his face. "I have information."

Zac paused. "Spit it out before I change my mind."

"The Hunter... she's here."

"What?" He suddenly realised why Regulus had sent him here of all places. It was personal, which meant Zac would get everything he needed out of this guy using any means necessary. The real test was who he would bring the information to.

"She's here with the Irish one, Tristan. He double-crossed Regulus."

"Tristan was working with Regulus? For how long?"

Garrett looked up at him with confusion. "You didn't know?"

"How long?" he roared, hauling the vampire up by the front of his T-shirt.

"Whoa, no need to get angry, mate. Tristan's been one of them for a hundred years, at least. Maybe more. If he's with the Hunter, then he's gone for good. He's got a hard-on for her... if you know what I mean."

For his own good, Zac ignored that comment. "What are they doing here?"

"They're lookin' for information about Victoria. Snoopin' around. They were seen at the British Library."

"Why?" he asked, knowing it had something to do with his blood.

"Victoria was a witch." He tried to twist out of Zac's grasp. "At least, that's what everyone thought."

"If she wasn't a witch, then what was she?"

"Oh, she was a witch, but she was somethin' more..."

"*Keep talking.*" He let Garrett go, pushing him back.

"That's all I know, I swear."

"Oh, Gary." He rolled his eyes with a laugh, "you and your lies again."

"All right, all right." The vampire held his hands up, palms out. "She was descended from a powerful line of witches who claimed to go back to the beginnin'. Untainted blood, they said. Her coven was hidin' somethin'. Probably still are. Somethin' old and powerful. They said if the Hunter found it, it would be the end. Shit'd hit the fan 'n all."

"The end of what?"

"I don't know."

"What are they hiding?"

"I don't know!"

"You better not be telling anymore lies, Gerald."

"It's Garrett!"

"Where is the coven?"

"Somewhere in London."

"Where?"

"I don't know! I don't know if they're still even here. No one has heard from them in decades."

"Well, something has stirred them up if you of all people know about them. Where did you get this information?"

Garrett looked at him warily and glanced towards the door.

"Don't think about it," Zac warned him. "I'll beat you every single time."

The vampire sighed, resigning that he wouldn't get away. "I know this guy who's on the in with some witches in Hoxton. He got the info from them."

Zac turned and walked around the room, running his finger along a stack of DVDs, reading the titles of a few books that were stacked on the mantle over the fireplace. Catching Garett's eye in the mirror, he said, "So, who makes the biggest cut?"

"What?"

Turning, Zac laughed. "C'mon, Gerry. Selling secondhand information to two founding vampires who would pay shitloads for it? Fifty-fifty? Seventy-thirty? Or were you telling your mate that you were only selling it to one of them? Making a little more on the side." Garrett was looking at him with wide eyes, giving away that Zac was right on the money. "Which one are you more afraid of?"

"Why the hell do you care?"

"It doesn't matter either way to me," he said with a shrug. "But you should care."

"Which one sent you?" His eyes darted to the door again, like he could escape. Could he be that desperate to take his chances out in the sunlight?

"*Guess.*" Zac deliberately let his lips curve into a smirk.

"*Shit.*"

Zac knew that if he was going to cross one of the founders, he would cross Arturius. Although he was now dead, he was a lot less scary than Regulus. He'd been arrogant, and that'd made him stupid. No, Garrett knew Regulus was behind this little visit.

Zac snorted, not taking his eyes off the vampire. This one was a runner. "You know you've been double dealing, Gerrard. And you know I can't let it continue."

"I'll do anythin'. *Anythin'.*"

Zac turned his head, looking the vampire up and down. "Anything, you say?"

"Yeah," he nodded his head furiously, "just name it."

He contemplated this for a moment, dragging it out, watching the desperation on Garett's face. Running a hand over the mantle, he picked up a wooden stake, turning it over in his hands before putting it back. "Well," he said, turning his gaze back onto the vampire, "there is this one little thing…"

"Name it."

"*How about dying?*"

Before Garett could bolt, Zac grasped the stake and lunged for him, fangs bared, his eyes consumed with darkness. His hand grasped the vampire's head in seconds, smashing it down onto the floor. Blood poured from a gash on his forehead and Zac's other hand came down, ramming the stake into his back and clear through his stomach.

Garett screamed, trying to wrestle himself free, but Zac was too strong, pressing a knee hard into his back.

"What's the matter, Gary?" he sneered, reaching into the vampire's mouth and grasping his tongue, tearing it from his mouth. "Cat got your tongue?"

Garrett writhed on the floor, blood pooling beneath them on the polished floorboards. He was trying to scream, but only strangled gurgling sounds came from his throat. Tearing the stake from his back, Zac flipped him over and stared down at the vampire with black eyes, knowing he couldn't leave him alive. Garrett had to go.

Without a second thought, he positioned his fingers directly over Garrett's heart and dug his fingers into the vampire's flesh, blood pooling from the entry wound and soaking into his shirt. He was so intent on burying his hand into the chest cavity, he couldn't hear the muffled screams that filled the surrounding air. Zac's head may as well have been stuffed with cotton wool for all the attention he paid.

Pressing his palm heavily into the annoying rib bones, they splintered with an audible crack and suddenly, his hand was grasping Garrett's still beating heart. As he squeezed the warm, slippery organ, blood and flesh oozed between his fingers with a satisfying squelch. The vampire's body jerked beneath him and desiccated inch by inch until the vampire let out a strangled gasp.

The room fell silent.

Zac knew he was blocking off his emotions. It was the only way he could deal with this. Already, he felt his sensitivity dulling and he wasn't sure if it was a good thing or not. His humanity was slipping away, and it hadn't taken much at all. The ease of letting go should've alarmed him after all the time he'd spent working towards the opposite, but he found his care factor at absolute zero.

Killing Garrett in such a theatrical way had been a little fun, hadn't it?

Leaving the body where it was, Zac climbed the stairs and went into the bedroom. Wrenching open the closet, he pulled out a new shirt—a long sleeve black button-up number. Garrett was stupid. He ran with rouge witches and didn't even have a sunlight spell, but at least he had excellent taste in clothing. Like that was a redeeming quality.

Rifling through the rest of the clothes, he pulled out a heavy woollen black coat that looked like it was from one of those upper-class boutiques. That would do nicely since his was stained with the blood of two vampires. Garrett wasn't going to miss them now, was he? May as well take advantage.

Stealing off a dead guy? This was a new low, but he'd been lower. This time, he'd just arrived a lot faster than usual.

Sighing, Zac wandered through to the bathroom and turned on the faucet. If he was going to go around killing vampires all day and night, he was going to tire of washing blood off himself. Sooner rather than later, he had to report back to Regulus. Had to be presentable for the boss, right? And he hoped the information he'd gotten from Garrett was up to scratch.

He'd find out soon enough.

CHAPTER 11

The British Museum was heaving with tourists. Aya looked up at the old stone building with its fancy columns and sighed. How she loathed crowds... especially ones full of oblivious slow walkers.

To her annoyance, Tristan took her arm and led her up the stairs and through the doors. The foyer was dimly lit, but light spilled in through the archways from the modern interior, drawing her eye. There was a gift shop to one side and a cloakroom to the other, and in the centre was a perspex box filled with all kinds of money—donations left by the hordes of humans who milled about with cameras in hand.

To the left was a grand staircase that looked just as old as the building's façade—a hundred years or so, perhaps. At the foot was a stand filled with maps. Wresting her arm free from Tristan, she walked over and picked one up, disregarding the suggested donation and immediately looked for the Middle Ages rooms.

"Here." Tristan pointed over her shoulder. "Europe AD 300 to 1100. Closed until late December."

Without looking at him, she slapped the map into his chest and walked up the staircase to the left, weaving her way through the clumped groups of slow walkers and unruly children.

They saw the first room as soon as they reached the upper floor.

Just as the map had stated, it was closed for renovation. All the entrances had been blocked off with panels of white chipboard and posters declaring as much. A walkway was set to one side to allow access to the rooms beyond, so they continued along to find a less travelled area.

Around the corner was an adjoining room that split off into another gallery ahead. A museum worker stood to one side, a walkie talkie clipped to his belt, watching people walk by. To his right was a makeshift doorway into the closed medieval gallery. That was where they'd get inside.

"Excuse me," Aya called out, walking up to the man.

He looked up at her and did a double take. He thought she was pretty, so that would make this a little easier and perhaps, a little more fun, too.

Leaning against the wall, she looked him up and

down with a smile. "Go away," she hissed under her breath.

The man's expression fell as the compulsion took hold and he wandered away looking sheepish.

Tristan came up from behind and gave her a look. Shrugging, she pushed through the door before anyone else walked through from the adjoining galleries.

The room was empty, save for the signs of the advertised renovation. Glass cases lined the walls and there were several freestanding cases around the room covered in white sheets—artefacts had been removed and put into storage for the duration of the works.

A fresh paint smell hung in the air, giving away the fact that the room had been painted a few days earlier. Flat cardboard boxes leaned against the wall and she guessed they probably held plaques that were yet to be placed next to their chosen items. They weren't far from finishing this gallery.

Sensing movement in the next room, she held Tristan back and silently moved forwards. The air hung heavy with something else, something that was very familiar.

The stench of witches.

Stepping into the next gallery, she knew a man stood at the opposite end amongst the empty cases, his shadowy form standing out starkly against the white backdrop. There was no mistaking what this man was. Aya was across the room before he could take another breath, slamming his face up against the wall, her hand wound into the hair at the back of his head.

"This better not be a trap, *witch*."

"It's the middle of the day and there are thousands of people in the museum," the man said. "I'm not that stupid."

"Like that's mattered before." She narrowed her eyes and smirked when his own widened.

"I can see you've had a very interesting life."

"Understatement of the millennia," she said and let him go.

"I prefer the term, warlock, actually," the man said, rubbing his face. "People think you're a girl if you say witch."

Male witches were rare, but Aya still saw them all the same. She'd call him what she wanted.

"Why have you brought us here?" Tristan interrupted before she could retort.

"This has been a long time coming," the warlock said. "We have access to information you want and are willing to help you get it in exchange for some assistance."

Aya thought as much. Nothing came for free and where she was concerned, they always wanted the infamous Witch Hunter to hunt someone down. "We'll see," she said suspiciously. "It depends on your terms."

"Of course."

As an afterthought, she asked, "Who was that man? The one who sent us here."

"Ahh," the warlock said. "You must mean Julian. He's human and sympathetic to our cause. He's our book man."

"He's very..." Aya tried to think of an appropriate word, "rumpled. And what are you called?"

"Joseph."

"Start talking, Joseph. We haven't got all day."

Joseph shuffled from foot to foot, giving away his uneasiness. Had he come here confident, he wouldn't have ended up on the receiving end of her malice. Had she blown all his carefully laid words out of the water? She hoped so.

"There's a coven of witches in London that's been making some outrageous claims," he said, looking warily at Tristan, who was watching the door. "They claim they're the custodians of something powerful. They also claim their line is unbroken from before the beginning."

"From *before* the Five?" Aya raised an eyebrow.

"Yes. They claim to be something more than just witches," he said, looking pointedly at Aya. "Their coven is known to many and is thought to have been disbanded over two hundred years ago. Many thought they were just a myth until now."

"And what does that mean?" she asked, her patience beginning to wear thin.

"They have a reputation for extremism. What they are is not for me to explain," Joseph said. "I'm not one of them."

"Then how do you know any of this?"

"We have an insider. Someone who is a part of them but disagrees with many of their views. Someone who wants to be free."

Aya mulled over this for a moment, thinking about the priest and the man that'd followed them from London to Salisbury. They really had a little network going, didn't they? The Anti-Witch Network.

"Who is this informant?" she demanded.

"I won't say just yet, but she is one of the blood. A half-breed."

And there it was. Blood. Half-breed. Did this woman have the same blood as Victoria? If Aya fed from her, would it have the same effect? Her gut told her yes.

She wanted to ask, but she didn't want to reveal her cards. "What is this *coven* hiding?"

"That, I don't know. It's something only the most trusted in their circle know anything about. We are not even sure they have located it."

"And why are you and your little friends so eager to form a resistance against them?"

"We may not know what it is they're working towards, but there has been a lot of talk about waking something. Don't misunderstand me, Hunter. The Coven has no good intentions. We fear the worst if they succeed."

"And this has something to do with me," she mused

out loud. "More than the mere fact that I am a witch hunter and you want my help."

Joseph shook his head, surprised. "People say you carry the abilities of a witch."

"I'm a vampire, Joseph."

"And we both know that's only part of it."

Her lip curled up into a sneer. "Clever little boy."

"Victoria's epitaph is a message to you, the hunter and the star. We knew that one day you would come looking, and we hoped it was sooner rather than later."

"You knew Victoria was after me."

"Yes. She was a part of the Coven until the Roman, Regulus, turned her."

Aya snorted. It all began to click into place. Victoria was part of this Coven that had something powerful hidden away that they didn't know how to wake. These renegades had counted on her following the trail back to Salisbury so they could enlist her help in stopping them. It still didn't explain what Victoria was—what all the witches in this Coven claimed to be and why they needed her on their side so much. The only way she could find out for sure was to meet this insider.

"Can you get me a meeting with your insider?"

"Yes, but it comes with its risks."

She rolled her eyes. "Doesn't it always?" There wasn't much left she hadn't seen when it came to backstabbing, double dealing, and elaborate traps. "You witches and your cryptic messages. Why can't you just say what you mean and leave it at that."

"We play dangerous games, Hunter. A little care works well for our kind."

"And not one of you knows the entire story." She sighed.

"In case one of us is taken."

Deep below, sleeps a vicious sword. Beware ye who breaks the sleeping ward. Goddamn witches and their cryptic poetry. Now, she realised, it was obvious that the Coven was trying to find and wake up something powerful. In these situations, Aya had learned that it was better to leave these things well alone. The Coven was playing with fire and innocents would be burned... *badly*.

"So, all of this... was just to enlist my help?"

"Yes, we can't do this alone. There are others trying to uncover the Coven's secrets and take them for themselves."

Arturius and Regulus had been looking for something. Now she knew what. Regulus had hoped to use Victoria somehow, but she'd ended up hunting Aya and ruining Zac and Sam's lives. Something had gone wrong, but what?

Joseph continued, "We want to find what they have and either destroy it or hide it away for eternity."

She snorted. "You don't even know what *it* is."

"No."

"Then how do I know you and your little friends won't take it and use it for yourselves?"

"That you'll have to take on faith."

"Faith," she hissed, "is of little consequence where power is concerned."

"It's all I have."

Aya regarded Joseph and found he believed he was telling the truth. In the end, she would be there to make sure all of them kept their word—a truth they seemed to have already acknowledged.

"I will help you," she said. "But it comes with a price."

"And what would you ask?"

"No more lies, no more secrets. And if I see fit to kill you all along with the Coven, know that I won't hesitate." If Joseph knew even a quarter of her reputation, he knew that she made good on her threats. She had nothing to fear from this rag-tag group of renegades, but they had everything to fear from her. She could take their power with a single touch, after all. For a witch being ordinary... that was worse than death.

The warlock sighed, but he nodded his acceptance. "Then it will be arranged."

"When?"

"We will contact you."

Tristan had been awfully quiet since they'd left the museum.

Aya regarded him as they walked back to the

hotel as if she could read his mind. He was usually all for another witch hunt, but he was oddly shaken this time. Perhaps he'd gotten more than he'd bargained for? He'd only signed on for finding the truth behind Victoria's lineage, not infiltrating an entire coven of witches known for their extreme views.

"Tristan," she said as he unlocked the door to their room.

"What?"

"You don't have to follow me, you know."

He threw the room key onto the table inside the door and grinned. "It's always an adventure when you're around."

"Unfortunately."

"I'd follow you into the bowels of Hell, Arrow. Figuratively speakin'," he said, running a hand over his face. "I just didn't count on having to actually go there."

Aya smiled wryly. "Another scorching day in Hell, my friend."

"I don't go back on my promises, you know."

"I know. Chances are, you won't have to lift a finger."

"I'm not afraid of a fight," he said, offended. "I'm worried about what we'll find."

Aya shrugged and turned to the minibar, pulling out an assortment of tiny liquor bottles. "Who knows, Tristan? Who knows? Probably all manner of beasts. Regulus has his fingers in this pie as well."

"Then perhaps you can put him down at the same time."

"Here's hoping." Before she could sit with her miniature bottle of vodka, a white envelope shot under the door and came to rest in the middle of the entryway. *Witches.* With a frown, she was across the room, envelope in hand. Wrenching open the door, she scanned the long hallway, but found it empty. Stepping back inside, she tore the envelope open, letting the door close with a bang behind her.

"What does it say?" Tristan asked over her shoulder like an excited child.

"It's a party invitation."

"I can see that. What does it say?"

"Satan's Rout, a Halloween Ball in an abandoned picture palace," she read. "At *The Coronet Theatre.* Closest tube Waterloo or Elephant and Castle... What the hell is this?"

Tristan snatched the flyer from her and laughed, his earlier worries slipping away. "It's a theatre party. They have these rooms with different themes and people wander about in character. There's jazz bands and performances and people dress up."

"What for?"

"To get high, have a good time, pretend. You know, forget about their mundane, mortal lives and maybe get laid in the process." He took out his cell and typed something into it.

"What are you doing?"

"Lookin' up the place."

"On a cell phone?" she asked like it was the most absurd thing she'd ever heard.

"You really need one of these," he said, waving his cell in front of her. "Very handy. Have you heard of a thing called the internet?"

"Why would I want one? I've been doing all right without it, haven't I?"

"It's the twenty-first century, Arrow."

"So?"

"So, don't be such a technophobe."

She looked at him as if he were speaking a foreign language. "Technology doesn't sit well with me." She snatched back the flyer and turned it over. "What kind of thing is this anyway? A theatre party, or whatever."

"It's really an alternative Halloween Ball."

Aya snorted. "Halloween?"

"Yes, you know, dressin' up and giving out sweets to children. Trick or treat? They're big on that in America, aren't they?"

"Why would anyone want to dress up as..." she turned over the flyer to the front, reading the costume suggestions, "satanic whore mongers and naughty fallen angels?"

"I would expect all kinds of crazy stuff," he said with a chuckle. "It is London, after all."

Aya sighed dramatically. "And that means nothing to me. Why would anyone want to celebrate

Halloween by dressing up in costumes and eating sweets?"

"You've never heard of Halloween?"

"Halloween is a time when the veil between life and death is at its thinnest. All I know about it is that it's more trouble than it's worth."

Tristan gave her a confused look but explained the whole costume and candy thing anyway. "You seriously don't know about modern Halloween?"

Rolling her eyes, Aya said, "I was asleep for a hundred and fifty years, Tristan."

He seemed surprised. "Really?"

"Really."

"If you say so." He laughed, scratching his head. "You missed some quality stuff."

"Like Halloween parties?"

"I could think of better things," he declared. "Is there anythin' else in the envelope? A message or anythin'?"

Aya picked it up, but it was empty. "Nothing. It's from our friend Joseph, it has his stink all over it. I assume I'll know the woman when I see her. I have a sixth sense about these things, you know."

"Yeah," he said. "Though it would be nice to have a little more information. I feel like we're goin' in blind."

"Perhaps, but I don't need it for this."

"What if Regulus knows about the half-breed woman? They could be lyin' in wait for us."

"Chances are, he'll have some of his thugs there," she told him. "Could be a bit of fun."

Tristan looked worried. "I worked with him for a long time, Arrow. If he knows, then he'll send the Six."

Aya had met the group of vampires known as the Six on a few occasions. The last time she had been in Paris, they'd attempted to surround her in a crowd of humans come to watch the execution of the French queen, Marie Antoinette. She remembered snapping Victoria's neck before escaping. That was a few months before she set foot in America for the first time.

"Let them come," she hissed. "It's about time I put them in the ground."

"They aren't to be trifled with, Arrow," Tristan warned.

"And neither am I."

The Six were Regulus' most trusted lackeys. Six of the most highly skilled vampires she'd ever met, comprising of assassins, spies, fighters, executioners, soldiers... They'd all been vile things when they were human, and all of those traits and skills had carried over. Regulus had put them together almost five hundred years ago and not once had they come close to laying a finger on her, let alone capturing her. Aya wasn't afraid of them.

She would go to this Halloween party and meet with the half-breed insider and find out the truth. Who she was and what she was.

Then she would solve the mystery behind Zac's

blood once and for all and confirm what she suspected was true—that they had something to do with the Celestines.

It was something she hoped to hell wasn't true, since Joseph said they'd turned to evil. That was the ultimate kick in the guts.

She would find a way to infiltrate the Coven and find out what they were hiding. Then and only then, she would decide if they were to live or die.

Either way, Aya was about to do a lot of killing. Vampires, witches, it didn't matter, as long as someone's blood was spilled.

CHAPTER 12

Regulus kept a house in the highbrow neighbourhood of Hampstead. It was more of a mansion, and the outside resembled the exterior of a Roman temple, all columns and scroll work. Zac snorted at the irony. The Roman had an inflated sense of self, more so than Arturius.

Zac pulled his new coat closer around him and walked up the front steps and rang the bell.

He wasn't surprised when a human opened the door and looked him up and down with a sigh. He was an elderly man, perhaps about seventy human years, with grey hair and a crooked back. He was obviously the legal owner of the house, even though it belonged to the Roman.

"Another vampire," the man said with distaste. "You must be Zachary."

Zac raised an eyebrow at the old man and nodded.

"Well, you better come in. He's expecting you."

Once he'd received the invitation, Zac was free to step inside and the man closed the door behind him. Pointing up the staircase, he said, "Up the stairs, third on the right. I don't escort vampires."

Walking up the stairs, Zac took in the finery with a detached air. Old and expensive paintings hunt along the walls, and even the carpet underfoot felt like it was the best quality. Material possessions came easily for someone who could compel their way to anything they wanted. That, and being two thousand years old and truly immortal had something to do with it as well.

When he reached the third door on the right, he lifted a hand and lightly rapped on the door.

"Come in," Regulus' voice came from inside the room.

When Zac opened the door, it revealed a cozy study, not unlike his father's back at the manor in Louisiana. The walls were lined with floor-to-ceiling bookshelves with ancient books clogging every available space.

The Roman sat in a dark brown leather chair beside an open fireplace which someone had lit due to the cold snap outside. The small table beside him held a crystal decanter full of brown spirits and he held a matching glass in one hand that was almost empty.

It was lavish and over the top, but Zac had expected nothing less.

"Don't hover by the door, Zachary, it's rather annoying." Regulus waved the young vampire into the room, gesturing to a matching armchair across from him. As Zac sat, the Roman raised an eyebrow expectantly.

"Aeriaya is in London with the Irish knight," he said nonchalantly, using her full name.

"Really?" The Roman was suddenly interested.

"They've been spending quite a bit of time at the British Library."

"The library? Can she be any more boring?"

"They've been attempting to find out where Victoria came from."

Regulus couldn't hide his smirk. "She wants to know about your blood."

He wasn't surprised Regulus knew that secret. "Yes."

"Is there anything else?"

"Victoria's family comes from a very old and powerful line of witches, but I suspect you already know this. Garrett seemed to think they were hiding something sacred to them, something ancient and powerful. He seemed unsettled at the prospect of the Hunter finding it first. I pressed him for more information, but he knew nothing else. Everything he told me he believed to be the truth."

The Roman looked at him expectantly. "And what did you do to him?"

"I killed him."

"How?" His eyes sparkled.

"He had been telling lies," Zac said without

emotion. "So, he lost his tongue. Then he suffered from cardiac arrest."

Regulus was beyond pleased. "I hope you made it slow."

"Extremely."

The Roman was still for a few minutes, pondering the information Zac had brought back. He didn't move from the chair, waiting to be dismissed, but Regulus wasn't finished. "It's curious how you used her full name. Until recently, she was just Aya to you. Did her betrayal cut that deep?"

Zac stared at the Roman, his lip lifting slightly into a sneer.

Regulus smiled, cocking his head to the side. "You must forgive me for not thanking you before now, but I had to be sure." He handed the young vampire a glass of what appeared to be an expensive Irish whisky. "You helped free me from that insufferable witch Katrin. She had us all ensnared from the moment she turned us. That was the part she so conveniently left out of her bargain. There wasn't much we could do without her say so. Now I am free to do all those things myself and not rely on incompetent fools to do them for me." He looked at Zac with a note of regret. "I could have done with you a hundred and forty years ago, Zachary."

He didn't say a word, instead choosing to gaze into the fire rather than be sucked in too deeply by Regulus' silver tongue. One day he would have an opportunity for revenge, and he couldn't hesitate when that time came.

Suddenly thinking of Tristan, Zac asked, "Why did you send Tristan to warn her?"

Regulus narrowed his eyes. "You ask a lot of questions, Zachary."

"Is he still working for you?"

"I knew the moment I sent Tristan away that he would deliver my message and promptly switch sides. I'm not a fool."

"You did it deliberately," Zac mused to himself.

"Aeriaya needed to be smoked out of her fox hole and it worked. She's here doing my work for me. She can go places I can't."

Zac knew better than to keep asking questions and clamped his mouth shut. Aya was looking for something the Roman wanted and that meant it had to do with this mysterious Coven Garrett had told him about. Whatever Regulus was looking for, so was Aya.

"Come, I have some people you need to meet." Regulus gestured for him to follow as he stood and walked into the hallway. "They all know you had a hand in the death of my brothers. That has instilled enough misguided respect in their back hearts for them to follow you regardless." Regulus turned and stared at Zac, his eyes burning. "Don't misinterpret my intentions, Zachary. I haven't forgiven you for your part in that. You are merely a means to an end, my friend."

"Likewise," he murmured in return.

The Roman smirked and descended the stairs, leading Zac to a sitting room that was every bit as lavish as the study. There were more vampires in the house—he could sense their presence and guessed there were six in the room they approached. The human butler who had opened the front door earlier was hovering within hearing distance, but no one seemed bothered by it.

The six vampires—five males and one female—looked up as Regulus walked into the room and glanced at Zac with curiosity. They were all dressed in dark clothing like they were a bunch of thugs waiting for their next order... which was exactly what they were.

"Knew it," one man muttered, looking Zac up and down.

"Knew that he'd show up?" another asked.

"Of course," Regulus interrupted. "After watching him play with his food, where else would he go but where he belongs?"

Zac was still struggling with that one, so he said nothing, which was the best thing he could've done. The six vampires were looking at him with a mixed sense of awe and apprehension. He'd had a hand in killing two founders and the witch who had created them, after all. Not to mention Alistair, who they probably would've at least known by reputation—he was three hundred years older and a lot stronger. By rights, Zac should've been the one who was staked.

"They call this lot the Six," Regulus said, breaking him out of his reverie and walking across the room. Pointing to the first vampire who sat in the leather armchair, he said, "This one is Nye."

The man nodded with a wry smile, his messy brown hair falling in his eyes. He didn't look a day over twenty-five. Regulus was still speaking, talking for him. "He's an old bastard, but he's a follower. He'd follow you to the end and rape and pillage along the way if that's what you asked him to do. Ironically, he does have a sense of honour that we haven't seemed to iron out of him yet."

Nye shrugged as if to say, whatever. Zac couldn't help but notice the ugly scar that marred the vampire's face and wondered how he got it. It began at his left temple, across his left eye, and the bridge of his nose, ending in a deep red gash across his right cheekbone. Nye was lucky he kept his eye, but it was more to do with sheer luck or maybe his opponent's lack of skill. Either way, he still had both of them.

Regulus moved onto the next vampire, who was a tall, broad-shouldered hulk of a man. "Rixum, the bald-headed buffoon is nothing but a grunt." The Roman slapped him on the back of the head. "He's the bodyguard. The vampire shield." The vampire nodded his head at Zac, not taking his eyes off him.

"This one," he pointed to a wiry man, who was rather plain to look at, "is Maddox. He was an assassin in his last life. A sneaky little bastard who will gut you in your sleep."

"Hey," the vampire said with an air of caution that Zac didn't like. What had Regulus told them about him?

"Rob is a newborn." Regulus looked the next vampire up and down. "He was a cage fighter, so he'll hit you where it hurts, then bite your ear off." Rob was a tall, muscled man with a shaved head and an arm filled with Japanese-style tattoos. It didn't matter one iota that the man used to fight for a living—he was a vampire now and that meant a whole new set of rules.

"He replaced William after he was cut in half," Maddox said, not elaborating any further.

Regulus continued down the line, gesturing towards a tall, slim woman. The hood of her jacket covered her hair, but from the colouring of her skin— pale and freckled—Zac guessed she was a redhead. "Holly is your token female, but she fights dirty and that's what I love about her. She'll bite and scratch you to death if that's what it takes." As she pulled off her hood, wild, red curly hair tumbled out and her hazel eyes glittered at him in the gloom. She obviously liked what she saw, but Zac's hostile glare didn't falter.

"This one we call Pyke, because he used to stick heads onto pikes outside the Tower of London after the executioner chopped them off. He's macabre and sick," Regulus said.

Pyke was broad-shouldered and tall, dark-haired,

and wore a chin full of stubble. He had an air of nonchalance, but anyone could sense the underlying malice about him. He, along with the other five, all had a skill that was useful. They were all exploitable to some extent, and Zac wondered how often they were left alone to their own devices.

Regulus watched as Zac looked the Six over. "They're loyal, skilled, and know how to get things done... which is what I expect from you," the Roman said, the warning in his voice not going unnoticed by anyone.

Zac raised an eyebrow at the founder. "And what do you want me to add to the mix?"

"You were a military man, were you not? And I understand you had some very specific training."

"Is that what they call it?" He snorted, not liking where the conversation was going.

"Victoria had great hopes for you. She was foolish, but her eye was accurate, I'll give her that. You, Zac, are our next greatest player. We are going to do great things together, you and I." Regulus seemed pleased with himself.

Zac snorted, surveying the six vampires. "Be more specific."

Regulus laughed and slapped him on the shoulder. "What do all evil predatory bastards want? Blood, sex, and power. And we will start with your girlfriend."

Deep down, Zac knew they'd use him against Aya. The Roman was smart in pitting him against her so soon after her betrayal, striking while the wound was fresh. The Roman was hoping it would make a spectacle. Everyone was looking at him as if they were waiting for a reaction, but they wouldn't get one.

Regulus snorted, disappointed. "Do what you want. Work with them, tell them to do your bidding, I don't care as long as I get results. Now get out. I'll be in touch when I need you."

"C'mon, Zac," the vampire who was introduced as Nye gestured towards the door. "We've got a place not too far way."

Zac trailed behind as the Six filed out of the front door and into the crisp night. He supposed he would just go with it. There was nothing else to do for the moment. Regulus would use him soon enough, and he would have to be ready.

Who knew what would go through his head when he laid eyes on *her* again. Would he still love her? Of course, he would. Falling out of love with Aya would be one of the hardest things he would ever have to do.

Following the Six through the streets, they soon came to a populated area. A rail bridge spanned across the road, between old brick buildings, and was painted with the words, 'Camden Lock'.

Zac remembered this part of town. Camden had always been a little of an underbelly and seemed no different now. It was still early evening, but most of the markets and shops had closed for the night, though the bars and clubs were only just starting their trade.

The streets were alive with people and movement. Everyone was out looking for a party.

They passed pubs and live music venues, touts standing outside looking to buy or sell tickets for a profit. Tourists and locals milled about, searching for a club to spend the evening at. There were walls plastered with gig posters and a booth advertising the latest things to do in London. It was covered in its own array of advertising—ghost tours, days away to Stonehenge and Bath, walks detailing the 'secret' London, and Jack the Ripper tours. Watching the tourists and backpackers picking up leaflets, Zac idly wondered if Jack the Ripper was a vampire. It would make sense.

Pyke stopped beside him, noticing the posters. "His name wasn't Jack," he told him. "It was Arthur. And he was all the bad things about being a vampire. Arthur the Ripper doesn't quite have the same ring to it, does it?"

Well, there was that question answered. As Pyke moved off, Holly slunk up beside him, running her hand suggestively along his lower back.

"C'mon, Zac," she purred.

Annoyed, he pushed past, making her stumble back a step.

Descending from street level, they made their way past the Lock and away from the markets and pubs, continuing down the path beside the canal. This time of night there were few people. Those they passed seemed to be locals with homes backing onto the water, using the path as a shortcut.

A few minutes later, they entered a block of apartments and climbed the stairs to the top floor. The entire building was empty, except for the top levels where the vampires lived.

The apartment was quite large, with enough space for the seven of them, spread out over two floors. From the look of the place, they'd been living here for quite some time. There was no inbuilt human security system to keep other vampires out, but Zac suspected there were other safeguards. Besides, Regulus wouldn't leave him alone with a human in the house for obvious reasons.

"Make yourself at home," Maddox said, gesturing towards a door down the hall. "You can have that one."

Nye handed him a new cell phone. "When Regulus wants something, he'll let us know," he said. "Until then, we can do whatever we want, except leave town, kill in public, kill an ally, or kill ourselves."

Zac slid the phone into his pocket and said, "Understood."

Without another word, he went into the bedroom Maddox said he could use and slammed the door shut. He needed some alone time.

CHAPTER 13

The next evening, Zac was sitting on the roof, staring out over the grey city, when Nye found him. He'd had no inclination to socialise with the Six, preferring his own company than six potentially psychopathic vampires. He didn't need his downward spiral to hurtle any faster than it already was.

"Come inside, mate," Nye said, leaning against the door that led into the stairwell. "No one likes a sad sack."

Little droplets of water beaded on the coat he'd stolen from Garrett from the light, misty rain that was falling. Sighing, Zac said, "Only because it's raining."

As he passed the older vampire, Nye thumped him on the back. "That'ta boy."

Returning to the apartment, he found the others sitting around the lounge with at least a dozen bottles of alcohol on the coffee table. Nye picked one up and handed it to him. "Get that into ya. Looks like you need it."

Taking the bottle from him, Zac opened it and took a draught, the soothing burn of the liquor calming.

"We're on the same side now, Zac," Rix said. "Your shit is our shit."

Zac's only answer was to take another long draught from the bottle.

"Don't you wanna know about us?" Pyke asked. "It looks like we're going to be working together for a while."

"Tell me what you want." Zac sighed, slumping back into a chair.

"We've all worked together in one way or another over the past few hundred years," Maddox said. "Except for Rob. He's new."

"He replaced William after he was chopped in half," Rix said, grinning. Maddox had already told him this, and obviously, Rix had been a witness.

"How'd that happen?"

"Scythe. Very medieval, if you ask me," Maddox said, shuddering.

"We were hunting some vampire Caius had sent after us," Pyke began. "Arturius wasn't the only Roman Regulus was pissed with."

"They all hated Katrin in one way or another. Caius was trying to break her hold over him," Nye explained. "We were sent to kill off his witches and vampires, but he sent someone after us before we could think about laying a finger on his little network. Will got chopped in half, but that was nothing compared to what happened to the other guy."

Zac understood completely. Regulus felt he was the only one who was allowed to operate outside of Katrin's influence and had done all he could to stamp out the other Roman's efforts. Aya had simply completed the job for him.

"And before you ask," Nye waved the knife he'd been playing with at him, "the last time I saw the Hunter was in 1790-something. Paris, if I remember correctly."

"She snapped Victoria's neck," Maddox said.

Nye rolled his eyes. "She's definitely a piece of work."

"Quite brilliant, actually," Pyke said. "You know her, Zac. What's she like?"

The six vampires looked at him expectantly, like he was about to tell the most horrific story ever, but Zac didn't have the stomach for it.

"What else is there to tell?" he asked, glancing at Holly, who'd been staring at him appreciatively since he'd sat down.

"A lot," Maddox scoffed.

"There's a hell of a lot of stories out there about her. I want to know if they're true or not," Pyke said with a gleam in his eye.

Zac shrugged. "Well, they're all true. I've been told I'm bloodthirsty when I lose it, but I have nothing on her."

"What kind of level are we talking about here? Ten being the highest and one being the lowest," Maddox quipped.

"I just kill them. She tears them into tiny pieces."

"Cool," Rob breathed.

"Cool until it's you," Nye snapped.

"She must be something," Holly purred from her corner, her eyes sparkling.

Zac narrowed his eyes and looked away, not liking what she had implied.

"Somethin' else." Pyke winked at her suggestively.

Nye was watching Zac with a strange expression, the knife still in his hand. "Shut it," he said to the others, pointing the blade at each of them. "Our objective hasn't changed. Capture, not hero worship."

Regulus told the Six what to do, but Zac suspected that Nye was their unofficial leader. What did the Roman say he was before? A spy? Someone who dealt with manipulation and information was sure to establish themselves on top as soon as possible.

"Why do they call you the Six?" Zac asked, changing the subject.

"The Avengers was already taken." Nye stabbed the knife into the tabletop.

"There's six of us," Maddox stated.

"Seven now," Rob added.

"*Nah*," Nye said, looking at Zac with a raised eyebrow. "We're still the Six. This one's in a league of his own."

Zac grimaced. "I don't know if I should be offended by that."

"I would take it as a compliment, mate. Take note of it, cos I don't give 'em out that often."

He didn't doubt it. Zac dropped the empty bottle onto the floor beside him with a sigh. After his little killing spree two nights ago, he'd become bored. He didn't know what he was meant to do but sitting around drinking wasn't high on the list.

"What the hell do you do when he doesn't want anything?" he asked.

"All kinds of things," Holly replied with a sly smile. "I'd be happy to show you..."

"Yeah, all kinds of things, Zac." Maddox made a lewd gesture at Holly, who flipped him off.

"Regulus will have something for us soon enough," Nye told him.

And that something would no doubt have everything to do with Aya, who was lurking somewhere about the city as they spoke—looking for that mysterious Coven and whatever it was they were hiding. Regulus wanted it bad, and Zac was his link to Aya. How the Roman was going to exploit that was anyone's guess.

Zac didn't have the strength to think about it until he had to. Without a word, he got up and disappeared down the hall, the Six watching him go with an air of acceptance.

They'd obviously been warned about his behaviour and his recent conversion. Zac still had his humanity, but that was slipping away a little more each day and soon, it would be gone entirely. And that was the one thing in all his long years he'd never done—let go. It would be either sweet relief or eternal torture when he did... and he would know once and for all what he was meant to do.

Life or death would claim him, and he didn't care which.

———

Holly only waited another day before she made her move.

She found Zac in his room, sitting on the edge of the bed staring out the floor-to-ceiling windows that opened out onto the balcony. It was much too cold to sit outside. Besides, he wasn't looking at the view. He wasn't looking at anything.

Holly came up beside him, trailing a finger along his shoulder. He didn't bother to lift his gaze to meet hers, even when she stood in front of him, her sickly scent washing over his senses. She straddled him, his expression still darkness as she trailed a hand along his jawline, tilting his head towards hers. Kissing him roughly, she pressed herself into his body, trying to make him respond.

Annoyance and anger seared through him as he felt his hand snap closed around her neck, wrenching her away. Her eyes glittered with unshed tears as she struggled for breath.

"Never touch me again," he snarled, his eyes boring into hers and pushed her to the floor. He hardly registered the moment she left. He couldn't touch anyone like that anymore, not even for his own amusement... not after *her*. She'd destroyed him.

Abruptly, he pushed the door open, the bang it made as it collided with the wall silencing the five vampires who were seated around the room. Holly was nowhere in sight. Stalking across the room, he ignored their knowing looks. He had to get out of here and go do something destructive.

"Where are you going, Zac?" Nye asked when no one else dared speak.

"To kill something," he spat as he opened the front door.

Nye jumped out of his chair and grabbed his coat, motioning for the others to stay. Zac groaned at the obvious need Nye felt to babysit him. Regulus had warned them he was prone to going off the deep end, and he wished he could just lose himself already. All this anger was unnatural.

Striding into the hallway and down the stairs, he

felt Nye shadow his every step. "Do you have to follow me?" he hissed, pulling the collar of his coat up.

Nye raised his eyebrows. "Eat who you want, Zac. I'm just here to stop you from doing it in public or not coming back at all." He wasn't condescending about it, that was a bonus.

Turning without another glance, Zac disappeared into the night, the spy trailing him as he wandered from district to district—Camden to Soho, Oxford Street to Hyde Park. They walked the length of Marylebone and Kensington High Street. He wandered so far that he lost all track of where they were and where they'd been. He passed so many humans, so many who would've satisfied his hunger, but he didn't touch any of them. If Nye found this odd, he didn't say a word.

Zac didn't know where in the city they were, but the buildings were old and lined the streets in long banks of dreary grey stone. He let out an annoyed sigh. He couldn't see anything from down here. The city stifled him. They stood in a deserted laneway, the sounds of traffic washing over them from the adjacent street. Satisfied that no one was around, he jumped as high as he could, perched on a windowsill halfway up the façade and jumped again, coming to rest on the edge of the roof. Nye was beside him a second later.

"Regent Street," he said, eyeing Zac. "Piccadilly Circus is that eye bleed over there."

Zac's vampire eyes were offended at the neon glow

the electronic billboards cast into the night. He looked away, watching the night busses pass them on the street below and the black cabs that darted through the mist.

He felt better up here, away from the monotony of the humans and their dreary city.

"Want to talk about it?" Nye asked when he knew Zac wouldn't be forthcoming on his own.

"No." He sensed the words building up in Nye's throat regardless.

"Holly is a stupid little girl who thinks vampires should screw all day long," he said. "She can fight, though."

Zac snorted. "You slept with her, didn't you?"

Nye laughed, slapping him on the shoulder. "Who hasn't?"

"Rix."

"Yeah, that man is ugly." His eyes sparkled wickedly until his expression relaxed and fell into a frown. "You're still into her, aren't you?"

"Who? Holly? *Please*," Zac scoffed, annoyed at the conversation.

Nye laughed again, trying to hide a note of nervousness. "No, I'm talking about the Hunter."

Zac's expression darkened. "She betrayed me."

"Did she?"

"Nye," his voice was full of warning. "Whose side are you on?"

"Mine," he declared. "Look, she's not what she

seems. We can use it to our advantage. I don't believe she intended to use you."

"And you know this, how?"

"I knew her when I was human," he said, looking out over the city. "She may not remember me, but I remember her. I was a spy in the service of one Sir Frances Walsingham, under the ultimate command of Queen Elizabeth the First. It was my business to know everyone. It was 1588 and she was lurking about, sticking her neck where it didn't belong. I remember the year because it was when the Spanish were set to invade England in their little row boats."

Zac raised an eyebrow. "Row boats?"

"Yeah, one hundred- and sixty-foot-long row boats," Nye replied. "All one hundred and thirty of them. She pulled me from one of the fireships that decimated the Armada. Me and Captain what's-his-face... Raleigh. I wouldn't have made it. My face had been split open by some brute of a Spaniard." He ran a hand over his scar, scratching the stubble that he'd neglected to shave off for a few days. "She compelled Raleigh but left me. Probably thought I was on the way out, knocking on Heaven's door. They trained me to hold on to my wits, so I remember quite a bit. If I didn't, then I'd be as good as dead. I was a spy. I was right under Mary Stewart's nose for a long time. My head would've been on the block if they found me out, not hers."

"Mary who?" Zac really wasn't up on his English history.

"Mary, Queen of Scots. The so-called Scottish queen who plotted to have Queen Elizabeth assassinated so she could take the throne. Her head was cut off for treason. You can ask Pyke about that part."

"Sounds like you were on the side of the righteous once."

"I did too many dark things when I was human to be considered good." He grimaced at some old memory. "Even if they were done in the name of all that was good and righteous. Or so I was told by the Crown. Serving Regulus is as good as serving the Tudors. It's all the same to me. Don't mistake my story, Zac. That was another life and I owe the Hunter nothing. She pulled me from that fire ship, only for me to become this. Fact is, she has a soft spot for the downtrodden, and you, my friend, are *downtrodden*."

Zac didn't want to talk about how screwed up he was. "How did you become a vampire?"

Nye laughed wryly at his blatant question. He knew exactly what his associate was doing. "There was more than filth that stalked the deepest reaches of the Tower of London. Men were sent there to die, and many were taken by our kind as the executioner's axe. That's all I'll say about that." When Zac said nothing, he continued, "And how did *you* become a vampire?"

He raised an eyebrow at his unexpected friend. "Surely you know something about that?"

"Yeah, the *Reader's Digest* version."

He sighed, not wanting to think about things long past. "I was already dying, so I didn't really have a choice."

"I don't know many who came into this life willingly and that's what probably screwed you up," Nye said. "You'd made peace with your death and some bitch brought you back and neglected to teach you right from wrong." He laughed. "Just like my pitiful excuse of a mother. Cheapside was a cesspool to grow up in, even more with a whore like her telling me I was a no-good son of a bitch. She got the bitch part right, by the way."

"What happened to her?"

"I got to work for the Crown, and she got stuck with a knife for a slice of bread. The 1500s were a nice time. Golden Age, my arse."

Zac rested his forearms on his knees and watched the world go by below. Every vampire he'd ever met had their own sob story, even Nye, who didn't have the issues Zac did. Maybe that was his problem. He still hadn't decided if he wanted to continue living despite all of it.

Now wasn't the time to think about it. He had work to do. "Wouldn't Aya recognise you?"

"She wouldn't recognise the man I am now.

Vampirism has changed me, along with this ugly thing." Nye traced the ragged line of his scar from his temple, across the bridge of his nose, and to his jawline.

"You're still devilishly handsome," Zac said wryly.

"I can see you're feeling better."

He shook his head. "Ironically, you seem to know how to calm me down."

"Because I've been there. I'm four hundred and twenty. I know a few things," Nye said, tapping a finger on his temple.

He might have calmed him down, but Zac knew that it was only one time of many. Next time the vampire mightn't be here, and he couldn't let himself rely on someone else like that. He had to learn how to rely on himself.

"Do you have any idea why Regulus brought you here?" Nye asked.

"The obvious reason would be because of her."

"Yeah, but why?"

"He wants something she has access too," he said with a shrug. "That much I know."

Nye grunted, but didn't answer. Instead, he looked out across the city.

"Do you know what she's looking for?" Zac asked.

"Not a bloody clue. It's got to do with witches, though. Always does." Nye shivered, pulling his coat closer around him, even though he wouldn't feel the cold. "And witches give me the heebie-jeebies, if you know what I mean."

Zac raised an eyebrow.

"The creeps, mate."

He snorted. "It's always witches."

"That's what I say," Nye exclaimed. "People say it's us vampires who get into the most shit, but the way those witchy types can worm their way into your head... Bloody hell, they should come with a warning label or somethin'."

Despite his best efforts to the contrary, Zac found himself liking Nye. Perhaps one day they could become friends. The vampire had a way of explaining things that made the impossibly difficult sound easy.

"People change for two reasons," Nye said with a faraway look on his face. "Either they learn enough that they want to change, or they've been hurt enough that they have to. It's the same for us."

Zac laughed. "Nye, you're a bloody poet."

"I'd have given Will Shakespeare a run for his money," he drawled. "Seriously, I've been around almost five hundred years. I learned how to read people and pretend to be things I wasn't from the best of the best spymasters the English had to offer. It's hard not to be this awesome."

Zac stifled a groan, suddenly feeling a lot better. A lot lighter.

Nye clapped him on the shoulder. "If I can pass

some of that on, then I will. You bloody well need it."
He looked Zac over and asked, "Ready to go back?"

Looking down onto Regent Street as the dawn lightened the night into a dreary grey, Zac nodded. Time to screw his head back on and focus. He couldn't lose himself now.

Turned out, they got a summons from Regulus that same day.

Zac and the Six arrived at the house in Hampstead in the early afternoon, assembling in the downstairs sitting room. The Roman wasted no time laying out his assignment. "As you all know, there has long been a rumour about a coven of witches operating in London that has a bit of a nasty reputation. They have something I want, which the Hunter wants as well. She's been hanging around asking a lot of questions and having secret meetings with witches and priests. I want to derail her efforts and find out what she knows."

"Is Tristan still with her?" Nye asked.

"It would seem so."

"What do you want us to do with him?"

"Whatever you want as long as it results in him being in pain." Regulus pulled a piece of paper from his back pocket and unfolded it. "I'm sending you all to a party."

"A party?" Zac asked, a little surprised.

"*The Coronet Theatre* in South London," he said, flinging the flyer at Nye. "They have a meeting scheduled with a witch who is part of the coven. A defector. This Halloween Ball is meant to be a cover."

"What do you need us to do?"

"Find out what the witch has to say and what the Hunter intends to do about it. And if you can capture her and that little shit, Tristan, then all the better."

"And the informant?" Nye asked.

"Capture it. The half-breed will be useful to me."

Zac wanted to know what he meant by half-breed, but he knew better than push for answers to questions that weren't his to ask.

"When is this?" Maddox asked.

"Tonight." The Roman nodded towards the door. "You have your orders."

It was their cue to leave. As they filed out of the room, Regulus held Nye back. Zac faltered a moment, unsure if he should wait for him.

"Go," the spy said. "I'll catch up."

Following the others outside, Zac wondered what he was going to do tonight. It seemed he was going to face Aya in a matter of hours. Could he bring himself to capture her after everything they'd been through? He'd risked everything to save her, *twice*, and she'd died to save his life... then she'd stabbed him in the back.

Any sane person would plot their revenge against

the woman who tricked them into loving her to get what she wanted. But he wasn't sane.

As Nye caught up to them, Zac flipped up the collar of his coat. Looked like he was about to go to the party of the century.

CHAPTER 14

The frosty London air hung around Zac like icicles, the clear sky sparkling with stars only his vampire eyes could see—the light pollution was thick this deep inside the city.

Perched on the roof of the old *Coronet Theatre*, jamming his hands deep into the pockets of his heavy black coat, he could see the entire street laid out beneath him. The tube station to the left, with its steady stream of human commuters, the *Elephant and Castle* pub opposite, bathed in the neon orange glow of the lights that dotted the road. Directly below, the footpath was lined with revellers dressed in their Halloween costumes, waiting for security to let them into the theatre.

All kinds of characters were present, from the stock standard devils and angels, to zombies, fairies, vampires, and other random madness. He knew the crowd was also littered with the real thing, masked not only by their costumes, but by witch's magic.

Regulus had more than vampires in his employ. Sympathetic witches had met the Six earlier and worked their magic. Now they could move about the theatre with no trouble from outside interference. Even Aya wouldn't be able to sense them, though Zac wondered if his blood had been silenced by the spell. Maybe that was the point.

Zac was steeling himself for the moment he'd lay eyes on her. He'd proved himself to the Roman and it was time for him to go solo, to send a message to Aya and her half-breed friend—the 'informant' she was said to be meeting here. If he delivered it was another question entirely, but his presence alone would be warning enough that Regulus' reach was absolute.

Still, Zac was unprepared when his gaze locked onto Aya's familiar form hidden by the fake hanging plants dangling between the windows of the pub.

She wasn't alone.

The other form was also obscured, but he instantly recognised Tristan pressed close to her, talking earnestly in her ear. The sight of them together burned a hole through his heart. She refused him and trusted the knight with this task. He imagined his glare was so full of malice, they would feel it burning into them and look up to find him on top of the theatre.

But Tristan's arms wound around Aya's waist, his hands on the small of her back. Zac's anger was an inferno burning into what was left of his soul. She let her head fall into the curve of his shoulder, her delicate hand coming to rest above his heart... and Zac felt like he was dying.

She hadn't heard him yet. His tentative grip on his humanity must have dulled his blood. Well, in that case, he would just have to let it go. He couldn't take it anymore—the hurt, the longing. After all this time, seeing her with Tristan was the final straw. It seemed death was the one who would claim him. This life needed to be destroyed.

Zac imagined himself tearing Tristan apart as he stared down at them. He fantasised about ripping his arms off and plunging the ragged bones into his heart, killing the vampire who took his love away, relishing the life slipping from his eyes. The blood that would pool on the ground at his revenge, seeping into the asphalt, trickling down into the storm drains, staining everything with his hate.

Unable to watch anymore, Zac tore his gaze from them and went back inside the theatre.

And he turned his humanity off like he would a light switch, the ragged ends of it searing as they fell away.

Inside, he met up with Nye, who was standing on the stairs, watching the crowd of humans mill about. He raised an eyebrow at him. "You're different."

"They're here," he said, ignoring the spy's comment. "Have you seen the half-breed?"

"That's her." Nye nodded towards a young woman who was weaving through the crowd, looking over everyone she passed.

She was quite pretty for a witch. Alabaster skin, long, straight chestnut hair, big brown eyes.

Zac inhaled her scent as she walked past and frowned. She was oddly familiar, though he had never laid eyes on her before. She didn't turn their way. Whatever magic had been woven over them rendered them negligible.

"I'll shadow her." Nye elbowed him and disappeared into the throng of people.

Pushing past anyone who stepped in his way, Zac went back upstairs, content to watch from the balcony. Up here, there was another bar and almost as many people. A roving performer shoved a tray of drinks under his nose and he took one, downing it in one go. Zac had never totally let go of his humanity before and it was an odd sensation. Whatever was going to happen tonight, the thing that lived inside of him would take care of it.

Leaning over the balcony, he watched the half-breed mill about the crowd, following her erratic movements as she searched the theatre for Aya. Nye was shadowing her every move. The witch was oblivious to the predator on her heels.

Zac filtered out the music and the noise, feeling out the presence that'd become as familiar as his brother

Sam's. Zac let his gaze scan the crowd and it wasn't long before it settled on a familiar form.

She wasn't wearing a costume—it would've been pointless. Aya was unmistakable. Tristan hovered behind her a ways like a perverted bodyguard.

The old Zac, of thirty minutes ago, would have seethed in anger at the sight of them together. Now, he couldn't care less. Now, he would capture and kill.

That was the moment she looked up and saw him leaning over the edge of the balcony, her blue eyes noticeable even from the third floor. His expression didn't change from the menacing scowl that had become his default as recognition flooded her features, then confusion as she realised his blood was masked.

No, not masked. Silent, *gone*.

He let his gaze flicker to the half-breed and back, Aya inclining her head as if she were thanking him. *If only she knew.* Nye was directly behind her mark, camouflaged by magic. Regulus knew Aya would trust him, and that trust would lead her into their trap.

He wondered how smart she really was.

Her heart skipped several beats when Aya laid eyes on Zac. He was the last person she expected to see here... not for a long time.

Casting out her mind, expecting to hear the familiar soothing sound of his blood, she frowned. She couldn't hear anything. His eyes flickered to her right and she inclined her head, acknowledging his gesture.

Letting her gaze wander in the direction he'd indicated, she noticed the woman staring at her. *So, this was the half-breed Joseph had sent us to meet.* The insider.

Forcing Zac from her thoughts, she strode towards the woman and grasped her arm. Leading her off to a dark corner, Tristan trailed them, his eyes scanning the surrounding people.

"I'm Coraline," the half-breed said.

"Start talking," Aya hissed, not caring for her introduction. "I want answers. All of them." The half-breed shrunk back against the wall and Aya sighed at her sudden fearfulness. "I'm not going to hurt you, Coraline. But understand that I am annoyed. This," she gestured to the surrounding party, "is an enormous risk." One that she feared was already about to pay out... in full.

"I know, but it's the only place that we could come to hide from them."

Aya didn't really believe her. "You're a member of the coven."

"Yes."

"What does that mean?"

"The coven, my family, is ancient. Our history tells that we were born out of the remnants of war. Our mother was branded the Betrayer of her people and our father was the Tyrant King. The story is so old, many believe it now to be a myth."

"Human witches have only existed for the last two thousand years."

"No, they haven't," Coraline said firmly. "That's the coven's claim."

"You also claim to be something more," Aya said, forcing her to explain further.

"We are, that I know for sure. We are like you."

Aya's eyes widened. Like her? Celestine? It wasn't possible. But it would explain the potency of Zac's blood—why it reinvigorated her power, why it sung to her like starlight. *Victoria had Celestine blood. But how?* It had something to do with the ones Coraline had called the Betrayer and the Tyrant King.

"Victoria was one of us until Regulus took her," Coraline continued. "A far distant cousin, but of the same blood. We knew she was looking for you and hoped that with her death, something good would come of it."

Aya scowled. "Well, for you, at least."

"You have a stake in this, Hunter. They are witches foremost, and they have become a greater threat than we'd imagined. Even in the way they treat their own. Those without the blood are cast out. They're killed on sight if they dare return."

"You speak of them as if they were not your kin."

"Blood links us, but that's all. I don't want any part in a single thing they have their hands in. Insanity, greed, and power drive them, and it will destroy everything."

Aya sighed. "*Lovely.*"

"Far from it," Coraline said. "They need to be stopped. The centuries of trying to keep bloodlines pure have only driven them insane."

"Inbreds," Tristan interrupted, shaking his head. "Genetics at its finest."

Aya elbowed him sharply, turning her annoyed glare back onto Coraline. "What are they looking for?"

"I don't know," she said with a shake of her head. "Only the inner circle knows. And I'm not inner circle."

"Then we need to get inside and find out."

"You want to infiltrate the coven yourself?" Tristan asked in surprise.

"Why are you so shocked, Tristan?" she hissed. "Of course, I do. Apparently, this is a lot closer to home than we first thought. Coraline has implied that we share the same blood. If that is true, then I have to see it for myself. I have to talk to this inner circle."

"You're goin' to expose yourself to them? Arrow, no. That'd be suicide."

She regarded the horrified look on the knight's face. Perhaps he was right, but there was no known way for her to truly die. If they killed her, she would resurrect.

"If you really want to go, I can get you in," Coraline said, eyeing the knight.

"How?"

"You must be one of the blood to enter their sanctuary."

"If I am like you," Aya narrowed her eyes, "then I don't need you to get inside."

Coraline nodded. "Technically, no."

"Where is their sanctuary?"

"In Bloomsbury. There's an abandoned tube station near the museum. They use the abandoned tunnels, but the whole place is warded against outsiders. There's no chance of getting in unless I'm with you. I can guide you through safely."

Aya regarded this for a moment. "How can I contact you?"

Coraline dipped her hand into the pocket of her jeans and pulled out a card, pressing it into her hand. "When you're ready, you can contact me here."

The witch backed away, melting into the sea of people. It seemed the meeting was over.

Looking at the piece of paper in her hand, all it contained was a number. Aya assumed it was to a cell phone and memorised it. Sighing, she ran a hand over her face, unsettled at the tension that had built inside her.

"Tristan," she said, leaning in close so he could hear her over the music. "I need some time."

"But what if the Six—"

"If the Six are here, then let them come and play." Taking in his worried expression, she rolled her eyes. "Give me some time to think, then I will meet you at the bar upstairs. Twenty minutes. I just need to process this."

Thankfully, Tristan nodded and backed off, leaving her alone.

Hoping to see Zac, Aya scanned the crowd, but couldn't sense him. It worried her to think what he was doing here, not to mention what Coraline had just told her. Thoughts flew through her brain so fast she couldn't grasp onto any of them for long.

Regulus took Victoria because she was part of the coven. He'd hoped she would be his way to whatever the witches were hiding—her blood was his key to their sanctuary—but somehow, it'd backfired. The Roman was going to stop the coven, then take whatever they were embroiled in and use it for his own gain. Of course, he was.

The coven claimed to be of the same blood as Aya, which seemed like an impossibility considering the first witches weren't gifted that much power by her family. Still, Victoria was one of them, which meant her blood had carried over to other vampires she had made. That made Zac and his brother Sam vampires with Celestine blood... if what the coven claimed was true.

And Zac was inside the theatre, in London of all places, and he knew she was looking for Coraline. When she'd seen him looking down from the balcony, it'd felt like he wasn't even there. His blood was silent, and she was afraid to think about what that meant.

Letting out a slow breath, she turned in the

opposite direction to Tristan, trying to find a quiet corner. Alcohol and blood would soothe her for now.

Zac wandered down the stairs to the first floor, not in any hurry. There was a band playing onstage—some kind of jazz ensemble done up as zombies—and most of the humans present were watching the performance. Lingering in the shadows, he saw who he was looking for. Aya was talking to the half-breed and Tristan was standing to the side, looking horrified.

As he watched their fevered exchange, he knew something big was going down. The way she was reacting to whatever the half-breed was saying made him wonder if she had a personal stake in what the coven was plotting. More so than there being witches involved. He wondered what it was.

As the half-breed woman walked away, he watched as Nye followed her. He was going to take the witch once she'd left the theatre. His job was to shadow Aya while the rest of the Six were there to help take her down if it came to that. Maybe they would do his job and kill Tristan for him... or maybe he would do it first.

Aya leaned over and said something into Tristan's ear and he nodded, wandering off in the opposite direction. She watched until he disappeared, then stalked into the hallway that ran along the side of the stage.

Zac ducked into the opening behind him and waited. The hall was lined with khaki-coloured camouflage nets and fake spider webs, and a multitude of costumed humans passed him by. When he saw her approach, oblivious to the fact he was watching her, he froze. She stood out like the brightest star in the universe. How he hated and loved her all at the same time. He knew what he had to do.

As she stood beside him, he grabbed her arm, pulling her across the hall into the dark corner of a room that'd been decorated to resemble a Japanese garden. Her surprise didn't pass unnoticed, but he ignored it, casting his gaze around the room to see if they'd been followed. All he saw were drunk humans and occasional performers dressed up as geishas.

"What are you doing here?" Aya asked, confused and horrified at the same time.

Zac was pained, his eyes closed, fighting what he knew he had to do. *Unless...* There was only one way out, one way where she wouldn't be caught.

"You need to leave," he whispered in her ear. "It's a trap. Upstairs, there is a door that leads to the roof. All other exits are being watched."

"I already suspected as much," she replied.

He let his gaze drop and saw her hands tremble. Why was he warning her after what she'd done to him?

"This is the only time I will help you. After that, you're on your own," he snarled. There was only one explanation why he was here of all places, and she looked like she had finally gotten it.

"You're with him, aren't you?" She shook her head in disbelief, her eyes wide. "You're with Regulus."

He shrugged, glared, then looked away. "You need to forget the half-breed and get out. This is your last warning."

Aya's expression fell and Zac knew she'd finally understood why she hadn't sensed him. His blood wasn't masked—his blood was silent, his humanity gone.

"Zac, *no*," she whispered, not trying to cover the shock in her voice. "Come back."

"You left," he said. "You made a choice... and so did I."

"Regulus has gotten to you." She shook her head in disbelief. "He's turned you into the thing you loathe."

"He only helped me see that fighting it was pointless."

"No, Zac. It's not pointless. Come back. It's not too late."

"Why would I want to?" he scoffed. "After what you did to me?"

"I did it to keep you safe," she breathed into his ear.

"*I don't believe you.*"

Zac turned to leave, to melt back into the crowd, but she pinned him against the wall, using all her strength against him. Letting her body meld into his, she pressed her knee between his legs, forcing them apart, grinding herself against him. Leaning up, she tentatively kissed his bottom lip, coaxing his mouth to hers. He didn't have the strength to turn away, his body tensing under her touch.

As Aya kissed him, he couldn't fight anymore. The burning need for her seared the jagged threads of the last of his humanity—the echo of what once was. Her mouth found his, the tip of her tongue coaxing him to part his lips. His hands found the back of her neck and face, and he pulled her close, crushing his mouth to hers, kissing her with all the longing and pain he'd felt since she'd left. It consumed him to where he almost lost control, his tongue clashing with hers, their lips bruising.

All at once, he pulled away. Aya allowed him to push her back, breaking physical contact.

"Zac," she whispered huskily, "I know you're still in there."

Sighing heavily, he leaned his forehead against hers, restraining himself at the contact. "I saw you," he said, carefully guarding his voice. "If you don't leave and take him with you, I will not hesitate. I will kill him." He was oddly satisfied when he watched her face contort into horror. Why the hell did she care so much?

She grasped the lapels of his coat. "Zac—"

"Leave," he said without emotion. "Leave before I kill him."

She took several steps back, a look of pain contorting her pretty features. Then she was gone.

Zac had to let her go. If he didn't, the Six would corner her and Regulus would've won. This was her last free pass. Next time he wouldn't lift a finger to help her. As long as Nye got the half-breed, then they would've satisfied the Roman enough. Aya would keep.

Besides, this wasn't about her. It was about murdering Regulus.

Zac waited a few minutes before peeling himself away from the wall and ascending the stairs to the third floor. Seeing no signs of the Six, he began to worry. Pushing through the door, he stepped onto the roof and stifled a surprised gasp.

The Six were circled around Aya and Tristan, their heavy black coats flapping in the icy breeze. *They knew.* They knew he'd warn her. There was no other explanation for the deviation in their plan.

"Look what we caught, Zac." Maddox laughed. "Just as planned."

Zac said nothing, his gaze darkness as he took in the two vampires in the centre of the roof. He couldn't let on that he'd tipped them off, or he was as good as dead. They assumed, but none of them had any proof... and he couldn't give them any.

He turned his glare onto the Six, who'd quickly come to know that it meant trouble of the greatest kind.

"Alive, dead, or maimed?" Nye asked, frothing at the mouth for some action.

"Alive," Zac snarled. "The condition doesn't matter."

Before the Six could move, all hell broke loose. Rob and Holly were dead in under a second, their bodies grey and decaying as they suffered their true deaths.

Zac let his eyes swirl into fury-ridden black orbs as he lunged for Tristan, the image he'd conjured earlier teasing the monster within. Maddox had him at a stalemate, their skill evenly matched.

Zac lunged from behind, grasping the vampire's right arm and wrenching it with all his might. He felt the bone pop from its socket at the shoulder, bones crunching under his hands, but it didn't come free from his body. Tristan roared in pain, alerting Aya to his plight as Zac sunk his fangs into the joint, attempting to sever the limb.

Maddox was thrown over the edge of the roof, the vampire screaming as he hurtled to the street below. He would survive—it was only four stories. Then Aya was on Zac, pulling him off Tristan.

Turning on her, blood dripping down his face, Zac flung her away, her body colliding with the brick wall behind. To any bystander, he would've looked positively demonic—lips pulled back in a feral snarl over his bloodied fangs, eyes black as the purest night.

Aya faced him with a calm expression, her blue eyes full of sadness. Zac realised then that he was the only one left and he would either prevail or die. Nye and Rix, he noticed, were dead, but not desiccated, and Pyke was impaled on the iron barrier at the roof's edge. They, along with Maddox, might still revive.

Then the question that'd haunted the back of his mind came to the surface. Did he want to die or go back?

"Zac," she hissed, bringing his attention back to her. "Stop this."

"Kill me," he sneered, wiping the blood from his face with the back of his sleeve. "That's the only way I'll ever stop."

"Arrow." Tristan grimaced, holding his limp arm. "He's gone. There's no saving him. Not right now. We need to go."

"Yes, go, Tristan. Go, so she can ruin you, too," Zac spat at them, glaring through his eyelashes. "Or perhaps I shall just kill you now to save you the pain."

"*Zac*," Aya took a step forwards. Tristan tried to pull her back, but she shook herself free.

Zac lunged for her, his anger taking hold, but her arms were around his neck in an iron grip that left him breathless. All she had to do was tear and he'd be dead. Perhaps that'd be better than the life he'd resigned himself to.

"I'm sorry, Zac," she murmured into his ear before everything went dark.

CHAPTER 15

I t was Nye's face Zac woke to some time later

The spy's messy brown hair and pale face were spotted with dried blood, telltale signs they'd been fighting. He was looking at Zac with a concern that annoyed the hell out of him. It wasn't like Zac hadn't had his neck snapped before. Sitting up, he pushed Nye away and rubbed some feeling back into it.

"Thought we were goners then," Pyke said, scratching the new skin on his stomach where it'd healed over.

"Why'd she leave us alive?" Maddox asked. Obviously, he'd survived his fall.

"She still has a soft spot for Zac." Nye nodded in his direction.

Zac glared at the four vampires with such force that they shut their mouths and looked away, knowing better than to push him further.

"Holly and Rob are gone," Pyke said.

Zac didn't even care. "I suppose that makes you the Four now."

"Until we get two more," Pyke said.

Maddox groaned. "We screwed up."

"Not entirely." Nye grinned mischievously. "We were out of it for a while, so I hope she's still there."

"*Nye...*" Zac hissed through his teeth.

"Take a chill pill, Zac Attack."

The first signs of dawn were staining the horizon, the dull grey glow of another miserable day was lightening the night as the five vampires jumped over the side of the old building down to street level. The entire area around the theatre was oddly deserted— nothing moved, human or vehicle. Nye led them to where he'd parked his car the night before, down a side street away from prying eyes.

Fishing out his keys, he unlocked it, the indicators flashing orange. Then he threw open the trunk with a flourish and proclaimed, "Ta da!"

The half-breed woman was bound and gagged in the trunk, her cheeks blotched red and stained with tears. She looked up at the sudden light and cowered back when she saw the five men looking down at her.

"Do you want to know what she told the Hunter? I know that, too." Nye was almost dancing on the spot with excitement.

"You know everything, don't you?" Zac drawled, jamming his hands into his coat pockets.

"I was a spy, Zac. Cut me some slack, mate." He

closed the trunk and rapped his knuckles on the top, nodding to the others.

"We'll take the other car," Maddox said, getting the hint. "Consider the bodies dealt with."

"Get in," Nye said to Zac, opening the driver's side door.

Climbing in beside him, Zac cut straight to the chase. "What did she have to say?"

"A great deal," Nye said, turning on the engine.

"Spit it out."

"Settle down, mate," he said, pulling out from the alley and onto the road. "She said the coven is of the same blood as the Hunter. I'm guessing she meant whatever she is a hybrid with, because I can't see it having anything to do with Arturius' blood. She didn't even know what they're hiding. Apparently, she's planning to get the Hunter inside their sanctuary."

"Did she say where this sanctuary was?"

"Bloomsbury. There's an abandoned tube station near the museum somewhere. From what the half-breed told the Hunter, the place is warded up to the eyeballs with all kinds of nasty spells. Only one of the blood can get in."

One of the blood.

Victoria was one of the coven before she was turned. Her blood ran with his and if what this half-breed woman said was true, then it was Celestine blood. That was why it was potent to Aya, but it also meant he could get inside the sanctuary.

Zac wondered how sure Regulus was of this, but perhaps he already knew. Maybe that was the real reason he'd been recruited. The Roman wanted into the coven and if he couldn't manipulate Aya to get in for him, he would either use the half-breed or his new protégé. He was Regulus' failsafe.

"She's Regulus' ticket inside," Zac mused.

"Bingo."

"I wonder what he plans to do once he's gotten in?"

"I guess we'll find out. I mean, if he wants us to go. He's been trying to find out more about the coven for a few hundred years. He never told me, but I assume that's where Victoria came from. I also think you have something to do with it as well." Nye glanced over at him as if he was trying to break through his poker face. The spy really was good with information. "Regulus does have a penchant for the bloodthirsty, but he's paid more attention to you than he has me or any of the others in the Six over the years. That leads me to believe that it's personal."

"I think we both know you've already worked it out," Zac said evenly, looking out the window as the grey streets passed by.

"You're of Victoria's blood."

He rolled his eyes. "Hallelujah."

"But that means... If what the half-breed implied was true... You also have the same blood as the Hunter."

"Which is why I get all the attention, apparently."

"I would keep that to yourself if I were you," Nye warned. "Say nothing to the others. Say nothing about it to me again."

"Wasn't planning on it," he said dryly.

He didn't intend to let anyone control him ever again.

It wasn't long before they arrived back at the apartment block where Maddox, Rix, and Pyke were waiting inside the parking garage.

As the outer door folded upwards, the car shot through and pulled into an empty spot at the rear. Popping the trunk as they got out, Nye dragged the half-breed out and dumped her unceremoniously onto the concrete floor.

She scrambled to her feet as best she could with her shins gaffer-taped together and let out a muffled cry as she came face to face with the five male vampires.

Nye reached out and pulled her to his side, half carrying her across the garage to where a door was set into the wall. He opened it and led Zac into a storage area, as the others entered the stairwell going back up to the apartment. When Zac stepped into the room fully, what caught his eye was the large steel cage in the middle of the room. The scent of stale blood filled his head and he gave Nye a look.

"What?" he asked, feigning innocence. Pulling the half-breed hard into his side, he smiled. "Sometimes we need to take extraordinary measures with our house guests."

Zac watched the witch's face fall into an expression of horror as she quaked. "Enough," he said. "Put her in and get out."

"Fine." He sighed. "Just don't go overboard." The spy pulled open the door of the cage and pushed the witch inside, none too gently. She fell to her knees and let out a sob, the tang of blood from her scraped knee filling the air.

"I'm calling this in," Nye said, closing the cage door. "If you want to question her before Regulus gets here, you better do it now. I doubt he'll be as merciful as you."

Zac nodded, not taking his eyes off the half-breed, who knelt on the concrete floor, hands and legs bound with gaffer tape and a gag stuffed in her mouth.

Nye had been good to him so far. It was easy to forget he was one of the Six and one of the bad guys. Nye was still capable of doing horrible things in the name of Regulus... they all were.

Once the spy had gone, Zac opened the cage door and stepped inside, not in the least bit worried about the half-breed's power. He was protected against her from the magic that'd been placed over him and the Six the previous evening. As he approached her, she tried to scurry away from him, but he knelt and caught her hands. Regarding her for a moment, he ripped off the gaffer tape from her wrists with a sigh.

She looked up at him in disbelief, allowing him to pull the gag from her mouth, though he left it hanging around her neck.

"What's your name?" he asked, still crouched in front of her.

"Coraline," she said slowly, the distrust in her voice clear as day.

"Coraline," he said, testing the sound of it. "Pretty name."

"What do you want?"

"Oh, I think you know what we want."

She frowned at him, rubbing her wrists. "No, what do *you* want?"

Zac stood and took a step back.

"You're being... *nice*," she said.

His eyes narrowed in warning and he caught the sound of her heart skipping a few beats. Allowing his lip to curl into a sneer, he said, "I can do this the hard way if you prefer." Coraline visibly cringed away from him, her back hitting the bars on the opposite side of the cage. "Thought so."

"You've bigger things to worry about than the Hunter," she said.

"Oh, you mean the coven? I already know about them." He didn't wait for a reply. "What are they hiding?"

"I don't know," she hissed.

"How were you going to get the Hunter inside?"

"Go and die," she spat.

"Sorry," he said. "Already did that."

"Do you even understand who you're dealing with? Who the Hunter really is?"

Zac glared at her. "I know what she is. I know who she was."

"Then... Are you one of them?"

"No," he scoffed. She was stupid enough to think he was one of the Romans.

"Then you work for them," she clarified. "That's just as bad." Them? The half-breed didn't even know that Regulus was the last remaining founder, did she? She didn't know shit. "They will all die, you know. With or without her help."

"Do you even know how 'they' plan to kill them?" he pressed.

She glared up at him, her jaw set in defiance. "If I knew, I wouldn't tell you."

"You know nothing," he scoffed. "You're only a glorified blood bag to the Romans. You're only the way in and when they've got what they want, then you'll die."

"Wait—"

"You know nothing, Coraline."

Striding from the cage, Zac slammed the door closed, driving the deadbolt home. Coraline knew nothing that interested him. She was useless.

She watched him, her heart racing as he secured the chains and padlock.

"We are like her," she stated. "She can kill them... and *so can we.*"

He looked at her with a raised eyebrow. Well, this was something new. Without a second glance at the witch, Zac turned and left the storage room.

"They will kill her," she shouted after him, her pleas falling on deaf ears. "Once they've got what they want, she will die her true death!"

Aya didn't stop running until she'd crossed London Bridge and South London was behind them, across the Thames. Standing in front of Monument tube station, she let her head drop into her hands. As Tristan came to a halt beside her, he pulled her into his side, his left arm still hanging awkwardly.

"I'm sorry, Arrow," he murmured into her hair.

"What have I done?" Her voice was muffled against his shirt and she pulled away.

It was barely dawn. The street around them was empty and the tube station was still closed with heavy metal doors pulled over the entranceways. Other than the flock of pigeons perched along the roof of a building across the street, they were alone.

Regulus knew Aya would go to London to search for

Victoria's family. He could only know that if he understood how she had enough power to destroy Arturius. That was why he wanted Zac. He was a link to her, and he'd inherited a version of Celestine blood. It was diluted, but he wanted to use it as an in to the coven. Zac was his fail-safe. How had she been so blind?

She'd left Zac heartbroken back in Ashburton, and maybe Regulus had known she would leave him that way. He'd taken advantage of her stupidity.

"Did you know?" she asked abruptly, turning on Tristan, her voice dangerously low.

He took a step back at her sharp tone. "No, I swear I had no idea."

"You better be telling the truth, Tristan."

"Cross my heart and hope to die." He held his hands up, palms out as if he were trying to calm her. "The last I heard of Zac before I met him that day in the bar, was when Victoria sent Regulus word that she'd turned him. I swear to God."

Aya stared into his eyes and felt the truth in his words. Letting out a long breath, she turned her back on him. So many things had happened in such a short space of time. So many secrets uncovered that'd only led her to even more.

"If you want to go after him, I will help you," he said with a grimace.

"I can't," she said. "You were right."

"About what?"

"I can't save him just yet. He's gone."

"You're goin' to abandon him?"

"No," she spat. "I could never abandon him. *Ever*. I need to get into the coven and find out where their true intentions lie. Only then can I figure out what to do about him. This is bigger than... It's—"

"To do with your true self," Tristan finished for her.

"The Tyrant King and the Betrayer..." she murmured. Who was the Betrayer? Somewhere along the line, a Celestine had betrayed them, but why? Only when she could meet with the coven could she get the entire story. Whether it was the truth still remained to be seen.

Tristan was frowning at her as the icy morning wind whipped around them.

"Tristan," she reached out and placed a hand on his arm, "it's time you knew the truth."

CHAPTER 16

When they finally sat in their over-the-top hotel room did Aya begin the overwhelming task of telling Tristan her story. She began by explaining who she'd been before Arturius had turned her, and how important it'd been for her and her brother to guide the witches in their first generations. Then she explained Katrin's betrayal, why she'd created the Romans, what Arturius had done to her, and how she killed Titus and escaped her prison, only to find her family dead.

She spoke long into the day, all the while Tristan listened with an unreadable expression, his gaze never leaving her. When she was finally done, silence descended upon the room and she was almost certain that something terrible was going to happen. Some kind of retribution for giving away her secrets like she had always been led to believe. But there was no sound other than the muffled roar of traffic passing by on the street below.

Finally, Tristan shuffled in his seat. "Shit, I had no idea, Arrow. I'm sorry."

Aya stared across the room into space and shrugged. "For a long time, I believed that something terrible would happen if I told anyone the truth of who I was. Not until Zac. He proved there was no consequence to letting the secret go. He told his brother when he thought I was truly dead."

"You gave him your blood to save him?"

"Yes. Katrin had cursed him. I couldn't let him die, so I saved him. What I didn't expect was for Arturius to rip my heart out."

"Shit, Arrow. I've seen you come back from other stuff, but a heart? I still can't fathom it."

"Well, it happened and it's not very pleasant."

Tristan scratched his chest. "Well, I suspect not."

"Now you understand why this is so personal," she told him. "If they claim to be part Celestine, then I need to know for sure. It would explain so much."

"I can't imagine what it means for what they're hidin'."

"I know it can't be good, which is why I need to go to the sanctuary sooner rather than later. If it has something to do with the Celestines, then I might be the only one capable of stopping it. These witches might be descended from one of us, but I am more pure blood than they are."

"Arrow, you know this might be a trap, right? What if they need you and this has all been an elaborate ruse?"

She shook her head. "No, I believe Joseph and Coraline told the truth. Maximus, too. One thing I've become good at is deducing people and their intentions. They all want to see the coven stopped. The inscription on Victoria's headstone was a warning. Even if they don't understand what it means, someone at some point did and still does."

"What do you want to do?"

"Contact Coraline. I want to get in there as soon as possible. Tonight, even."

"What about Regulus?"

"Regulus will die regardless of what happens. I haven't decided about the coven yet. That all rests on what they have to say for themselves. Either way, someone is going to die." And either way, she was going to like doing it.

"Do you want me to call?" Tristan asked, conveniently changing the subject.

"Dial the number then give me the cell," she said, not wanting to admit she didn't exactly know how to work it.

Tristan punched in the number from the card she'd stuffed into her pocket the night before and passed over the cell. Placing it up to her ear, Aya waited as each ring sounded out with a beeping sound. After about ten or so, the line made a clicking sound and went dead.

"No answer," Aya said, looking at the screen. Pressing the redial button, she waited, but the call rang out again.

"Nothin'?"

"If she's not answering, then she must have run into trouble trying to leave the theatre," Aya replied.

"Then the Six took her. I told you we should've killed them while we had the chance."

"Well, there's nothing I can do for her right now."

"You're just goin' to leave her?"

"For now." When Tristan narrowed his eyes and sighed, she said, "Look, Tristan. She knew the risks involved in agreeing to meet with me. There's no doubt now that Regulus wants into the coven, and Coraline is his ticket. He won't kill her. Not yet. That means we've got time."

After their run-in with the Six and Zac, she'd assumed Coraline had gotten away before they could take her. They didn't know for sure, but now everything seemed to point to her being in Regulus' hands.

"I can get into the coven myself," Aya declared. "I don't need Coraline to get through their wards."

"Then why did you bother contactin' her?"

"Because she has inside knowledge of the place and if worse came to worse, then I could use her as a bargaining chip."

"That's a little heartless . . .."

Aya glared at the knight. "I wouldn't let her die. I'd get her out. She is part Celestine, even if it's only a drop." She rose, grabbing her leather jacket and shrugged it on.

"You're goin' now?" Tristan stood sharply, grabbing her arm.

She pulled away, turning for the door. "Stay here."

"No way, Arrow. I'm comin' with you." Tristan grabbed his jacket and made to follow her.

"No," she said firmly. "This is my task. If I bring a vampire into their sanctuary, they'll kill you on the spot. You need to stay."

He dropped his jacket onto the seat and she was relieved she didn't have to fight him this time. "How will I know you're all right?"

"If I'm not back by this time tomorrow... start to worry. If I'm not back in another day, then I'm gone."

"Arrow..."

"Tristan," she said. "I'm a million times tougher than you, ser knight. I won't go down without a fight and besides, I never go down in the first place."

Before he could retort, the door slammed closed behind her and she was gone.

Aya hadn't slept in two days and most other vampires would be dead on their feet, but she was wide awake.

She sat on the roof of a building opposite the British Museum as the early evening traffic drove by on the narrow street below and humans walked the pavement back and forth. Sunday evenings usually saw cities slow down, but not London. It seemed it was busy all day, every day.

Coraline said the sanctuary was located in Bloomsbury in an abandoned tube station. The map she'd located pinpointed it on a street near the museum and it'd been aptly named Museum station. Apparently, they'd closed it in the 1930s because there were two other stations close by—Russell Square and Holborn—and the line would've been too short and crowded for the amount of trains that used the network.

Below her, an *Off Licence* was open, its light spilling out onto the street. People went in and out as they brought cigarettes and booze on their way home.

Somewhere along here on Bury Lane was the concealed entrance to the old station. It looked like the witches had masked it with glamour when they'd moved in, and Aya suspected that unless one knew exactly where it was located, then it could never be found.

Aya hoped that an unsuspecting member of the coven would come along and show her, or she could feel it out when a passerby stepped too close and set off a ripple of power from the ward. Until then, she had to wait.

Across the way, there was a camera shop and a bookstore that were still lit up with people inside. Wandering along the rooftop, she gazed down into an alleyway where several buildings had security entrances—these were apartments. Underneath all this clamour had to be the disused tunnels Coraline had spoken of.

She could feel something in the air, but it was vague. Every time she tried to focus on it, it slipped away into nothingness.

Aya watched as a man walked down the alleyway beneath her. He was human, but she watched him anyway, hoping his movement would uncover something. The air shifted slightly as he passed a blank, windowless wall. The man kept walking, oblivious. As soon as he rounded the corner, Aya was at street level, staring at the wall.

She could always sense the sickly-sweet residue of witches' magic, but here she could feel nothing. It was just a wall. If she hadn't seen the ripple, she wouldn't have suspected otherwise. No length of searching would've uncovered the entrance to the sanctuary.

The coven were smarter than she gave them credit for.

Placing her hand on the wall, she felt a vibration through the brickwork. Coraline had said only one of the blood could get inside. She'd come across similar wards on many occasions. Difficult spells to master, they were highly prized by the covens who cast them.

Trailing her hand across the painted brickwork, the wall shimmered, and the faint outline of an old heavy door appeared before it melted back into nothing.

Looking around, Aya found she was still alone. No one had passed by the mouth of the alley yet. Feeling for the door handle, she grasped metal and twisted, the door opening inwards with a slight creak. Before she was discovered, she slipped inside into the darkness.

It didn't take long for her eyes to adjust to the lack of light and she made out the beginning of a staircase spiralling downwards.

It appeared this was a service entry. The main entrance to the station would've sat along the main road, a block away on the surface.

Without another thought, Aya descended, feeling the air for any wards that might be hidden along the shaft, but nothing was amiss. If any spell was in effect here, it'd dissolved a long time ago... or someone had removed it.

The stairwell opened up into a long hallway, and since there was no other direction to go, she followed it. A few minutes later, she stood in the ticket hall.

It was dark, the only light pooling in from a dozen skylights that'd been set into the celling high above. As it was night, the dull orange glow of the streetlamps inched through the dirty glass.

The walls of the open hall were tiled in a pale green, with the word 'Museum' set into the mosaic in a contrasting dark brown hue. The floor was made of shiny speckled concrete—a style of building that was unfamiliar to Aya. To her left, another staircase descended towards the main platform, and she headed this way—the other entrance led back up to street level where the way was well and truly blocked.

So far, Aya had felt no wards and wondered if Coraline had been telling the truth, or if the 'inner circle' had already noted her presence.

Stepping out onto the platform, she stilled, casting her mind along the silent tracks. The rush of air that traveled down the tunnel ruffled her hair and the muffled sound of trains on other lines echoed dully through the bedrock.

There was no other sound or movement, so she took a tentative step forwards, but before she could take another, the shadows lengthened. A light glowed at the opposite end, warm and inviting. *Witches.*

Readying herself, Aya waited as the light revealed the shapes of several women walking towards her. Thirteen in all, and by the feel of them, she thought this must be the infamous circle.

The lead witch smiled at her, the picture of friendliness, her arms spread open in welcome. Not the picture of horror and evil Coraline had painted, but none of that meant anything. Experience had taught Aya that everything and everyone was deceiving in some way. She took no one at face value.

"Welcome," the woman said, her voice echoing across the platform. "I am Alisandra. I am the matriarch of the coven." The witch glided forward, her long skirt trailing over the dirty floor. A ball of yellowish light hovered above her shoulder—magic lit her way. "And you are Aeriaya."

Well, Aya snorted to herself, *they already seemed to know a lot more than they should*. Alisandra was tall and pale—her skin was the colour of the cream wall that'd concealed the door above—and her hair was as long and straight as Aya's, and just as dark.

Looking her over, Aya could see the resemblance between this woman and Coraline, even if was only slight.

Alisandra smiled when she didn't reply. "We hoped that one day you would seek us out, sister."

"Sister?" she scoffed as the thirteen witches came to a halt beside the matriarch. Thirteen to a coven, thirteen to a circle. It would be spectacular if she had to fight them, and she almost wished she had to.

"You must have many questions to ask of us," Alisandra said. "And I will be glad to answer as many as I am able." The witch gestured to the women standing behind her. "These are the Circle, my sisters and confidants. Come, we mean you no harm."

Warily, Aya stepped forwards, following the matriarch through the middle of the group, conscious of their reserved gazes. This had been way too easy, and she had at least been expecting some kind of resistance. The coven had welcomed her home like a long-lost sister.

When they left the platform and entered the tunnel, the twelve women bade Alisandra farewell as she led Aya on alone, a small blob of light separating from the matriarch's orb and floating with them.

Alisandra stopped in front of a door that'd been set into the wall of the tunnel and opened it. Inside, was what appeared to be an industrial fuse box, all wires and pipes. Across the front, yellow and black tape was crisscrossed, warning people not to tamper with it.

The witch looked back at Aya and smiled, then stepped through the doorway and disappeared, leaving a rippling image behind her.

Of course. The coven were smart enough to mask their sanctuary further and tightly enough that even she couldn't sense it.

Aya followed the matriarch through the ward and emerged into another well-lit passageway. Here it felt more lived in and homely. Several doors were spotted along the corridor at irregular intervals before the path turned a corner ahead.

"Welcome to our sanctuary," Alisandra said. "Granted, it's not much to look at, but it's safe and it's home."

So far, Aya had only uttered one word to the witch and her only response this time was to raise an eyebrow.

"Come," the matriarch beckoned. "My chamber is not far."

Chamber? More like storage closet, Aya thought.

Alisandra's room was decorated with rugs and paintings and was less like a storage closet that Aya had expected. Despite the lack of a window, it was warm and inviting.

Witches tools lay on an altar to one side—a silver bowl, dagger, and assorted herbs—and the back half was separated with a Japanese-style folding screen that was covered in cream rice paper. Aya supposed the witch slept behind the partition.

The matriarch offered her a chair, and she sat opposite, folding her hands in her lap like a seventeenth-century lady.

"I could tell you everything from the beginning," Alisandra began, "but I'm sure you have some specific questions you would like to ask. Perhaps that would be easier? Ask me what you will."

"I am led to believe that you and I share the same blood," Aya stated.

"Yes, that is correct."

"How?"

"I think this might be better explained if I tell you the history of our beginnings."

"I have time," Aya said. "I have a right to know."

"So be it." Alisandra nodded. "In the beginning, the first witch was created from a Celestine woman named Aoife. She took a human woman and created our coven."

"Aoife?" Aya asked slowly, not recognising the name.

"In the stories, Aoife was a member of the Tuatha de Danann royal family. She was a fae, sent to marry the king, known as Lir, to solidify an alliance."

"The fae?"

"Another supernatural race, long extinct in this world," the matriarch told her, mistaking Aya's surprise for ignorance, "but in truth, Aoife was truly a Celestine. Her marriage would serve to put an end to the feud between the Tuatha and the Celestines, but she didn't want any part of it. She was one we call the Betrayer. She created the first witch from her own blood, and from that first witch the coven was born."

The Tyrant King and the Betrayer. Lir and Aoife? Aya shook her head. "You're saying that there was a witch before the Five?"

"You see, Aeriaya, we are descended from the *original* witch, purely separate from your Five. We existed for a full thousand years before you were even born."

For once in her life, Aya was truly driven to silence. The things Alisandra said rung true. Even she knew about the feud between her kind and the Tuatha—it was a part of her people's history that was long dead.

But the supposed act of Aoife creating a witch? That was new.

If all this were true, there would be one fundamental difference between the Five and Aoife's original witch. Aya's family had held back that part of themselves that would've given them a conduit into a realm of power that was too great for a human mind to comprehend. This original witch, whoever she'd been, would've been driven to insanity by the things Aoife's blood conjured.

It explained a lot, actually.

Aya tried to sense Alisandra's emotions but couldn't feel any emanations from her. It was a strange sensation. She could tell something was missing but couldn't quite place her finger on it. The witch had either blocked her from using her ability or she didn't have any emotions at all.

"I know the history," Aya said cautiously. "But not of what you speak."

"No, you wouldn't." Alisandra shook her head. "That kind of betrayal would've sunk deep, wouldn't it? I can imagine your leaders would've wanted to keep it a secret at all costs."

"If the story is true, then why would Aoife want to create a witch? That's the part I don't understand."

Alisandra sighed. "That's the great mystery. As with all things, time erodes memory and what was once important becomes lost."

If there was any truth to this story, then the matriarch was referencing a time that was over three thousand years ago. For a coven who prided themselves in their heritage and pure blood, they sure forgot a lot of important information. Aya was positive she wasn't getting the entire truth, but she couldn't just compel the entire Circle—that was impossible—neither could she force it from them. No, the witches were playing a dangerous game of wits with her.

"There's been a lot of talk about something that your coven is hiding," Aya said, measuring Alisandra's reaction.

"Dear, there has always been a lot of talk about what we do. Not all of it is true. Much of this *talk* is malicious slander from those who oppose us, but I assure you, Aeriaya, we don't oppose anyone. We do not want enemies. That's not why we continue to exist."

"Then why do you?"

"Because we are tasked with keeping the balance." She said like Aya has asked the most absurd question she'd ever heard.

Aya snorted at the blatant dodging of her question. They were hiding something, and they didn't want her to find out what it was. Alisandra was telling her what she thought she wanted to hear.

"We have been searching for a way forwards for centuries," the matriarch continued. "Some time ago, our order was splintered and in chaos. No one seemed fit to follow the old ways anymore. Some of us turned to evil, and the result was less than pleasant. It took a long time to bring the coven back to its former glory. For that to happen, the Circle at that time had to search out our history and rediscover our true heritage."

"And how did they do that?" Aya asked, not liking where this story was leading.

"They had to go back to a place of power and find a sign."

It was then Aya knew the coven had been to her home. They'd entered the clearing. They had Celestine blood and it was the only prerequisite. What had they taken?

Rising to her feet, she snarled, "You've been to my home?"

"No one alive," Alisandra said, holding up a hand. "Almost a thousand years ago, the highest in our coven went to your ancestral home. They hoped to find a sign there, anything to help point us in the right direction. To help us find our true calling."

Aya eyed her suspiciously, not liking what she was hearing. "And what did they find?"

"Bones hanging from the trees, bones in the house... and fields upon fields of white flowers."

Of course. No one had been there since she'd left the night they were killed. *Bones.* Her family and friends had been reduced to bones.

And the flowers. They were one of Aya's strongest memories from her life before. The white flower that'd grown so abundantly around the house. She remembered taking long walks through the forest, the bright green moss that coated the trees, the lush grass, and the flowers. On warm summer days, the sun would make the little field come alive with small white blooms, their yellow centres bright and happy. Often, she'd gather as many as she could carry, knowing they were her mother's favourite.

"Aeriaya, I want to offer you a gift. I understand that with your affliction," she gestured to her, "it doesn't allow for true death."

Aya was violently snapped out of her reverie. They knew how she could die. *Truly die.*

"How?" she asked, trying not to sound desperate.

"The Circle soon found the flower was poison to one not truly Celestine. To those of us who had become infected with vampirism, it delivered them to a true death, where none could be found before."

Aya almost didn't dare to ask, already suspecting the answer. "How did they discover this?"

"They experimented on their own. Barbaric, I know, and I don't condone what they did in the coven's name."

"How did they do it?"

"At first, they made witches ingest the flower whole. Later, they added it to blood and when the vampires fed, it entered their bloodstream. Then the flowers were dried and crushed into a fine powder and the tips of weapons were dipped into it. An oil was distilled... and it was the most effective of the experiments."

It seemed those so-called 'experiments' had gone on for some time.

Alisandra watched her absorb this information carefully. "I know that one day you want to die," she said. "Being truly immortal must take its toll on a creature. Being taken from your true calling and turned into something dark. Becoming something inherent with evil. The Celestines were pure and cared for life deeply. I cannot imagine the things you have been through, Aeriaya. I truly cannot. But know this, if you want to end your suffering, end the torment... you can come to us. Our door is always open to you. You are the one remaining link to an extinct race. Your blood is ours."

After all that time Aya had spent trying to end herself, the solution had been staring her in the face from birth. If she'd had the stomach to go home, would she have worked it out? Would she have ended it there and then, sparing herself two thousand years of suffering? There was no way of knowing for sure.

Still, Aya was worried. Her life was different now. The stakes were higher, and she was sure Alisandra was hiding something. And now the witch was encouraging her to commit suicide? Did the matriarch really believe she would do that?

Aya had to admit she'd been tempted, how could she not? She'd said it to Zac. One day she wanted to return to the Earth, but it would be on her own terms, not the coven's.

Now there was the option, but it also meant that if the coven wished it, they wouldn't hesitate in killing her if she became a threat.

This game just became deadlier than she could've

ever imagined... and she had to keep playing it if she wanted to walk out of the sanctuary alive.

What was the coven trying to wake? Everything Alisandra had said pointed to the original witch. If she could sleep for a hundred and fifty years, it stood to reason that a human witch made with Celestine blood could do the same. It was those parts of herself that allowed her to do as much.

"I have dedicated my existence to fighting those who abuse their gifts," Aya said carefully. "You must understand this is a decision I must consider carefully."

The witch nodded. "I understand."

"I must deal with the remaining Roman vampires. This is my task and once it's done—"

"Of course. We seek to bring an end to the Romans as well. If you require our help, all you have to do is ask."

Aya nodded. Did they know that Regulus was the last? It seemed, by her statement, that they did not, and she wouldn't be the one to correct them.

"When you are ready," Alisandra said with a gentle smile. "Come to me and I will hear you. Whatever you decide, we will be here to help you."

CHAPTER 17

Aya walked for miles across London after leaving the sanctuary, mulling over everything Alisandra had told her, trying to sort the truth from the lies. There was no doubt in her mind that the coven was up to something and that something was not good.

She thought the matriarch was aloof, secretive, and vague about almost everything. The only thing she was clear about was that Alisandra thought it was the best thing for everyone if Aya took her own life.

The moment Aya went back to the sanctuary and told her she wasn't interested in dying anytime soon was the moment they'd do the job for her. She wasn't afraid of her true death. She was only afraid of it coming before she was ready.

What she needed to do was meet with Joseph and find out what'd happened to Coraline... then get more information out of the 'warlock'. Someone had to know something about the original witch. If that's who the coven was trying to wake, then someone must know where she was sleeping.

And what the hell was she going to do once she found out? Aya didn't have a clue, but something had to be done. The original witch would be insane at best, and an insane witch only meant trouble in all capital letters. No wonder that little rag-tag group of witches had gone to so much trouble to find her.

It was still early morning when Aya finally returned to the hotel to put Tristan out of his misery. As she walked through the door, she saw him sitting in the same chair she'd left him in. His gaze snapped up and his expression relaxed into one of relief.

"Arrow." He shot across the room and took her in his arms.

"Have you been sitting there this whole time?" she asked, shrugging him off.

"No," he said slyly.

"Liar."

"What happened?"

"I met with the matriarch of the coven. Seemed they were expecting me."

"Someone betrayed you."

"I don't think so. Witches are a crafty bunch. They probably sensed me walking through their front door."

"What did they have to say for themselves? Are they like you?"

"Yes, it would seem so." She sat on the edge of the bed. "Some fairly outrageous claims were made...

some of which I'm not even sure are true. They seemed to believe they are descended from a witch who was created a full thousand years before the Five."

"What?" Tristan exclaimed. "How is that even possible?"

"It's entirely possible. We all had the ability. This witch was said to have been made with Celestine *blood*."

"That's insane."

Aya snorted. "They *are* insane, if that's what you're asking. There was a reason my parents never gave their blood when they made the Five." Her thoughts went back to the conversation with Alisandra. "The matriarch is hiding something. She dodged any questions I asked about what they were doing. And she said she knew how I could truly die and told me how I should end myself sooner rather than later."

"Arrow." Tristan pulled her into his side, an arm around her waist. "*No*."

"I do want to die someday, Tristan. At least now, I know how."

"You can't be serious?"

"I want to have the option," she said calmly. "One day, I want to pass on. Is that such a terrible thing to want?"

"But the coven are encouragin' you to take your own life... *today*."

"I know."

"They're manipulatin' you."

"Tristan." She sighed, laying a hand over his. "I know exactly what they're trying to pull. If I didn't play along, I wouldn't have left there alive. They're threatened by me and what I represent."

"They think you can stop this weapon they're tryin' to resurrect?"

"Yes. Though, the deeper we get into this, the more I think it's who, not a what."

Tristan frowned. "Who do you think it is? I mean... if it's a who."

"Alisandra kept speaking of the witch the Celestine, this Aoife, had created. She had a lot to say about it. So much, in fact, that I think they believe it's her."

"They're tryin' to awaken the first witch ever created?"

"Possibly," she said, leaning forwards. "Tristan, this witch is nothing like the Five my family had created. Celestine blood is too overwhelming for a human, even in small doses."

"I see..."

"And they've kept their bloodline so constricted, they've forgotten about a thing called the gene pool."

Tristan shook his head, looking conflicted.

"I'm not sure, but everything points to it," she told him. "The one thing I do know is that I have to go back there and at least try to convince them to reconsider."

"And what if they don't?"

"Then..." She shrugged.

"You'll kill them."

"Before they kill me." Usually Aya wouldn't be worried about that, but this time was different. They had the flower.

"But you'll come back... Unless..."

"Probably." She shrugged. "Tristan, we've been in trouble before, but this is the worst kind. I've asked you once already, and now I'm asking if you're entirely sure. This has the potential to become messy, and I can't guarantee that you'll come out alive at the other end... me either."

Tristan's eyes widened. "You're givin' me an out?"

She nodded. "I'm giving you an out. I won't blame you if you wanted to take it. I'll understand."

"Arrow, this is the second time since we got here that you've told me this and I haven't left yet."

"Okay, but don't blame me when you wish you had."

The knight shook his head and changed the subject. "Do you really think they'll listen to you?"

"Maybe, maybe not, but there's only one way to find out."

"I'm goin' with you this time."

"They'll kill you on the spot."

"Not if you're there."

"*Tristan*," she scolded, but he interrupted with such passion, she faltered.

"I won't stay here in this goddamn hotel room while you go out there and fight a bunch of insane witches. You can't do everything on your own. Stop goddamn pushin' me away. You said it yourself. They know how to kill you, for good this time. I won't let it happen. Let me help you."

Aya laughed at his sudden outburst.

"Goddamn, Arrow. You can be so annoyin', you know that?"

She smirked. "It's my mission in life."

It'd been six hundred and sixty years since she'd let someone help her, and that person had been Tristan. It seemed fitting they'd do it again.

Aya frowned. "I am worried about Coraline, though. If she was picked up by the Six or the coven, then she's probably in a hell of a lot of trouble."

"Do you have any idea how we could contact Joseph?"

She shook her head. "I'm sure when someone finally misses her, they'll come running. I want to deal with the coven first. If she's there, then it'll be two birds with one stone."

Tristan didn't look happy about it, but he asked, "When do you want to go?"

"Tonight."

"They hide their door in a brick wall?" Tristan exclaimed when they stood on the darkened alley hidden in the shadow of the British Museum.

"Yes," Aya replied, raising an eyebrow. Placing a hand on the wall where she knew the door hid, the air shifted and the glamour fell.

Opening the door, she looked back at the knight, who was watching her uncertainly. "Are you coming or are you just going to stand there?"

"I'm comin'," he said with a groan and followed her into the dark passageway.

As before, Aya sensed no wards in place as they descended the spiral staircase to the ticket hall. She guessed they'd be met on the platform once again.

"This place gives me the creeps," Tristan whispered behind her.

"Just wait until you meet Alisandra."

"The leader?"

"Yeah, she's a big ball of sunshine and flowers with the venom to match."

"If she tries anythin', I'm—"

"Let's just play it by ear." She elbowed him into silence and led him towards the platform. "Through here."

Just as she'd expected, she sensed Alisandra when they stepped out of the passage and into the open. Aya hadn't noticed before, but the roof stood higher than was needed to take an average-sized train car, even those the humans would've used back at the turn of the century. The platform also stretched longer than was needed to take a modern grouping of twelve or more carriages. The space suddenly seemed overwhelming and it was full to the brim with the cracking energy of the thirteen witches of the Inner Circle.

"Aeriaya," Alisandra crooned, her voice sickly sweet. "We did not expect to see you so soon."

She nodded. "Alisandra."

The witch regarded Tristan, looking him up and down with distaste. "And who is *this*? Why have you brought a vampire into our sanctuary?"

"He is my friend and companion. He had no choice in what he was turned into, and neither did I."

"All vampires should be eradicated. Your companion may not have gone willingly, but what he once was is gone."

"Well, this escalated quickly," Tristan murmured.

Aya ignored him. "Oh, so is that what you're trying to do?"

"Do not underestimate us, Aeriaya. Our ambitions are none of your concern."

"I think they are," she drawled. "You're part Celestine. I was born pure Celestine. That alone makes it my concern."

"We are our own and we work towards our own ends. If you'd returned to your family as you are now, they would've done the same. They would've killed you to end your misery. A creature of power should never have been turned."

Arturius had said the same thing to her not that long ago, but Aya had come to terms with what she'd become well over a thousand years ago. Who was Alisandra to tell her otherwise?

"As witches, you have a duty to heal the Earth," she declared, not falling for her poisonous words.

"We are not bound to your duty," Alisandra scoffed.

"This is not what the Celestines stood for," she said. "I should know. *I was one of them.*"

"Perhaps not, but perhaps not all Celestines were like you."

"You share our blood. I cannot let you continue down this path. You will destroy us all."

"You do not understand what you are dealing with!"

"Maybe not, but I can have a good guess," Aya spat, eyeing the matriarch. "Who are you trying to wake? What are you hoping to do once you've succeeded? Kill all vampires?"

Alisandra's lips curled into a maniacal grin, but she didn't deign to answer.

Aya's jaw tightened as she attempted to keep herself under control. "I will not die by your hand, Alisandra. Not now, not ever. Who are you trying to wake? Answer me and I might spare your life."

Alisandra laughed at her threat. "Your continued existence is an insult to your ancestors, Aeriaya."

"No, your existence is an insult to *me*," she seethed. "I may have been turned, but I am more Celestine than you and your cover ever will be."

The witch let out a long sigh, closing her eyes. "So

be it," she murmured. "You brought this fate upon yourself, Aeriaya. This must be done."

Aya felt the buildup of power immediately. Reaching inside herself, she felt the familiar coil of power at the base of her spine spring to life.

Alisandra's head fell forwards, her hair obscuring her face. *"You are an abomination and you must die."*

"Arrow." Tristan grimaced beside her. *"I can't move."*

Alisandra stepped forwards with a look of triumph on her face, and Aya moved in front of Tristan.

The matriarch had the twelve witches of the Inner Circle behind her and who knew how many witches hid in the shadows. When she drew a silver dagger from under her robe, Aya knew exactly what they'd laced the blade with.

Tristan fell to his knees behind her, gasping for breath.

"Do not panic," Aya hissed. "I'll protect you."

She let go of her power and felt the fire burn down her arm. It pooled in her palm, the entire length of the cavernous platform glowing iridescent blue. The smug look on Alisandra's face faded and the witches faltered.

Aya said a silent prayer to the stars, hoping her plan would work.

Slamming her open palm down onto the platform, the tiles cracked under the force of her power as she fed it into the earth below.

For a sickening moment, nothing happened, but then the ground quaked and a long crack, shining with blue light, split the platform apart... and went straight for the witches.

The thirteen witches threw up their hands all at once, stopping the fissure from pulling the ground out from under them. Roaring in annoyance, Aya pressed even more power into the earth, making it quake enough to dislodge sections of the celling. Dull booms echoed through the tunnels and a thick layer of dust was kicked up into the air.

The witches were forced to drop their makeshift shield as her power slammed into them again, and a few stumbled and fell from the force. Alisandra screamed with rage, obviously not counting on this at all. So, there *were* a few things the coven didn't know.

Tristan gasped next to her and stumbled to his feet—whatever spell they'd cast on him, breaking. "*Arrow...*"

Aya knew she couldn't fight them. Not right now.

Pushing the knight back along the platform, she cried, "Tristan, run. I'm right behind you."

He turned and bolted the way they'd come, not stopping for anything. They had to get out of here before the coven put their wards back up or they would both die here and now.

As Aya ran through the tunnel towards to the ticket hall, she skidded to a halt at the end and summoned her power again. This time, instead of moving the earth, she slapped her hands against the walls of the tunnel. The structure shifted with a violent crack and with an almighty boom, collapsed in on itself. The rush of air and grit pushed her back into the ticket hall and she turned to run, making for the staircase to the surface... but something had changed.

"Tristan, stop!" she screeched.

He skidded to a halt, arms bracing either side of the doorway, breathing heavily.

"Get back, the door is warded."

"It wasn't before," he said, stumbling back.

Ignoring him, she looked around for another way out, but everywhere she flung her mind was barred tight against them.

Looking up in desperation, her gaze halted on the thick glass skylights embedded in the sidewalk above. They hadn't thought to cast a web over the roof, but was she strong enough to break through?

"Tristan," she beckoned, pointing to the roof, "give me a lift."

"Are you strong enough? Because I know I can't break through God knows how many feet of glass and concrete."

"Just give me a lift," she said, pointing towards the tunnel she'd just caved in. "That won't stop them for long."

They were running out of time and she hated to admit it, but that little show had just drained her power considerably, and she'd have to call on it once more before they could get out of here.

Tristan linked his fingers together, bending over so

she could anchor her foot in his hands. "Ready, go," he said and pushed her up with as much force as he could muster.

Aya sailed up through the air, her hands shimmering with blue fire, and pressed against the glass with so much force it cracked and shattered like a thick layer of ice. She came back to land a second later, pushing Tristan out of the way of the falling shards.

"Bloody hell," he cursed.

Ignoring him, she asked, "How high can you jump?"

"Me? What about you?"

"I can make it on my own."

"Fine, give us a lift."

This time, Aya used her strength to give Tristan the extra height he needed to reach the hole she'd just blasted in the street above. He shot through into the night air with a yelp and she didn't wait to see if he'd landed safely before following him. She made it halfway through before he grabbed her shoulder and heaved her up and out.

Not wasting a second, Aya grabbed Tristan's arm and led him down the mostly deserted street, away from the gaping hole in the sidewalk. There'd be some confused human emergency workers descending on Bloomsbury at any moment... not to mention the coven.

"Do you suppose it's safe to go back to the hotel?" Tristan asked once they had gone several blocks.

"Yes." Aya looked back over her shoulder. A moment later, when she was satisfied they weren't being followed, she said, "They won't dare to come after me. Not outside of their territory. It's too much of a risk."

"Then let's get out of here before they come lookin'."

"With pleasure."

CHAPTER 18

Aya and Tristan didn't stop running until they reached the park next to the Ritz. They walked into the foyer of the hotel, the doorman looking at them perplexed. Both vampires were covered in dust and their faces were smeared with it.

"Well, that didn't quite go to plan, did it?" Tristan leaned back against the wall as the elevator slid down the shaft towards the ground floor.

"Not exactly, but at least I know what needs to be done."

The elevator dinged and the doors slid open. An attendant usually stood inside, but it was empty tonight, and Aya was grateful she wouldn't have to compel the poor human. She was too tired for it right now.

"Have you ever done that before?" Tristan asked as the doors slid shut.

"What?" she asked, pressing the button for the fourth floor.

"The hand thing. It was like a bloody earthquake."

"Not in a long time," Aya told him. "Not since before and never like that." If she relied on her power to get her out of unpleasant situations all the time, then she would have no power at all.

When she opened the door to their room, she saw another envelope sitting innocently on the carpet. Joseph had tried to contact them again while they were out smashing holes in the sidewalk.

"The warlock?" Tristan asked, stepping around her.

"It would seem so." She picked it up and ripped the seal open.

Inside was a piece of paper with the words: *Tomorrow, noon. You know where.*

Slapping the note against Tristan's chest, he took it and flipped it over, scanning the message.

"I'm taking a shower," she said before he could say anything.

Of course, she was going to meet him. He had a hell of a lot of explaining to do.

Aya didn't know whether it was stupidity or adrenaline that pushed Joseph to arrange their first meeting here at the British Museum of all places, but to force them under the nose of the coven was foolhardy and it annoyed the hell out of her.

She looked up and saw Joseph staring at them from where he stood on the steps of the museum. With a snarl, she strode towards him, but he took a few steps backwards and disappeared through the main entrance.

"Arrow," Tristan called out after her, "let him be."

"Like hell," she said, and barged inside.

Again, she felt Joseph's presence in the Medieval gallery and couldn't find it in herself to be calm.

"Did you know?" She pushed him hard into the wall, not caring if she had hurt him.

"Know what?" he asked, eyes wide with fear. An angry vampire was one thing, an angry Celestine-hybrid was a whole new kind of horror.

"What they can do to me?" she demanded.

"W-what do you mean?"

"Arrow, he doesn't know." Tristan pushed between them, severing her contact with the warlock. How many times had he held her back in situations like this? Too many to count.

"And I don't want to if that's how she reacts," Joseph said, straightening the lapels of his jacket.

Aya didn't know who he intended that comment for, but she hissed at him like a cat, her hackles raised.

"You went to the coven," he said to her.

"Oh, and what a lovely reception it was," she

retorted, the sarcasm dripping from her words like honey.

"Did you take Coraline?" he asked, the worry plain in his voice.

"No," she tilted her head to the side with a sneer, "I took myself."

"What did they say?"

"They said nothing. They're psychotic, that's what they are. They suggested suicide was my best option and denied hiding anything, but then again, it's not a *thing* they're hiding. It's a *who*."

"A who?" Joseph asked, paling.

"They wouldn't tell me, but I believe it's the original witch."

"The original witch? You mean the first of their line?"

"The one and the same."

The warlock glanced at Tristan. "How is that even possible?"

Aya rolled her eyes. "She was made with Celestine blood, not human, not like the Five. Who knows what she could do."

Joseph seemed to be frozen to the spot, totally lost for words at her tirade. "What about Coraline?" he managed to get out.

"What about her?"

"We haven't heard from her since she left to meet you that night at the Halloween Ball... She never came back. We tried to contact her, but we couldn't reach her. We hoped she was with you."

"Nope." Aya shook her head. "She left after we spoke with her. In a bit of a hurry, if I remember correctly."

"Shortly after, the Six cornered us on the roof," Tristan interjected.

"What?" The last bit of blood drained from Joseph's face, leaving him with a sickly pallor.

"The Six might have taken her," the knight mused.

"I think you mean the Four," Aya corrected with a sly smile. "Well, the coven doesn't have her. That we can be certain of."

"How do you know that?" Tristan asked.

"I would've sensed if she was there."

"Then Regulus must have her," Joseph interrupted. "You have to save her."

"I *have* to save her?" Aya asked with a raised eyebrow. "When am I going to do this?"

Joseph didn't seem to hear her. "You can take on Regulus. You can get in and get her out."

She shook her head. "Even if I could get in, there's no way of knowing if she's there. Not to mention I have no idea where *there* is."

"She could be in any number of places," Tristan said. "Regulus has houses scattered across the country, not to mention the Six have their own hiding places."

"So, you're just going to leave her?" Joseph cried. "After the risk she took to meet you?"

"She knew what she was getting herself into." Aya narrowed her eyes at the warlock. "Besides, they need her to get into the sanctuary. Wherever she is, she'll be safe for now."

"But—"

"But nothing," she interrupted. "I'll help Coraline, but in my own time. I won't let her die."

"You know what has to be done, Aeriaya," Joseph said. "The coven needs to be destroyed and Regulus needs to follow."

"Oh, don't I know it," she huffed.

"Regulus has been looking for a way into the coven for three hundred years. Victoria was the closest he ever came. The moment she was changed, her blood was useless. The matriarch knew what she was going to do, and she was blacklisted. If she came back and used her blood to enter the building, she would've been killed instantly. Regulus would never have gotten inside regardless. And now Coraline will suffer the same fate. When he can't use her, she'll be dead or turned into a vampire, neither fate she would want."

Aya looked at the warlock, wishing he'd told her this *before* she went to see Coraline. "What else do you know about Victoria?"

"Nothing that concerns you."

"*Everything* concerns me," she hissed. Her hand shot out and grasped the warlock around the throat. "Especially when it involves my kind." Joseph's heart was beating a hundred miles an hour and she let her gaze flicker to his neck where the flow of his blood called out to her vampire side.

He gulped. "I'll tell you whatever you want to know, just don't take my power."

Aya let her hand fall away, but not before shoving him one last time. Tristan placed a hand on her shoulder, a useless gesture designed to calm her down.

"I don't know much," Joseph began. "It's a secondhand tale. I only know what Corrie told me."

Aya tilted her head to the side. She supposed Corrie was short for Coraline.

"Victoria was born of the coven, as you know, but she was born with a talent so small that the circle almost missed it. It was that tiny spark of power that saved her life as a child and they never let her forget it. As a result, she grew up bitter and hard, and won no friends or husband... until Regulus came along. She knew exactly what he was and went willingly with him, knowing what would become of her. He showed her one sliver of kindness and she was his. The coven brought her defection upon themselves, but they had enough sense to realise what she was about to do."

"She was going to let Regulus into the sanctuary?"

"Yes. I suppose he wanted whoever they were hiding away, but even Victoria didn't know. I mean, why would they tell her?" Joseph shook his head. "The coven had blacklisted her, but she had no idea until she smuggled Regulus inside. The coven almost killed him and her, but he escaped and took Victoria with him. Corrie said she was dying, that's why she begged Regulus to turn her. I don't know the real reason why, but Victoria thought he loved her. I suppose you met her after that."

Something inside Aya almost felt sorry for Victoria. The coven, her own family, had shunned her and Regulus had manipulated her for his own end. The monster that she'd turned into had destroyed Zac and his brother and had hunted her halfway across the world. She couldn't feel sorry for that. The brothers never wanted to be vampires.

Aya would never be sorry for setting foot in America, despite the doubts she had, but it was a silver lining kind of sorry. Zac would've been human, and he would've died in the American Civil War at the too young age of twenty-three. But now he was a vampire and she'd had the chance to love him—and hoped she would get a second chance at it if they all came out of this alive.

"I don't know what'll happen next," Aya murmured. "But it won't be good. I'll do whatever I can, but I can't make any promises to you, Joseph."

Without another word, she strode across the gallery and back out into the museum proper with its stream of tourists.

Aya believed Victoria didn't understand what would happen when she made the brothers. No member of the coven had been turned and lived to tell about it, let alone turn another human being. From what Zac had told her, Sam hadn't completed the change before he tore off Victoria's head. If anyone figured out that she turned Zac's brother as well, then Sam wouldn't be safe. Liz, Alex, and Gabby would be collateral damage. Their existence had to be kept secret.

Unless Coraline was no longer useful to them, Zac was next in line. Aya couldn't let that happen.

Outside, the day had darkened and the air was crisp with frost. Winter saw the sun set at the ungodly hour of three-thirty p.m. and it made the grey stone city seem even more dreary.

Pausing around the corner by a shop front, she rested her throbbing head against the cool façade. A monumental task had been set before her and she didn't know where to start.

She felt Tristan stand beside her and was suddenly glad he found it necessary to follow her like a shadow. His presence was reassuring when nothing seemed to be going her way.

Turning around and leaning against the wall, she listened to the street around them as much to clear her mind as to wonder. If Regulus was so desperate to get into the sanctuary, would the Four be hovering around the edges of it? Listening with everything she had, she heard it. Or, at least, she hoped she did. Last time it hadn't been there at all.

"Tristan, we have to get Zac back," she suddenly declared.

"Why? Because of his blood?" It was like the knight had been reading her mind.

She glared at him. "That's not all and you know it."

"You can't hear him anymore. How do you expect to even find him?"

She leaned against the wall of the shop, watching the entrance to the museum. Witches weren't the only supernaturals she'd seen hanging around Bloomsbury. Regulus' thugs had caught a whiff of what was going on, she was sure of it. The concealed entrance to the old tube station was being watched by more than its inhabitants. The witches were careful who they let see their movements, but nothing escaped her.

Her attention shifted to the side of the museum, Montague Street, where the road was lined with hotels crammed into old grey stone buildings. Just as she had suspected, the Four stood there bickering amongst themselves. They were probably still annoyed that they'd given them the slip at that Halloween Ball, and she didn't bother to listen in.

"Arrow," Tristan scolded her, but she put her hand over his mouth to silence him. She pointed towards the four vampires and his eyes widened. He knew it, too. Where the Four were, Zac wouldn't be far away.

"You knew, didn't you?" he asked, shaking his head.

Aya nodded and looked back towards the Four, who had now begun to move off in the opposite direction towards Russell Square. They'd been milling outside of a hotel at the end of the street and once they'd disappeared out of view, the door opened and Zac appeared, scowling after them.

Aya's heart skipped a beat and she pushed away from the wall, dragging Tristan into the *Off Licence*, the man at the counter looking at them suspiciously. Zac walked towards them, his head low and the collar of his black coat pulled up. He made a sharp left, now travelling away from where they stood concealed in the shop's doorway. He hadn't seen them.

"Are you buying anything?" the attendant grumbled.

Aya ignored the man's question and grabbed Tristan's arm, pulling him back out onto the street.

The knight snorted. "You're goin' to follow him now?"

She rolled her eyes at him. "You can go if you want, but who knows when I'll find him again." She stalked off down the street, leaving Tristan frowning after her.

Zac walked fast, much faster than the surrounding humans, but no one seemed to notice. They all had their heads down, intent on getting where they were going, oblivious to the others around them.

Even in the throng of people, Aya could still sense him. He'd always had an imposing presence and even without the sound of his blood to guide her, she had no trouble keeping up with him.

Tristan was following and she was glad he kept his

distance. The last thing she wanted to hear was his disapproval. She knew they had bigger problems than Zac's humanity, but this was just as important to her. Tristan would step in if he was needed.

Aya followed Zac for the next hour, until time seemed to fade. She suspected he was just walking, trying to distract himself with no actual destination. They passed many famous landmarks and beautiful sights, but he didn't stop to look up at any of them. His head hung like he was defeated.

When they eventually came to the river by Westminster, Aya knew she had to make her move or risk losing him again.

It'd become late, about two or three a.m. by her guess, and the streets were mostly empty. The air was heavy with mist, the threat of early snow heavy around them. Zac stopped by the stone wall that marked the edge of the Thames and turned his head sharply. He'd finally caught on that he was being followed.

Tristan stopped beside her and nodded.

Before she could change her mind, Aya appeared behind Zac and grasped his head in her hands. Before he could wrench himself away, she twisted, the snap of his neck sounding dull in the heavy air. His limp body fell against her and her arms locked around his shoulders to ease him to the ground.

How many times would she have to snap his neck before he would come back?

"Come," Tristan said, appearing at Zac's feet.

"There's an underground place near here where we can take him. It's safe."

Aya was glad he had nothing smart to say about what she'd just done. The knight simply picked up Zac's feet and helped her carry him away into the night.

CHAPTER 19

Darkness.

After a world of suffering, it was calming.

It covered everything like a thick blanket. So close, refreshing. The best night's sleep he had ever had.

It was quiet. He was alone and without fear. The ever-creeping blackness would eventually take his thoughts, his soul. Was this what true death was like?

Slowly, the edges of his vision cleared. Hazy at first, but the surrounding room was coming into focus.

Disoriented, he moaned, but no sound came from his parched throat.

He saw her then, nothing but a small, blurred form.

Blinking hard, he lifted his hands to rub his eyes, but was met with resistance. He pulled against the force only to realise chains with shackles were wrapped tightly around each of his wrists. Looking around wildly, he saw that his ankles were also lashed to the chair he sat in.

He panicked, pulling harder against the chains with all his strength. The woman touched his hand lightly with her long, pale fingers. Not a hallucination, after all.

She was slim and shorter than a grown woman, and it was impossible to tell her age. She was so familiar to him, though he couldn't place her in any of his memories, but when he looked at her, he only felt pain.

"Release me!" he yelled with such fury she stumbled back a step.

"Zac," her calm voice murmured. "It's Aya."

The fog in his mind seemed to cling tighter as she spoke. He didn't know where he was. Who was this woman? He yelled at her again and thrashed against his restraints.

"I'm sorry it had to come to this," she said, "but it's for your own good."

So, he was a prisoner.

"What do you want?" he snarled at her.

"I want to bring you back. You've lost your way."

"I don't want to be found," he hissed. Dropping his head, he gave it a shake, feeling woozy. "What the hell did you give me?"

"Don't worry, it's not permanent."

He groaned, shaking his head again, trying to

loosen the fog. Did she slip him a vampire roofie while he was out? *Damn it.*

"Why the hell do you care?" he spat.

"Of course, I care about you, Zac."

He laughed, his head lolling backwards. "You want to bring me back? That's the stupidest thing I've ever heard."

"I never stopped loving you, Zac."

"How can you stop something that hadn't even started?" He scowled at her, flexing his muscled arms against the chains.

"It started the day I first saw you."

"No, it didn't."

"Yes, in 1863," she stated, leaning back against the far wall.

1863. He'd been human then and deployed north to Virginia. An image flashed in his mind of a raven-haired Englishwoman in a blue dress. *Her.*

"You should've killed me then. At least one of us would've enjoyed it." When he heard her heart falter, he smirked. "Chain me here for eternity, I don't care. When he comes for you, you will die over and over and no one will be there to stop him."

"You would let him take me?" she asked quietly, the disbelief in her voice amusing to him.

His head dropped forwards and he laughed again, shaking his head from side to side. He hadn't realised just how far he'd come. His humanity was practically non-existent. If he could go back and change that night in the theatre, he would've taken her the moment he grabbed her arm. Aya was so desperate to save him, she would've followed him anywhere. Pathetic, really. The infamous Witch Hunter, brought to her knees by a man.

"No, I don't believe it."

"Can you hear that?" he whispered, glaring up at her. Aya just stared at him, seemingly unable to formulate a response. "It's sweet, sweet *silence*."

He watched as her eyes swirled with tears and he snorted at the irony. Now he'd made her cry. With a gust of air, she stalked from the room, the door closing with a dull boom that echoed through his stone prison.

Closing his eyes, he breathed in the damp air, the chains around his wrists rattling as he curled his fingers around the armrests. It hadn't taken much to get to her, and he was left disappointed.

How far would he have to push her until she resorted to physical harm? He had no idea, but he was going to have fun finding out.

Zac didn't know how long he'd been locked away in the prison Aya had created for him. His thoughts still hadn't cleared entirely and when he drifted off, his head fell to the side, jolting him back into wakefulness. Hissing, he blinked hard, trying to stave off sleep.

The room about him was stone, and the light had a

green tinge like a swamp full of slime in the sunshine. Water trickled between the cracks in the wall onto the earthen floor and the air was heavy and cold with moisture. If he was still in London, he had to be somewhere underground near the river.

Zac tried to bend his fingers around enough to catch the metal fastening on the manacle that bound his wrists but couldn't create enough slack to undo it. Defeated, he slumped back and fell in and out of consciousness.

The sound of metal crunching on metal stirred him awake and his gaze focused on the door to his right. It edged open and he gasped when a figure walked through the opening. There stood his love, just as the day he last saw her. Beautiful, *glowing*.

She walked towards him, an expression of hope etched onto her features, but his memory grasped an image of her turned back—her reluctance and betrayal. She left him when he needed her the most.

Letting out a slow breath, his eyes rolled and he looked away. What was she going to do this time? When he drew in another breath, there was another scent on the air and it stunk like betrayal. Glancing back towards the door, he realised that she wasn't alone.

Something inside him snapped when he laid eyes on the male vampire. His lip curled into a feral snarl as his fangs elongated and he lunged with so much force, the chair almost tore from where it'd been welded to the steel floor. The shackles tore into the flesh of his wrists and blood ran over his clenched fists.

She wanted a reaction? This was one for the history books.

"Get out, Tristan," Aya said through her teeth as he backed out hastily, the heavy door closing behind him with a thud.

She hauled Zac backwards, slamming his body back into the chair, not caring if she hurt him or not. Wrenching his head to the side, her fangs sank into his flesh. He tried to struggle, but she held her arm across his chest in an iron grip that he couldn't break.

The sickly scent of blood filled the small room and almost drove him mad, except he was too weak to do much about it. He was so hungry and Aya was taking what little blood he had left. If she took much more, he would desiccate. Except he wouldn't die, he'd burn from the inside until he fed.

Groaning, his head lolled backwards, eyes rolling into his head. Why wouldn't she just let him die? He didn't have the strength to fight her when she grasped his face, making him look her in the eye.

"Zac," she whispered, her gaze searching his as she knelt in front of him.

His eyes were heavy, what little energy he had was leaving him. Slumping forwards, his head came to rest against the crook of her neck, his ragged breathing the only sign that he was still conscious.

He was a fool. He wanted her back.

He shuddered as her cool hands caressed his burning face and neck. "I can't stay," he whispered into her neck.

"You can't go back to him, Zac," she reasoned. "He's destroying you."

"No," he rasped. "You don't understand."

"What I understand is that he turned you into the monster you never wanted to become. He took you to the edge and pushed you over. He took your humanity."

"Aya," he whispered, raising his head so he could see her face. "I let go of my humanity because I couldn't take the pain anymore. I didn't know what was wrong with me until you."

"Zac—"

"I need you," he interrupted, not wanting her to convince him otherwise. "You want my humanity so much? Then don't piss all over it. You think you're doing me a favour? A kindness? A true kindness would've been driving the stake into my heart yourself."

She shook her head defiantly. "You and I both know that it's not your true self saying that."

"I am death without you." He went to raise his hand, but the chain held him back, it's rattling echoing off the stone walls. Aya took a step back from him, knowing he was still unstable, his blood still silent. "Instead, you're drawing it out, starving me. I might be unhinged, but this is taking it to a whole new level."

"I don't want to hurt you, Zac, but you're leaving me no choice."

"I'm not coming back." He was losing his grasp on his temper. "Kill me."

"No." Aya glared at him, not backing down.

"Kill me!" he roared, lunging for her, the chains holding him back a mere inch from her face. *Kill me.*

She pushed him back onto the chair roughly, the chains clashing against the metal chair.

"Why did you leave?" He couldn't help but ask.

"I left to protect you," she replied. "This is my task, and mine alone. If anything happened to you because of me..."

"If it's your task alone, then why is *he* here?" When she looked at him wide-eyed and silent, he scoffed, "Your silence is deafening, Aya."

"Tristan knows things," she murmured. "He's helped a great deal."

Zac tilted his head to the side, his lip curling into a snarl. "Do you love him?"

"What?" She seemed surprised by the assumption.

"It's a simple question," he spat. "Do. You. Love. Him?"

"No," she snapped. "Do you love me?"

She knew it would conflict him and he clenched his jaw, grinding his teeth together. He glared at her, the edges of his vision clouding as his rage simmered.

"Have a think about it, Zac," Aya said, walking towards the door. "You've got all night."

As the door closed behind her and the bolt drove home, he roared his anger after her but it fell on deaf ears.

So, he was left to his thoughts and the ever-increasing madness that was driven by his hunger.

Zac was jolted awake violently, the potent scent of fresh human blood filling his senses. With a grunt, he jerked his head from side to side, unable to focus on where it was coming from.

"Want this?" Aya stood in front of him, waving a glass filled with thick, red liquid.

Blood.

Zac felt his teeth tighten and his jaw set in defiance. She was playing dirty.

"You can have some if you do one thing for me."

"Give up already," he rasped, trying to ignore the burn in his throat.

"Feel one thing. *Anything.* I don't care if it's blind hatred for me. Just feel one thing."

He just stared at her, trying not to let the blood get to him.

"If you don't let your humanity back in now, it will be so much more difficult later."

"No."

Aya sighed and dipped a finger into the glass and walked over to him. Before he could turn away, she smeared blood across his face and over his mouth. Jerking away, he held his breath, pursing his lips together. Just one taste would drive him mad. He was so hungry he would do anything for more.

She watched as he tried to fight his natural impulse to breathe. "Don't fight it," she said. "Take a deep breath."

Before long, he couldn't bear it anymore and hissed. Sucking in breath after breath, he cursed her as the blood took him, his eyes changing.

"Do you hate me? Are you angry with me?" she asked, kneeling at his feet. "Do you want to hurt me?"

"I feel nothing for you."

Her hand flew to his neck and squeezed. He stared at her defiantly as he drew in rasping breaths. Why wouldn't they just stop trying to change him? First, it was his brother, now it was Aya. Why couldn't she just let it go? Did she really love him like she had said, or did she just want to see him suffer?

Resigning himself to whatever fate she had in store, he let his body relax, his expression slackening. Aya's hands dropped away and he drew in a sharp breath through his crushed trachea.

"I never knew how sadistic you really were," he drawled. "When do we start with the bloodletting?"

"Zac..."

"As long as you finish with the heart, go nuts." His head snapped to the side as her palm connected with his cheek. "Not hard enough." This time, her fist connected with the edge of his jaw and there was an audible crack as the force of the impact fractured it. "Much better."

As the bone knitted itself back together, he saw something in her hand. *Ahh, there it was.* He wondered when she would bring out the stake. She brought it down faster than his eye could follow, and he roared in pain as it shot clear through his hand.

He laughed, stifling a grimace, the stake well and truly imbedded in his flesh. "I felt that, but that's not right, is it? Physical pain isn't an emotion."

She must have decided it wasn't quite enough when she tore the stake from his hand and imbedded it in his thigh. Zac threw his head back, gritting his teeth together, stifling another cry.

"How about now?" she snapped.

"Nope."

Grasping the end, she twisted the piece of wood, grinding it deeper into his flesh until it scraped against bone.

"*Ahh.*" He laughed shakily, filtering out the pain. "That's the spot."

Suddenly, she wrenched the stake away and flung it across the room. "Enough."

"But I was having such a great time."

"Is that what you really want? You want me to hurt you?"

"If I'm going to feel something, it may as well be pain. I can relate to pain."

"I don't want to hurt you, Zac. *Please*."

"Emotional pain is so overrated."

"What do you want from me?"

"What do I want from you?" he scoffed.

"What do you want?" she yelled.

Zac sighed. He wasn't sure if he'd ever heard her raise her voice at him before. If she had, he didn't remember.

"The truth," he said, watching her closely. "There was something you couldn't bear to tell me. Remember?"

Aya was silent so long, he thought she wouldn't let go of whatever had pulled them apart in the first place. She had nothing to worry about. They were already broken and maybe it was irreparable. Whatever repercussion she was afraid of didn't matter anymore.

"When I killed Arturius," she said, her voice quiet in the small room, "something strange happened."

He didn't dare say anything. Was this finally the truth?

"My power doubled back on itself and splintered through my mind..." She let out a sharp hiss, shaking her head. "And for so long, I thought it'd broken me. He made me what I am, and who knew what would have happened when... I was afraid of losing control and hurting you."

"You could've told me," he said. "Look what happened when you didn't."

She shook her head, leaning back against the far wall. "It was my problem."

"I would've stood by you," he said almost condescendingly. She looked up at him, her gaze full of pain and regret, and he understood. "Nothing happened, did it? All of this was for nothing."

Aya's silence was all the confirmation he needed. She was as she always was. This thing that'd happened when she killed Arturius? Nothing had come of it and he felt... His eyes snapped up and met her blue gaze. *He'd felt.*

"Zac?" she asked, her voice hopeful.

"You can hear it," he stated. Despite his best efforts, his humanity had begun to come back and all he wanted to do was slam his head into the bluestone wall of his prison.

"Yes."

"I don't want to." He shook his head, the chains around his wrists rattling. "*I don't want to.*"

"You have to." She was back in front of him, a hand caressing his face.

He loved her, he always would. He could never fall out of love with her. And he realised that's what she'd been counting on to bring him back.

"I love you," she whispered. "There has been no one else and there never will be. I love you. *Forever.*"

A tear slid down his face and she was on her knees, her hands wound in his hair.

"I know," she murmured, pressing her lips to his clammy forehead. "I know."

Reaching behind the chair, she brought back a bag clad in a hospital emblem. It was full of blood and he couldn't help it when he let out a strangled moan. She set the bag on his lap and retreated across the room, giving him some distance. "It's not your issue, Zac. I wanted to keep you out of it. The last thing I wanted was to drag you into my mess."

He leaned over and held the blood bag to his mouth, drinking greedily. "It became my issue long before I ever met you," he said, gasping for air. "From the moment I died, it became my issue."

"No." She shook her head. "If I hadn't set foot in America, Victoria wouldn't have followed. Then—"

"Stop," he said. "I don't care who pissed off who first. It's not a competition."

"What can I do?" she asked, watching him sate his hunger.

Ignoring her, he asked, "How long have I been here?"

"Almost a week."

His expression fell. A week?

"Aya, this is important," he said. "I need to go back."

"You can't be serious?" she exclaimed.

"I know who the Coven are, Aya. I know everything."

She slumped back against the wall. "Seems like I didn't give you enough credit."

"You never did." He couldn't help it.

"If you know everything then you know what they can do."

He was silent for a moment. He knew. He found out right before she'd jumped him on the street. It'd been too easy following them in the museum. So easy, at first, he thought it was a trap, but with his blood silenced, he was far too sneaky for his own good.

He'd heard everything that the witch had told her. How they believed the Coven was trying to awaken the original witch, how the defectors were plotting to kill Regulus, and how Aya was plotting to kill them all.

And Victoria. How could he feel sorry for her after what she did to his family? What she did to him? He couldn't.

Later, after telling the Four the useless information, he'd split off from them and walked, not knowing what to do. Looking down into the cesspool that was the Thames, he was set upon and he'd woken up here.

"I may have turned myself into a heartless monster, but I have a plan," he said, but did not elaborate. They had Coraline and she'd implied she could do the job for him. "If I don't go back, there's no hope in hell you'll be able to get within five feet of Regulus. Aya, I'm so close. *There's another way.*"

She stared at him in disbelief. "*No.*" She shook her head. "If there was, I would know."

"I hate to be the one who tells you this, but you don't know everything."

"You don't hate it," she scoffed. "You're loving this."

"Let me go."

"If I let you go, you'll never come back."

Zac sighed and looked away, not trusting himself to look at her. "We keep coming back to this?"

"What?" she asked like she didn't already know.

"Trust."

Her head dropped into her hands.

"You have to let me go," he whispered, his gaze taking in her eyes that sparkled with unshed tears. "I don't know what will happen, but this time, you need to trust me. For once in your life... *trust me.*"

Tentatively, she reached down and undid his restraints. Standing back, she looked at her feet, gesturing to the door.

"Go," she whispered. "Go before I change my mind."

When Zac walked into the apartment, Nye was sitting on top of the kitchen counter giving him a look that said he'd almost written him off.

"What the hell happened to you?" the spy asked, looking him up and down.

He was still wearing the same clothes he'd been in when Aya and Tristan had snatched him from the street, and they were caked with his sweat and blood, his coat missing. He looked like he'd been dragged through Hell and the story he was going to tell Nye was only nine-tenths of the truth.

"I had a run in with my ex," he said wryly.

Nye's eyebrows rose. "The Hunter did this to you?"

"They jumped me not long after I left you and the others by the museum."

"That was like a week ago. She had you that long?"

Zac grimaced.

"So that's what was different with you at the party the other night."

"What do you mean?" he asked, knowing exactly what Nye meant.

"She couldn't bear to let you go without your humanity."

"Nye, the fact that you're a bloody genius makes me want to punch you in the face."

The spy laughed and tapped his temple. "I've got an IQ of 106."

Zac leaned against the kitchen counter, picking up a bottle of scotch someone had left out. Truth was, he felt strange. It was like he could feel the edges of himself tingling, like his nerve endings had been dulled to feeling and were slowly returning with pins and needles. His humanity was igniting, but it would still take time for it to come back entirely.

"How did she do it?" Nye asked, watching him.

He shook his head. "She told me the truth."

"Looks like she tortured it out of you."

Zac grimaced. "She tried, but it would never have worked."

"Mate, death wishes are dangerous when you're a vampire."

"I know nothing else."

Nye gave him a look and snatched the bottle of scotch. "No offence, but you need to have a shave, mate. You look like a hobo, and you stink like one, too."

Zac grunted, pushing off the bench and wandered down the hall.

Aya had become afraid of so many things since they'd met. Zac knew enough about her that she'd never ever felt this way. Maybe she was right when she left, but she did it for the wrong reasons. And maybe he'd tried to cope with it in the wrong way, too. He hated feeling emotions he couldn't handle, but it was better than the alternative. Turning his back on his humanity had been an ill-advised move on his part. The way he'd goaded her on made him feel sick. What would he have become after a week? A month? A year? Hell, even a decade?

Stripping off his filthy clothes, he turned on the shower in the en suite attached to his room. Glancing at himself in the mirror, he grimaced at the sight.

Aya had really done a number on him, hadn't she? He was covered in dry blood, sweat, and dirt, and a week's worth of stubble covered his chin. Why the hell did he still have to shave when he was dead? Hell, why did he still have to breathe when he was dead? *The mysteries of the universe.*

Once Zac had showered and made himself presentable, he went back out to the kitchen where Nye still sat on the countertop looking at his cell phone.

"Regulus wants to see you," he said.

"Where is he?" Zac asked, knowing the spy had called the Roman while he was in the shower.

"The pub," Nye said. "*The Good Mixer.*"

"Fine," he said, grabbing Nye's coat from the back of the sofa.

"*Hey.* Get your own."

"Get a new one," Zac retorted, slamming the door behind him.

The Good Mixer was a little pub just off Camden High Street that had been there for forever and a day. It was packed with alternative types—goths, punks, rockers, and a few old men who'd probably been drinking there for their entire lives.

A punk girl behind the bar eyed Zac as he came in —she had black and blue hair, and large tattoos on either arm. From the look on her face, he knew she was a sympathiser who knew what he was. She inclined her head towards the rear of the pub, and he moved past the bar, not acknowledging her gesture.

Regulus sat at a table in the back, flanked by two men and a woman Zac had never seen before. Half a dozen bottles of hard liquor sat before them, mostly empty.

When the Roman laid eyes on Zac, he stood, his expression unreadable, and led him across to the opposite side of the bar. Sitting at a free table, he gestured for Zac to sit.

"Zachary," he said thinly. "You have some explaining to do."

Zac said nothing, he just sat and faced the Roman.

Regulus' eyes narrowed and he tapped the top of the table. "What I want to know is how you gave four very skilled vampires the slip and what you think you were doing once you did."

"The British Museum is a hive of activity these days," Zac said nonchalantly. "All kinds of unsavoury people hang around there."

Regulus gazed at him, waiting, his expression unreadable.

"Witches, vampires, *hybrids*," he went on. "I'm guessing they don't go there for the history, but you already knew that."

Regulus snorted, taking his cell from inside his coat. He typed a message and dropped it back into his pocket. He stood without a word and walked through to the front of the pub. Zac didn't have to ask. He knew that the Roman wanted him to follow.

It was quiet out on the street. Almost everyone was inside the pub or on their way to somewhere that wasn't out in the cold. Frost was thick in the air and the threat of snow loomed in the darkness above.

Walking down the street a ways, the Roman turned side on, his breath vaporising in the frosty night air. He looked calm, but Zac knew better. His jaw was tight and even in the darkness, he could see his eyes had changed. This would not be pretty.

Still, he wasn't prepared when Regulus appeared in front of him, his fist hurtling through the air. Zac stumbled back a few steps from the force of the blow, hardly aware that blood gushed from his broken nose. It took a few seconds for the synapses in his brain to grow back together and when his head snapped up, it was just in time to see Regulus' fist hurtling towards his face again.

It connected with a sickening thud of bone against flesh and he doubled over, clutching his face, pretty sure his cheekbone had just shattered.

"Do not think I am someone to be trifled with, Zachary. I make good on my threats. *Every single one.* Who are you to question me? *Hmm?*"

Zac grimaced, stifling the urge to curse out loud at the throbbing pain in his face.

Regulus was still shouting at him, not waiting for a response. "I could just kill you to teach you and the others a lesson in obedience. Or I could just get Nye to put an end to you. You've become great friends, have you not? Imagine having to murder your best friend. Do you think he would care? Would you?"

"That would imply I still had a heart," Zac sneered, spitting blood onto the pavement. "You saw to put an end to it the night you made me kill that girl."

"I made you?" Regulus scoffed, his eyebrows raised. "I didn't *make* you do anything. All I did was simply offer you the opportunity. You're the one who took it, Zachary."

Zac's jaw set and fought the urge to grind his teeth.

"You are *not* my equal. You will be nothing more than you are now. *Mine.* Do you understand?" When he didn't answer, Regulus shoved him. "*Answer me!*"

If he didn't say something to please Regulus, he was as good as dead. "I understand," he said, unable to hide the strain in his voice.

The Roman grabbed the front of his shirt and pulled him close. "Screw with me again and it will be the last thing you ever do. I do not kill traitors mercifully, Zachary. Know that I will drag it out for days, weeks, years if I have to."

He stared the Roman down until he pushed him away. Wiping the blood from his nose with the arm of Nye's coat, he spat, "Fine. I get it."

"Now," Regulus said, "I want answers. Where were you for the last seven days?"

"Locked in a dungeon."

Regulus' eyebrows rose and it looked like he didn't believe him in the slightest.

"Aya," he explained. "She snapped my neck and locked me up."

"What was she doing with you?"

"They tried to turn me."

"They?"

"Aya and Tristan."

Regulus seemed to mull this over for a moment, his expression total darkness. "And did they succeed?"

Zac knew the right answer, and it was the truthful one. He'd never been turned in the first place. "No."

"What did she tell you?"

"She told me nothing that you don't already know."

"Then why did she take you?"

"She knew I'd turned off my humanity and she wanted it back."

Regulus scoffed, shaking his head, "I never thought she had a heart."

"Stranger things have happened."

The Roman looked him up and down, his carefully guarded expression suddenly falling. For a moment, Zac saw something akin to jealousy. "What the hell does she see in you?"

He'd said it to himself, but Zac answered anyway, "I ask myself the same question."

Regulus frowned, looking away and after a long minute, he snapped, "Get out of my sight."

Zac knew better than to linger. He strode away towards High Street before he could be called back.

Weaving his way through the slow walkers and drunkards on the street, Zac walked and walked, not wanting to go back to the apartment just yet. He couldn't face Nye and the rest of the Four. They'd ask him questions he didn't want to answer. They would want to know what Aya had said and done to him. He still couldn't fathom it himself.

She'd abandoned him, telling him all those brutal things. How she didn't really love him, how she'd used him. And for what? To protect him? She knew nothing about what he wanted. If she did, she would understand it was the worst possible thing she could've done.

Her power had folded back on itself? What the hell did that even mean? It didn't really matter. She'd said nothing had happened and it was the biggest joke he'd ever heard. She'd pulled away from him for *nothing*. Even if something had happened when she'd killed Arturius, it wouldn't have mattered. It was the truth when he said he would have stood by her. A vampire's intensity dial was turned up to a billion and everything he felt for her was overwhelming... and he would've done whatever it took to help.

When his cell vibrated in his pocket, he wrenched it out with an annoyed groan, looking at the screen. The number was blocked, which probably meant it was Regulus, and he hoped the Roman hadn't changed his mind.

"What?" he snapped.

"Zac?" It was a female voice. Definitely not Regulus.

Was it...? "Gabby? What the hell?"

"Hello to you, too," she said.

"How did you get this number?"

"Give me some credit, Zac. I am a witch."

"You know I don't buy that."

"I put an APB out in the universe, and I got a tipoff." He could hear the shrug in her voice.

"What do you want?"

"I see you're still grumpy."

"Gabby, I'm not in the mood for a chat. I've got things to do."

She laughed at his tone, which only fed his annoyance. "You've only been there two weeks and already you have a reputation."

"I have a reputation?"

"People like to talk, Zac."

"People talk about me? Why would they bother?"

"They bother because they're afraid of you. There was a lot of talk about two very particular killings a while ago."

Vince and Garett. "Good. Then maybe people will stay the hell away from me."

"*Zac...*"

"Can we talk about something else?" he asked, pinching the bridge of his nose.

"If you want."

"Sam?"

"Oh, so you still do care. Word on the street is that you gave up your humanity."

"Gabby."

"He's fine. He and Liz moved to LA."

"Liz got into college?"

"Yeah. UCLA."

They were silent for a moment and he wondered... "Is he happy? Are they happy?"

"Yes."

"Good," he declared sharply.

"Sounds like something's still in the on-position in there."

Was it that obvious? "Aya locked me in a dungeon and tortured me into it."

"*Wow*," Gabby exclaimed. "I knew she had guts, but *wow*."

"Are you taking a dig at me?"

"Shut the hell up, Zac."

"What were you saying about guts?"

Gabby's laughter came down the line and his mood lifted slightly.

"Why are you calling me?" he asked, fed up with the small talk. "I know this isn't a courtesy call."

"I know how to kill Regulus. For good. And I need you to do it."

Zac's eyes widened and he felt his heart skip a beat. "Start talking."

CHAPTER 21

As far as insane schemes went, Gabby's was at the top of the pile.

When they were trying to find a way to end Arturius, Zac had suggested to her that she could replicate Aya's ability, but she'd scoffed at the notion. The one thing they hadn't counted on was the Coven. A Celestine's abilities couldn't be replicated, but they could be transferred.

Only one person had the ability to receive. Zac shared the same blood as the Coven through Victoria. He would be the one to do it.

Until now, Zac had been negligible. Someone had figured out his blood was potent to Aya and her abilities, and that information had found its way to Regulus. That was the only reason he'd shown up in Ashburton. He'd been manipulated into becoming the thing he loathed all for the Roman's own gain... and now his time of death was closing in on him.

Zac was grateful that no one knew the truth of who Sam really was. There was no way anyone could know they were true brothers or even vampire brothers, not unless someone went digging. Gabby would make sure he and Liz were hidden and safe. He'd never uttered Sam's name to anyone, not even Nye, and if they had an inkling, he would become a target as well. There was no way in hell that was going to happen.

Gabby's plan was brilliant, but there was one hitch. Zac knew he was linked to Regulus and if he actually killed him, he would die along with the Roman.

He was willing to do it, knowing what would happen. After all, he'd turned into something dark and didn't even have enough trust in himself to readjust—he'd been struggling with it for his entire vampire life. If this was to be his end, then he better make it mean something.

For their plan to work, Zac needed Coraline and her power. It'd been over a week since he'd seen the witch and wondered what condition the vampires had left her in. There was no doubt in his mind that she was alive since Regulus needed her to get into the Coven's sanctuary.

Walking into the apartment, he wasn't sure what he would come back to. Any respect he'd garnered with the Four might be misplaced now that a girl had captured him. The Hunter, but still a girl.

"Hey," Rix said as he walked into the kitchen, "heard you got tortured by a girl."

Case in point.

"Gimme that," Zac said, snatching the beer the vampire had just taken from the fridge.

"*Hey,*" Rix exclaimed, but Zac had already walked away.

Nye was draped over the sofa watching something on the television, beer in hand. Looking up, he grimaced at Zac, pointing to his nose. "Missed a spot."

Shucking off Nye's coat, he flung it at the spy, hitting him in the head.

"Aw man, you got blood on it," he cursed, flinging it aside.

"Don't worry, it's only mine." Zac shrugged, sitting across from him.

Nye raised an eyebrow.

"Regulus has a mean right hook."

"We good?"

"For now." Taking a swig of beer, he asked, "Where we at?"

"The half-breed's still downstairs and in one piece, if that's what you mean."

"What are we doing with her?"

"Nothing yet. No doubt Regulus will want to move her. I don't know why he hasn't told us to yet. A week is a long time." He raised an eyebrow. "Maybe he was waiting for you to come back... alive or dead."

As if on cue, Zac's cell rang. Looking at the screen, he nodded. "Master beckons," he said with a roll of his eyes.

"Careful, mate."

"Hello," he said, walking down the hall.

"Zachary," came Regulus' voice, "I need you to do something."

"When?"

"Now," he snapped. "I need you to move the half-breed. Think you can manage that without being abducted again?"

"Yes," he said thinly, holding back the urge to say something sarcastic.

"I have a house just outside of Andover," the Roman said. "Take her there. It's guarded and secluded."

"Understood."

"Take Pyke and Maddox with you. They know the way. Oh, and Zachary?"

"Yes?" he asked warily.

"Do not screw this up."

Oh, he was going to... and royally. Hanging up, he walked through the apartment and called out to the two vampires, "Maddox. Pyke."

"What's up?" Maddox stuck his head out into the kitchen.

"We're taking the half-breed to Regulus' house in Andover."

"Now?"

Zac narrowed his eyes at the assassin. "Now."

"Fine," the assassin said, grabbing his jacket. "Pyke! C'mon, Regulus' orders."

Zac strode into the living room and snatched up Nye's coat again.

"*Not again*," the spy protested.

"Back later."

Nye watched him thoughtfully as he left the apartment but said nothing.

Zac joined Pyke and Maddox, who were already down in the garage. As he crossed over to the car, Maddox came out of the storage room a moment later with Coraline flung over his shoulder. He hadn't bothered to bind her hands and when he set her down, Zac glared at him and the assassin pulled the roll of gaffer tape from his back pocket. Snatching it away, he bound her wrists and ankles together. The whole time she just stood there and took it, not making a sound. Zac narrowed his eyes at her, but she didn't look up at him once.

Pyke popped the truck and opened it up, watching as he tossed Coraline inside. Zac watched her gaze pass from him to Pyke as if she was trying to work something out, and he wondered if she knew something was about to go down. With a sneer, he lifted a hand up and slammed the trunk closed.

Maddox went to open the driver's side door, but Zac stepped in front of him, shoving the assassin out of the way. "I'm driving."

"You don't know where to go," he argued.

Turning around, he spat, "So give me directions."

Maddox backed away, hands in the air. "No

problems," he said, looking at the ground or anywhere that wasn't in direct eye contact with Zac.

Pyke got into the front with him, neglecting to put his seatbelt on. "You want to go west on the A30, south on the M40, and west as far as she goes on the M3. There's signage from there for Andover."

Zac raised an eyebrow. "Or you could put the address in the GPS."

"Could never get that thing to work."

The engine roared to life and Zac pulled the car out of the parking garage and onto the road, squealing the tyres on the asphalt. As the buildings of the city thinned out into the trees and fields of the country, his mind rolled over the different ways he could get rid of the two vampires in the car without killing them in the process. The possibilities were endless, but he'd have to be careful not to hurt Coraline too much. When he threw her into the trunk, he noticed there were a lot of blankets stashed away. No doubt for the countless bodies the Four had to dispose of, but in this case, it would be enough padding for the witch to ride this out.

The roads were mostly empty at this time of night. The M40 was only travelled by them and a few trucks and b-doubles hauling cross-country deliveries. All he needed was an embankment or a ditch. Idly, he wondered what the safety rating was on this car, but it didn't matter as long as he didn't snap his neck. Up ahead, a sign stated it was six miles to Andover. Time was running short. He had to do it now.

As the road rose slightly, a ditch pronounced itself to the left and he swerved violently to the side, the car smashing through the barrier.

"What the hell?!" Pyke cried out, his hand shooting out to grab the wheel, but as the car hit the corner of the embankment, it dropped on one side, causing it to flip over and roll several times. The vampire wasn't wearing a seat belt, so the first thing that happened was his body flew forwards into the windscreen, cracking it where his head collided with a sickening thud.

Zac let go of the wheel, took his foot off the gas, and braced his arms against the roof, grimacing as Pyke's now unconscious body slammed into his side. The car flipped at least a dozen times before it finally slid to a stop upside down in a shower of crunching metal and tinkling glass.

The engine ticked as it cooled, a hissing sound coming from somewhere inside. After a minute, when the car didn't catch on fire, Zac grimaced and shook his head. It seemed he was the only one still conscious.

Unfastening his seatbelt, he turned and kicked out the driver's side window. Crawling into the night air, he stood with his hands on his knees and waited for the gash on his forehead to heal. Cursing, he lifted his shirt to see a blackened bruise already forming from his shoulder to hip where an unconscious Pyke had bashed into him at least ten times as the car went over. It only took a minute for it to turn a sickly yellow colour before finally returning back to normal.

Cracking his neck, Zac pushed against the wreck, flipping it right side up. Kicking open the mangled trunk, he found Coraline unconscious and bloody.

"Shit," he cursed, pulling her out and carefully laying her on the grass. Pressing an ear against her chest, he faintly heard her heart flutter. Slashing his wrist open on a piece of jagged metal, he pressed it against her lips, flooding her mouth with his blood. Her natural reflex was to swallow and when she inevitably did, he sighed in relief. If she died, then it was over.

Zac pulled the gaffer tape from her wrists and ankles, covering her with a blanket and walked around what was left of the car. Pyke was laying in the mud a full ten feet away, his neck at an odd angle, blood heavy in the air. Inside, Maddox was smart enough to wear his seatbelt and welts had risen on his skin where it'd pressed into his flesh, but at some stage, his head had hit the widow at his side. Blood still ran from a gash in his temple and Zac startled as the assassin groaned, his eyes fluttering as he tried to force consciousness.

Zac couldn't have that. It took all his strength to twist the door open and when he did, he reached inside and pulled the vampire from the wreck.

"What are you doing?" Maddox rasped, his eyes on Zac as he was dumped unceremoniously in the dirt.

Zac's only answer was to bend down and snap the assassin's neck before he could heal enough to challenge him.

He looked up as Coraline's sharp gasp signalled her return to health. Crouching beside her, he waited for her to get her bearings. She'd probably be pissed, but at least she was alive.

"What the hell?" She almost threw up, spitting blood on the grass.

"Sorry about the theatrics," he said as she glared up at him. "But it's hard to surprise these guys. They've seen it all."

"You're a mole?" Coraline asked, sounding surprised. "But..."

"But what?" he turned to face her, his eyes dark. "You want to give Regulus and the Coven the middle finger. What I want out of this is none of your business. I got you out of there, so just be grateful."

"You gave me your blood?"

"Don't sound so surprised."

"But..."

"I crashed the car, let's just call it even."

"If you're not one of them, then why are you so—"

"Mental?" he interrupted. "That's the word you're looking for, right?"

She cringed away from him, wiping her mouth on the blanket.

"I am not a puzzle for you to solve, Coraline," he drawled. She shrunk back even farther from him and he should've felt bad, but there was nothing inside him. "You're getting what you want." He pulled her to her feet and dragged her out of the ditch.

"Where are we going?"

"To see your little boyfriend."

"What?"

"Maximus," he spat.

"How did you know?" Before he could retort, she said, "The witch told you, didn't she?"

He shrugged, knowing she meant Gabby. How those two came to be buddies was beyond him.

"How do you know her?"

"Oh, we go way back," he replied sarcastically. "How do you know her?"

"She came to me while I was in that cage."

"She came to see you?" Zac asked, his brow furrowing.

"Not like that," Coraline said. "She spoke to me through meditation."

"I'm just going to pretend I know what that means."

"She spoke to me in my mind. She told me help was coming, but I didn't expect it to be from you."

"Sorry I disappointed you."

"I should have guessed it after you spoke to me."

"Shut up," he snapped. "We've gotta go."

"Where are we?"

"Just outside of Andover."

"If we're going to Salisbury, it's still a fair way," Coraline said, hugging her arms around herself. She didn't even have a jacket. "Did you even think about how we would get there?"

"I'll carry you."

"Oh, no, you won't. You almost killed me in that car!"

"I healed you."

"Luckily for you, I was still alive."

"If you won't let me carry you, then you can walk." His eyes darkened and he turned away before she could push him any further. "You have legs," he snapped. "*Use them.*"

Coraline only groaned and walked down the side of the highway. She looked past him back down the road, but it was empty and uninspiring, save for the broken barrier the car had flown through.

They'd only walked half a mile when Zac looked back and found she'd fallen behind. "You walk too slow," he huffed, his breath vaporising in the icy air.

"Not all of us have super vampire strength, you know," she said sarcastically as she caught up.

"Here," he said, beckoning her over. "Jump on my back."

"What?" She hugged her arms around herself, turning a shoulder towards him.

"I said, get on my back. It'll be faster."

"No way."

"Coraline." He rolled his eyes, annoyed at her

reluctance. "I'm not going to eat you and I'm not going to hurt you. I swear you won't catch a horrible disease by touching me."

She looked at him warily, glancing back down the road.

"Yeah, they'll be coming soon enough," he said, but she still didn't move. "For God's sake. It's freezing, you'll catch your death standing out here."

"If you're not with them, then who are you with?" she asked quietly.

"Is that what this is all about?"

"Who?" she demanded.

Zac sighed loudly, running a hand over his face. If he was on a side, he supposed it would be hers. "We're on the same side, Coraline. Now get on my back."

Reluctantly, she jumped up onto his back, curling her arms around his neck, and he hooked her knees around his elbows.

"Hold on," he said sharply. "If you fall off, I'm not going back to pick you up."

"This is it," Coraline said, tapping Zac on the shoulder.

He shrugged her off his back and she almost fell on her backside.

"Hey!"

"Thirty minutes is better than six hours, huh?" he said, ignoring her.

They stood out the front of a small cottage, warm light glowing from the downstairs windows. A thin layer of frost had already settled on the grass and Coraline was shivering, despite wearing his coat—well, Nye's coat. She shucked it off and threw it at him like it was laced with poison.

"A thanks would be nice." He cocked his head to the side, watching her in the half-light.

"Thanks." She rolled her eyes and walked up to the front door, rapping on it sharply. A moment later, the door inched open a crack and a man peered out at them.

"Coraline?" he exclaimed, throwing the door wide open. A second later, he saw Zac loitering in the shadows, and the man swallowed hard, looking him up and down as the witch ducked inside.

Zac laughed at him, shaking his head. "Invite me in, Maximus."

"I'm not even going to wonder how you know who I am," the priest said. "Thank you for freeing Coraline. I assume that's what you did, vampire, but I can't let you in."

"You can and you will."

"Compulsion won't work on me."

Zac laughed again. "I'm not trying."

"What else could you possibly want from us?"

"You want to finish the Coven, and I want to finish the Romans."

Maximus' eyes widened.

"Let him in, Max." Coraline placed a hand on his shoulder. "He's an arse, but he's with her."

He frowned at her, confused. "Fine, come in."

Zac pushed past him into the house. "I need to go back to London, but you have to do something for me first, Coraline."

"What?" she asked warily.

"You will help me put an end to Regulus once and for all."

"And how am I meant to do that? If I have to go back with you, then why did you bother bringing me all the way here in the first place?"

"No." Zac shook his head. "You need to give me something."

Understanding flashed across her face. "You mean...?"

"He's protected against you."

Coraline's eyes widened. "But not against you."

"I can see your brain cells are rubbing together."

"You're not much of a people person, are you?"

"Firstly, I'm not a person."

"Guys," Maximus interrupted their bickering, "I know witches and vampires are not the best of friends, but we're on the same side here. At least, I hope we are, so hold your tongues."

Coraline sighed and led them through to a cozy sitting room where a fire burned merrily in the hearth.

"How is that even going to work?" she asked, sitting

in an old leather armchair and pulled a blanket around her shoulders.

"How is what?" Maximus interrupted. "What does he mean, Corrie?"

"He means to borrow my power," she told him.

"But I don't understand. Is that even possible?"

"Victoria was the vampire who turned me," Zac said, amused at the shocked expressions on their faces. Max and Corrie—something was going on there. "You can give me your power."

"You have Celestine blood?"

"Neat, huh?" He rolled his eyes, annoyed.

"But what about you?" Maximus seemed alarmed at the notion of her giving away her Celestine power, even as minuscule as it was.

"It's not a permanent thing," she reassured him. "I'm only giving him a strong dose of it." She turned to Zac. "You'll only get one shot at this, so make it count."

"Oh," he drawled, "I plan on it."

CHAPTER 22

Truth was, Zac was expecting the shit to hit the fan when he walked back into the apartment. Maddox and Pyke were on their feet when he came through the door, Rix not far behind.

"What the hell, Zac?" Maddox pushed him hard, his shoulder hitting the wall.

"What kind of stunt was that?" Pyke slammed Zac's head against the wall, cracking the plaster.

The warm trickle of blood that ran down his forehead was enough to darken his eyes and Zac pushed the vampire back with all the force he could muster, sending him hurtling across the room into the island in the middle of the kitchen. He landed with a grunt, holding his side. Rix took a swing and before his fist could connect, Zac grasped his wrist and squeezed, feeling the bone crack with a satisfying snap. Before Maddox could have a go, Nye was pushing him away, a hand on Zac's chest.

"Hands off," Nye snapped, holding them apart. "What the hell is going on?"

"This wise guy crashed our car and snapped my neck," Maddox seethed, pointing at him.

"And the half-breed witch is gone," Pyke exclaimed.

"Zac?" Nye looked him up and down.

"Get your hand off me," he spat, knocking the spy's arm aside.

"Hey, calm the hell down." The spy pointed a finger at him. "And you," he turned to the three vampires, "no blood in the house. You know the rules."

"Stuff the rules," Pyke spat.

"If he's double-crossed us, then we have more problems than blood in the house," Rix said.

"Leave this with me," Nye said sharply, staring down at the three vampires.

"If you can't sort this, Nye, then I'm going to Regulus," Maddox declared, waving a finger at him.

"Piss off, Maddox."

"If I find out you've helped him, so help me God, you'll go down with him."

"Get the hell out before I kick the shit outta all three of you idiots." Nye asserting his authority was something else. The three vampires backed down immediately, but not without a great deal of tension in the air. They stalked from the room, shooting glares at Zac before the front door slammed behind them.

Nye listened to their footsteps recede downstairs

and when they faded, he turned to Zac. "What exactly are you playing at, mate?"

"Revenge," he said simply.

Nye's eyes widened as he suddenly realised what he was doing.

"I thought you of all people would have gotten it by now."

"Obviously not," the spy said. "She turned you, didn't she? When you said she tortured you—"

"She didn't turn me," Zac exclaimed, offended. "I was never turned to begin with."

He watched Nye as he ran a hand over his face, whatever he was thinking carefully guarded. He would either hand him over to Regulus or kill him on the spot. Which one would it be? Zac's money was on turning him in. There was no way he could know that Coraline had given him her power. Then it would be done sooner than he thought.

"What did you do with the witch?"

"Coraline," he said, reminding the spy of her name. "She's safe."

"You're going to kill Regulus?" Nye looked up at him in disbelief when he finally put two and two together. "It can't be done."

Zac didn't reply. Instead, he waited for the inevitable, but deep down, he hoped that this semblance of a friendship he'd struck with the spy would win out.

"Zac, you can't be serious."

"He has no right to do the things he's done. He has no right to know the things he does. Regulus deserves to die, and I will be the one to deliver him."

"But, mate, you're linked to him. If you kill him, then you'll die as well."

"I'm aware of that."

"You'd really sacrifice yourself to end him?"

"I can't control this thing I am, Nye. Every time, every bloody time I lose it, I slip further away, and the corpses keep piling up. Innocent people who don't deserve to have their throats torn out. I've fought *wars* as an excuse to sate my hunger. One day I'll be so far gone, I won't come back."

"*Mate...*"

"If I die ridding the world of Regulus, then it will be worth it. All this time I've spent struggling with this thing inside would've been worth something."

For once in his life, Nye seemed lost for a comeback.

Zac looked away, shaking his head. "She was wrong to try to protect me."

Nye clapped a hand on his shoulder, making him look into his face. "No," he said. "Protecting someone you love is never wrong."

Zac snorted. "Maybe not, but there's got to be a better way of going about it."

The spy let his hand drop. "You've got some explaining to do, mate. The sooner, the better."

"I know, but it's a long story."

"We've got time," Nye said, glancing at the front door. "But let's go someplace else. Something tells me we don't need those three idiots listening in." He walked into the kitchen and came back with another coat on, since Zac was already wearing his. "Do you trust me?"

"Do you trust me?" He grinned wryly.

Nye looked him up and down. "Yeah," he said. "Strangely enough, I do."

<hr>

Nye didn't take Zac far from the apartment. They sat on a rooftop above a bar called *Gilgamesh*, which sat smack bang in the middle of Camden Market. It was broad daylight and thousands of humans swarmed below them, music and various food smells filtering upwards into the cool air. Everyone was too busy looking at the surrounding stalls to bother looking up. It hadn't rained so far, but the sky was heavy with promise.

"I don't know where to start," Zac said, fiddling with the buttons on what was now *his* coat.

"How about at the beginning?" Nye said with a chuckle. "Once upon a time..."

"It's just... it's too much, you know. The Romans and Aya. I mean, it's more than just who pissed off who."

"I understand Arturius turned the Hunter, but why? Zac, what exactly is she?"

"You don't know, do you?" Zac was a little shocked. "I thought you had it all worked out."

"Know what? I have no idea what she is a hybrid with, but I know it has something to do with the half-breed you busted out. Are they the same?"

"Kind of," he replied. "That's something I only know secondhand."

"Then what?"

"She was a Celestine."

"Celestine..." Nye said thoughtfully, testing the word out. "I've heard that before."

"You have?"

"Yeah, but I have no idea what it means."

"The Celestines were the ones who made the first witches. They were creatures of power," Zac said with a sigh. "Katrin was one of the Five and betrayed them. Aya was one of the last of her kind before she was taken by the Romans. Taken by Regulus."

"Oh, man. It's all starting to make sense now."

"Katrin wanted to know the secrets to their power and thought by creating the first vampires she could take whatever she wanted by force. Take from their blood."

"She obviously failed," Nye said, watching Zac with an odd look on his face.

"Yeah, when they all realised Aya couldn't give them anything, Arturius took it upon himself to turn her. She escaped, killing one of the Romans, but they killed her entire family as retribution."

"*Hell*," the spy hissed. "That's bloody brutal, and I'm guilty of some brutal stuff myself."

"They're all dead save for Regulus. After what he did to me through Victoria and what he's doing to me now... Can you understand why I want to end him? Not just for Aya, but for myself." *And for Sam.*

Nye grimaced and looked out across the market. "He never told us any of this."

"For the longest time, Aya believed if she gave away her secrets, something horrible would happen. I don't know what, some kind of curse maybe, but nothing ever did."

"We've hunted her ever since I was on the scene," Nye said. "But I never knew the reason for it."

"All this time Regulus never told you why? And why he wants into the Coven?"

"I can see it's got you all worked up," Nye said. "Explain the Coven part to me, then I might just help you in your crazy suicide mission."

"the Coven believe they are trying to wake the original witch. The first in their line. From what I understand, she was made with Celestine blood, which is why her decedents carry it. Why Victoria did and why I do."

"Regulus wants this original witch?"

"Aya said that this witch would be unstable. The

Five were never given Celestine blood, it would be too much for a human to handle."

"Oh *great*." Nye threw his hands into the air. "Another psycho witch? That's just great. My favourite thing."

"I trust Aya will end the Coven. I know as much. What I also know is that she'll never be able to get close enough to Regulus to kill him."

"Zac—"

"No, Nye, listen to me," he said sharply, not wanting to be convinced otherwise. "I'm the only one who can take Celestine power, and I'm the only one who is able to get close enough to finish it."

"So that's why you busted out Coraline? So she could give you her power?"

"Neat, huh?" he said dryly.

"Neat when you're dead."

"A matter of consequence."

"Zac, are you sure you're ready to die?"

"I already told you my reasons, Nye. Nothing is going to change." He looked over to the spy, gauging his reaction. "What I want to know is what you'll do. Turn me in to Regulus or kill me. It's up to you."

Nye regarded him for a moment and Zac was almost ready to fight him if he had to, but the spy let out a long, sharp breath, his head dropping to his knees. "Hell, Zac," he said. "You haven't thought about door number three, have you?"

"Door number three?" he asked with a scowl.

"The one where you get to say goodbye to the woman you love? You know? Hello? Don't just go and off yourself, mate. What are you going to do about her?"

"Nothing."

"Screw that."

"So, you're going to help me then?" Zac said to change the subject.

"I'm a man of the world. I've always been on my own and Regulus knew that he never had me. I stayed and took his orders because it was better than going at it alone. I needed someone to order me around in the beginning. It was all I knew. Soon enough, it was just easier to stick around. Then you came along with all your psycho Celestine shit and now it seems I've got something to fight for. Something right," he said, looking out over the market.

"Wow."

"Don't get a big head, mate. I've done some messed up shit in my time. Maybe now is my chance to repent for some of it."

Zac snorted.

Nye glared at him. "You believe in what you're doing. So does Regulus, but he doesn't have half the conviction that you do. And I like to think we're mates on some macabre level. I'd throw my lot in with a mate over a founder any day."

"I've never sworn fealty to anyone, Nye—"

"Mate, first rule of being a bad-arse vampire is

never to swear fealty to *anyone*. Not even the founders of your race."

"I suppose that makes me bad-arse then."

"Right on, brother," Nye declared with a lopsided smile.

Brother? Sam would kill him if he knew what his big brother was doing. He couldn't even stop to think about Sam. Poor Sam, who had had his life stolen as well. He would be shattered to hear of his death. And Liz... he'd loved her once, but now it was a different kind of love. She was with Sam and that made her his little sister. And then there was Alex. They'd never been the best of friends, had they? But he'd helped Aya when he couldn't and for that, he'd always be grateful.

Zac had fought it and fought it, but he'd really had a family in death, no matter how mismatched it was, and he would do anything to protect them.

"What do you think Regulus wants with the original witch?" he asked, desperate not to think about the people he'd be leaving behind.

"No clue." Nye shook his head. "I've been a part of the Six for close to three hundred years, and I don't even know a quarter of the things Regulus gets up to. It could be anything, and that's what worries me the most."

"Why?"

"Why?" Nye raised an eyebrow. "Because that man is capable of *anything*."

"All the more reason for him to die."

"We need to do something about the others," Nye said, standing. "They're going to want to know what I'm going to do with you."

"And about Coraline."

"Mate," Nye said with a sigh, "let's go get you an alibi."

<hr>

Maddox shot to his feet when he laid eyes on the two vampires. The apartment was deathly quiet, and the sound seemed to echo on forever.

"Sit down, Maddox." Nye rolled his eyes. "Where's Rix and Pyke?"

"Gone for takeout," the assassin said with a smirk. "What about him?"

"I'm taking him to help me fix his mess."

"We should take his head. If Regulus finds out, then we're all done," Maddox exclaimed.

"Mate, don't you trust me?" Nye was using his leverage over the assassin to get him to back down.

"Of course, but—"

"But nothing. The half-breed has gone into hiding and I have an idea where she might be holed up. If we're not back in twenty-four hours, then you tell Regulus."

"Why?"

"Because if we don't come back, then we're dead," Nye said like it was the obvious answer—probably because it was. In twenty-four hours, it would be over one way or another.

Maddox stood again and edged towards them, placing himself between the two vampires and the front door. "What are you playing at, Nye?"

"Don't try to stop me, Maddox," Nye said darkly. "Or do you want to end up on the floor again?"

Maddox shot a glare at Zac, but he reluctantly stood aside and let them pass.

"I'm going to fix this mess, Maddox. If I find out you messed with this," Nye shoved the assassin on the shoulder, making him stumble back a step, "then your arse is mine. Understand?"

"Understood," he replied, his jaw set.

Nye grabbed Zac's arm and shoved him out the door as much for show than anything. Neither of them were in a hurry to die.

"Where to now?" Zac asked once the door was closed behind them. Maddox could still hear them, and he wondered what the spy would say.

Nye opened the door to the stairwell and turned back with a sly smile plastered on his face. "Door number three."

CHAPTER 23

I t'd been two days since Aya had let Zac go and for two days, she'd done nothing.

Truth was, Zac had rattled her. He'd said there was another way to end Regulus, that he was working towards finding and executing it. Whatever it was, she couldn't fathom it. So far, she'd been the one to kill the founders. Five out of six. Why should Regulus be any different?

After everything with Zac and the Coven, Aya had lost her nerve. Everything had gone to hell faster than usual, and this time the stakes were about a billion times higher. Death—true death—was a very real possibility.

"You need to decide, Arrow," Tristan said, pulling her thoughts back to the present.

"Soon enough," she murmured.

It'd also been two days since she'd left the hotel. She'd wandered the halls, swam in the pool, compelled handsome young men in the bar to sate her hunger, and not once had she thought about the Coven.

It seemed like her choice was obvious, but it would need more thought before she did anything. Aya had said it to Tristan and to Zac—one day she wanted to truly die—but if she could get Zac back…

Tristan's cell phone rang and Aya shook her head at the sudden trill, thoroughly annoyed.

"Hello?" he asked cautiously. He listened for a moment, his expression falling into surprise.

Even with her enhanced hearing, Aya couldn't make out what was being said or who was on the other end.

"I'm listenin'," he said, annoyed. "Do you think that's a good idea?"

God, Aya was dying to know what was going on.

"She's safe? Understood… okay. The Ritz…. *Don't be smart*. Room 437."

When he put the cell back in his pocket, Aya asked, "Who was that?"

"Zac."

"You're kidding."

"I wish I was," he scoffed.

"What did he want?"

"He got Coraline out. He took her to Salisbury, to Maximus." He paused like he was going to say something else and thought the better of it.

"Tristan," Aya scolded, "what else is there?"

"He's comin' here. He wants to speak to you in person."

Aya collapsed back onto the bed and closed her eyes. She wondered what Zac had to say, especially since the last time she'd seen him, she'd tortured him into bringing his humanity back.

If he was coming here, it wasn't to declare his undying love to her, it was because he knew another way to end Regulus.

The bed dipped as Tristan sat beside her. "You're somethin' else, you know that?" He said it in a tone that she didn't like. *Reverence.*

"Tristan, I..." she began, trying to be diplomatic about turning him down.

"Look, Arrow..." Tristan sighed, scratching the stubble on his chin. "I would be lyin' if I didn't say that I wasn't attracted to you, but I obviously don't have whatever it is you see in Zac. I get it."

"Love is a difficult thing," she murmured. "It's the one thing I want to control but can't."

Tristan laughed, slapping his forehead.

"What?" she scowled at him.

"The control freak admits that she can't control everythin'."

"Wipe that smile off your face before I wipe it off for you."

"Ahh, now that's the Arrow I know and love."

Zac hung up his cell and stuffed it back into his pocket with a sigh.

Ever since he'd told Nye what he was going to do, he'd struggled with what he would say to Aya. He thought about telling her the truth, but she would immediately know what it would mean for him. After spending the better part of a week with her, he didn't doubt she'd try to lock him up again. This was, after all, Nye's idea. He wanted him to say goodbye. The spy just didn't count on it being this way.

"Are you sure you really want to do this?" Nye asked.

"Yes," he replied, glaring at the spy. They were already halfway across town and he was running out of time to figure out how he'd play this.

"What about the Coven, mate? I don't think you've thought this through."

"All I've done is think it through," Zac grumbled. "Regulus will see her coming from a mile off. I will be able to walk right up to him unchallenged. She needs to be in the dark. The risk is worth it."

"The risk of her being the one hating you for a change?"

"She needs to be out of the way," he said. "She might be old, but she's prone to terrible decisions as much as any of us. She'll never let me do this and I can't risk her trying to stop me. You've never seen her lose it." He remembered the first time they'd met back in Ashburton. He didn't know who she was, but she saved him from a pack of werewolves, tearing them apart with her bare hands and mutilating their bodies beyond recognition. How she'd stopped and not moved onto him was beyond comprehension. Any normal vampire would've kept going until nothing was left alive.

"If that's what you believe, then I'm with you, Zac," Nye said, watching him out the corner of his eye.

When Zac had told Gabby what he'd planned that morning on the phone, she'd ripped him to shreds. There'd been a lot of foul words said between them, and she told him to wait until she could undo the link between him and Regulus. The witch didn't count on him moving so fast with her plan. That was the moment she told him the Roman had forced her to cast the spell that could ultimately kill him. That went down a treat. And to undo it? She needed Regulus' blood. Like hell that was going to happen. She wasn't even in the country and by the time she got here...? It'd already be too late.

Gabby vehemently wanted to save his life, but the fact was that he didn't want it. Zac had already made his choice.

"We're here." Nye pulled the car into the long drive at the front of the Ritz and turned off the engine. "Here." He handed Zac an auto injector—a spring-loaded syringe—filled with a strange green-tinged substance. "Stick her with that and it'll knock her out long enough to get the job done."

Nodding, Zac took the injector and shoved it into the back pocket of his jeans. When they got out of the car, the valet took the keys off Nye as they walked inside, the doorman ushering them through the gold and glass entrance.

"Whose idea was this?" Nye whistled, looking up at the crystal chandelier that hung low in the foyer.

"I can't imagine it being hers."

"Tristan, the showy bastard."

Zac tensed at the mention of the knight's name but said nothing. He better look after her or... He snorted at the irony. Nye would make sure.

They passed the front desk unchallenged and Zac pressed the button to the elevator, bashing on it several times to make sure it worked.

"Pushing it won't make it come any faster," the spy said with a chuckle. "You'll break the button."

"I don't..." he began but stopped himself.

Nye placed a hand on Zac's shoulder. "Don't be in such a hurry to say goodbye, mate."

The elevator dinged and the doors slid open.

"What floor would you like, sir?" the attendant asked.

"Well, ain't this fancy," Nye proclaimed.

"Four," Zac said, pushing the spy inside the elevator.

The attendant raised an eyebrow, but didn't reply, pushing the button for the fourth floor. As the numbers slid past, it felt like forever and his stomach churned. What would she say when she saw him? Hell, what would he say? He'd said some horrible things to her and deep down, he knew he'd meant most of them.

As soon as the door slid open, Zac pushed through and strode down the hall before he lost his nerve. Nye was a heartbeat behind him as he scanned the doors for the right number, 437. Coming to a halt, Nye knocked him out of the way and rapped his knuckles on the door.

A second later, it was wrenched open.

"What are you doin' here?" Tristan spat as he laid eyes on Nye.

"Trying out the other side for a bit," he retorted, pushing past the knight. "Posh room, knight. The life of a traitor isn't half bad, huh?"

"If I'm a traitor, then what does that make you?"

Nye smirked. "To be a traitor one has to first be loyal."

"God." Zac rolled his eyes, walking into the room. "Shut the hell up."

Nye winked. "Aye, aye, Captain."

"Worst joke I've ever heard," he said and looked at Tristan. "Where is she?"

"Next door." Tristan eyed him with suspicion and nodded to the left.

"Take your time, Zac Attack," Nye called out, opening the minibar. "Tristan and I have some catching up to do."

Zac lingered out in the hall, unsure how he was

going to go about this. Would he talk to her first? Would she let him? Would she sense what he was about to do and stop him? If he had to stick her with the needle and run, he would regret it, but it had to be done. He'd made his mind up a thousand times over before he'd even got in the car to come here.

Aya would sleep and he would die. *For her.*

Regardless, his hand lingered on the handle a moment too long before he swung the door open.

Then she was there, perched on the end of the bed, just as he had remembered her.

Aya stood, a hopeful look on her face as she laid eyes on him. Every time, every damn time he saw her, she stole his breath. She was beautiful. Not just her looks, but her being. To him, she was beautiful in every way he could imagine.

Closing the door behind him, Zac looked at the floor, suddenly shy.

"Aya," he began, but she was already in front of him, her hand on his face.

The moment she touched him, it all came flooding back and whatever he was about to say died in his throat. God, he wanted her so much it was like an addiction. What he was about to do to her was a sordid joke. She'd be furious.

"It's always been you, Zac," she said. "Ever since the first day I saw you. I'm sorry. For everything. I only did it to protect you."

She was breaking his heart. Even when she wasn't trying, she still broke his bloody heart.

"I understand," he told her. "But it doesn't make it hurt any less."

"I know."

"Aya, I—"

"Do you know how comforting it is to hear your blood again?" she interrupted.

"I'm still trying to figure that one out," he whispered, suddenly realising he'd unconsciously leaned towards her. His gaze flickered down to her lips and back up to her eyes, eyes that stared right into his soul. He wondered how she didn't know that this was goodbye.

"Zac," she whispered, pulling him close before he could turn away. "*Kiss me.*"

He couldn't have said no, even if he had wanted to.

Thrusting his hands into her hair, he pulled her flush against him, kissing her deeply, his body responding when she moaned into his mouth. Her hands ran up his chest and eased the coat from his shoulders and he dropped his hands away, letting it fall to the floor.

"I've missed you so much," she murmured.

Zac eased his hands under her blouse, caressing her soft skin. "Don't say it. Don't say it if you don't mean it."

"I mean it," she kissed the corner of his jaw. "A thousand times over, I mean it."

Abruptly, he pulled off her blouse, her black hair tumbling over her shoulders in waves. He pulled her hard against him, his lips finding hers as she coaxed him backwards towards the bed, forcing him down on top of her.

He tore his shirt over his head and kissed her navel softly, trailing his lips up towards her breasts, her body writhing under his touch. When she moaned in pleasure, he settled between her legs and she tightened them around his waist in response, almost driving him mad.

Sinking his fangs into the crook of her neck, he ground his body into hers, coaxing another moan from her lips. Her blood was even sweeter than he had remembered. It was the most addictive thing he'd ever tasted.

Pulling away, she drew his face to hers, kissing her blood from his lips, her tongue running the length of his bared fangs. God, he wanted her so much.

His hand found its way between her legs, his fingers pressing into her through her clothes as she moaned into his mouth.

Starting to unzip her jeans, he stopped, letting his gaze search hers.

"Yes," she said without hesitation. "I need you."

They peeled off their remaining clothes and explored each other with lips and hands, her touch burning him down to his soul.

As he took her, the sensation overwhelmed him, and he was lost. He didn't want to be found. *Ever.*

He was an asshole. And he knew it.

It'd seemed like hours had passed as Zac lay next to Aya, his arms wound around her delicate frame. They lay against one another, skin on skin, like he'd wanted to so many times. He didn't want to move, but soon enough he had to. It was the only place he wanted to stay and the only place he couldn't. She'd finally given herself to him, finally trusted him, and he was about to betray her and die.

She shifted against him, turning over so they were face to face. He gazed at her, taking in every detail and committing it to memory. The curve of her cheek, the arch of her eyebrows, the clear icy blue of her eyes, the way her hair fell about her face as her head lay against the pillow. Wherever he was going, he wanted to remember it all.

Aya brushed her lips against his and he caught her in a soft kiss, dragging his teeth against her bottom lip.

She sighed. "Where've you been since…"

"Regulus'," he said, turning on his back. "I had to get Coraline out."

"How did you figure it out?"

"I had most of the pieces," he explained, looking at

the ceiling. "Gabby told me where Maximus was, and I delivered her."

"Gabby?" she exclaimed, propping herself up on one elbow.

"Yeah. She's not impressed with you right now."

"I kind of expected that. Is she here?"

"No. She's still at..." He was about to say home, but he clamped his mouth shut.

Aya pressed herself closer, her hand splaying across his stomach.

"Your half-breed friend is safe." He shrugged it off. "That's all I can do for now." *What a lie.*

Glancing at her, he saw she was frowning, her brow furrowed. Had she caught on that his mood was more than he'd let on?

"Can Nye really be trusted?" she asked. "He was one of the Six."

"He's one of us. And I think they call themselves the Four now."

"If he's defected like you say, then technically, it's the Three."

He snorted, turning back to face her. "Can we talk about something else?" He didn't want their last conversation to be about plotting death and destruction. "We have some time to think about those things."

"Of course." She leaned over, pressing her lips against his.

"This, I'd rather," he said with a smile and flipped

her onto her back, eliciting a sharp gasp from some unknown place inside of her. Before she could say anything, he kissed her again, sucking her bottom lip into his mouth and teasing her with the tip of his tongue.

"You've changed," Aya whispered, turning her head to the side as he nipped at the tender spot just below her ear.

"How so?"

"You're..."

Zac faltered. Could she sense what Coraline had given him? If she found out, then his plan would fail. "I'm what?"

"Stronger. Surer."

"I have a path and I'm following it," he whispered, suddenly morose.

"What—" she began, but he silenced her with another kiss, shifting his body on top of hers. Positioning his elbows on either side of her, he cupped her face tightly as she plunged her tongue into his mouth, and he let out a deep moan that shuddered right through him.

"I'll never be able to get enough of you," he said between kisses, grinding his pelvis against hers, making her squirm underneath him.

All Aya could manage was a tiny whimper.

When they could finally drag themselves from bed, Zac kissed Aya slow and hard one last time before turning around and picking up his discarded clothes.

"What are you going to do now?" she asked, and he looked up to find her gaze boring into him. She would expect him to stay now, wouldn't she?

"I have to go," he murmured, dragging his jeans on. "There's something I need to do."

"And you have to go back to Regulus to do it?" She sounded angry. Disbelieving.

"Aya." He sighed. "Remember when you said you'd trust me? I just need you to do it for a little while longer. Please?"

Shrugging, she turned her back to him and dressed. When she pulled a tank top on, covering her beautiful skin, he stepped behind her, winding his arms around her waist, his fingers splaying out over her stomach. She fit against the length of his body perfectly and he knew he'd have trouble letting go.

"Zac," Aya murmured, trailing her hands down his arms.

He kissed the spot right underneath her ear, right on the corner of her jaw, the one he knew made her shiver. "I'm sorry I can't stay longer."

"After this is over... After I deal with the Coven, after I deal with Regulus... I will be free. Then we'll have all the time in the world."

He closed his eyes, holding back his grief. If he let it out, she would feel it, too. Letting a hand drop, he pulled the auto injector Nye had given him from his back pocket. "God, I love you, Aya. I love you so much it hurts."

"Don't go," she said, leaning her head back against his shoulder. "We can do this together. You don't have to go back to him."

He almost faltered, but he buried his face into her hair and breathed deeply for the last time. "I'm sorry," he whispered. "I hope one day you'll understand."

Before she could pull away, he stabbed the needle into her neck, her cry of surprise forcing tears from his eyes. As her body became limp in his arms, he lowered her gently onto the bed as she tried to fight the drug.

"No," she said, her voice barely audible. She tried to push him away, but it was too much and her eyes fluttered closed, her hand dropping limply onto the bed beside her.

Brushing her hair aside, Zac kissed her lightly on the forehead, taking in her peaceful form one last time.

She'd be furious with him when she finally woke. He had to keep believing this was the only way. Otherwise, he'd falter at the last minute and Regulus would kill him before he got the chance to get close. And if he caught Aya... She was too important. To him, to the witches. She had a destiny far greater than loving him.

Pulling away, Zac strode across the room, closing the door behind him before he could change his mind.

Zac opened the door to the next room, eyes on the floor.

"Zac?" It was Nye.

"It's done."

"What's done?" Tristan was on his feet, seething with sudden anger. "What did you do to her?"

Nye scowled at the knight. "He put her down, that's what."

"You drugged her? What the hell? What for?"

"She needs to be safe while I do this," Zac murmured, looking up at Tristan. The knight was wild with fury, and rightly so.

"Do what?"

"I'm going to kill Regulus once and for all."

"But," he sputtered. "The link—"

"Will kill me."

"You're just goin' to leave her here powerless and die on her?" Tristan exclaimed. "It's the one thing she wanted to prevent by leavin' you behind."

"She's not powerless," Nye butted in. "You'll be here to guard her until she wakes up."

"You better do it, or..." Zac began.

"Or what? You'll be dead," he growled.

"I'm his fail-safe, knight." Nye cocked an eyebrow. "You'll have to tangle with me."

"What did you give her? Where is she?" Tristan was

wild and it was a wonder he hadn't tried to punch Zac in the face yet.

"Next door, safe and sound." Zac sighed, walking past the two vampires towards the minibar.

"It's a synthesised silver thing that Regulus had made up a few years ago," Nye explained. "It'd put a plain old regular vampire down for a week. In the Hunter's case, maybe a day or two, tops."

Zac rattled through the empty bottles and hissed. There was no alcohol in sight, and he might just break something before he found it in himself to calm down. With Coraline's power flowing through him, he didn't want to take any chances.

"Nothin' better happen to her because of it," Tristan was almost yelling at Nye.

Zac spun, striding up to the knight, a look of pure anger on his face. "When this is done, can I trust you to help her take down the Coven?"

"I know I will," Nye said, glaring at the knight.

"Fine," Tristan spat, backing down. "I'm doin' it for her, not you."

"I know you think I'm a selfish bastard, Tristan," Zac said. "But I have my reasons a million times over."

"She'll never forgive you."

"Perhaps, perhaps not. If one person understands sacrifice, it's Aya. In time, she'll understand."

Nye clapped Zac on the shoulder, sensing his uneasiness. "C'mon, mate. Let's get this show on the road."

Throwing one last glare towards Tristan, Zac strode from the room, Nye on his heels. There was no use stretching it out, no use buying time. The sooner it was done, the sooner the threat would be eliminated.

Regulus was about to die, and he wouldn't even see it coming.

CHAPTER 24

When Nye pulled up in front of Regulus' house, Zac looked up at the building with a sudden sense of dread. He didn't remember the house being so imposing the first time around.

"Keep it together, mate," Nye said, opening the car door. "It's D-Day."

Zac conjured up an image of Aya, holding it in his mind for a moment and he could almost believe she was there with him.

For her, he thought, *for Sam, for Liz, for Alex, for Gabby. So, they can be safe.*

Getting out the car with a grimace, he slammed the door shut and followed Nye up the path.

The spy didn't knock, he just pushed open the door like he owned the place. The lights were on in the foyer and for a moment, the house seemed empty, but in a blur of darkness, the Three were suddenly there, surrounding them with a snarl so ferocious they sounded like rabid animals.

"What the hell, Maddox," Nye spat, shoving the assassin who had stopped directly in front of him.

"I went over your head," he said darkly, tilting his head to the side.

Nye stepped forwards, stopping an inch from Maddox's face. He was eerily calm and in no way threatened by what he obviously considered his subordinate. "I don't remember you being such a pansy boy, Maddox. You sounded like a pathetic lap dog just then."

This seemed to piss the assassin off big time. "I can still rip your head off."

"I don't remember you being such a kiss-arse, either."

"It's over, Nye. Regulus knows about him." Maddox pointed at Zac, who stood behind them, tense and ready to kill if it came to that. "And he knows about you."

"About me?" the spy scoffed. "And what exactly does he know about me?"

"Traitor," Pyke said.

"Traitor?"

"We can take you down, if that's what you really want," Rix said, the threat clear in his voice.

Maddox sneered, "Three against two isn't that bad."

Zac went to step forwards, but Nye held up a hand to stop him. "Age has nothing to do with it, neither does strength. It doesn't matter one bit who we were before or after. It matters who we are *now*. You all know I could rip through you and come out the other side unscathed. Hell, Zac could do it with one arm tied behind his back."

"Then why don't you, Nye?"

Nye pointed to each vampire. "Her Majesty's assassin. Her Majesty's executioner. His Majesty's bodyguard. What makes you think that you're any less disposable now than when you all served the Tudors? Kings and queens seek to rule the world and Regulus sees himself to be king of the vampires. What a gaff. Have every one of you lost yourselves so much that you can't see what he's planning?"

"We have our orders, and we have our duty," Rix said.

Nye laughed, stepping away from Maddox. "He will be nothing but ash in the next ten minutes and if you don't want to end up in a neat little pile right beside him, I suggest you leave. *Now*."

"What the hell happened to you?" Pyke exclaimed. "Four hundred years, mate. Four hundred years we've fought together, and now you take *his* side after five seconds?"

The Three stared Nye down like he was the most despicable thing they'd ever seen. To them he was every bit a traitor for helping Zac. They were in every way thugs under Regulus' control. They were vampires and relished in it.

Nye was frozen to the spot, not in fear or anger, but it was like he was standing in the centre of a hurricane —calm and still. Now Zac understood why they'd been so afraid of him, why they defaulted to his say so. In this moment, Nye was unpredictable and capable of anything, and the Three knew it because they'd seen it.

"Get out of here." It was so quiet, Zac almost missed it. How four words could be so full of anger and mercy at the same time, he had no idea, but he knew he was glad Nye was on his side.

Maddox faltered, his expression falling slightly into something akin to fear. Rix grabbed his arm, pulling the assassin back. And just like that, the Three backed out the door and were gone.

"Remind me never to piss you off," Zac murmured.

"Consider yourself reminded," he replied, inclining his head towards the stairs. "We've been made, so its now or never."

Regulus hadn't come downstairs to confront them and Zac should've been worried, but there was nothing they could do about it now. He was upstairs waiting for an audience, just like the king he deigned himself to be. They would be walking into a trap, but the point of no return was long gone. Zac pushed open the door to the study with a violent jab, sending it inwards with a bang.

"Zachary," Regulus said, the calm in his voice unnerving. He was in the chair he'd first saw the Roman in when he'd come to the house after killing Garrett. He sat now as he had then—superior and callous, a glass filled with sickly brown spirits in his hand. A sneer crossed his face as he laid his dark eyes on the vampire behind him. "And Nye. How nice of you to pay me a visit."

Zac didn't hesitate. He strode into the room with Nye close behind. "Enough," he said. "Just enough."

"And why are you here? By that charming look on your face, Zachary, I can take a wild guess and say you're displeased with me."

"I'm not here to argue about why," Zac spat. "I'm here to end you."

Regulus rose from his chair, his eyes never leaving his. "And how do you suppose you will do that?"

Aya had told him that all it took was a touch. If Regulus tried to kill him, he'd get a nasty shock.

"You think you have it all tied up in a neat little package," the Roman drawled. "Beware the Coven, Zachary. They're not what they seem."

"And I guess you would know all about that," he replied. "You've never been able to get inside to get what you want."

"And what might that be?" Zac didn't reply, clenching his jaw instead. "Oh, come on," Regulus continued. "You must have some idea. Otherwise you wouldn't be so worked up about it."

"We know the Coven is trying to wake the original

witch. It won't work. I'm here to stop you and Aya will stop them. It's over."

"You think they're trying to wake the original witch?" Regulus scoffed. "Are you stupid?"

Zac didn't understand. The Roman was bluffing. Stalling. "Then what are they trying to wake?"

The Roman laughed, shaking his head. "*Something else.*"

He almost hesitated in his desire for more information, but he took a step forwards, refusing to believe his lies anymore.

"Do it, Zachary," Regulus goaded him. "Rip my heart out. I *dare* you."

And that's exactly what he did. Zac flew across the room with alarming speed and plunged his hand deep into the Roman's chest, the power Coraline had given him shocking through his arm and into Regulus' heart.

He didn't know whether it was the fact that the Roman didn't defend himself or the peculiar feeling of his dose of Celestine power, but his eyes widened with shock. Regulus drew sharp breaths through his teeth, his eyes dark and threatening and for a moment, he actually looked pleased, but Zac was not capable of noticing. In that moment, he was not himself.

Was this how Aya felt when she dissolved a life in her hands? How she felt when a founder's heart turned to ash in her delicate hands? If it was, then he finally understood.

The ash of Regulus' heart ran through his fingers

like the finest sand, but instead of the creamy white sands of paradise, it was the colour of the blackest death.

Pulling his hand away, Zac felt numb waiting for the inevitable. The Roman's dead body slumped to the ground and whatever life that'd been lingering inside him finally seeped away.

Zac looked down at his sickly grey corpse and couldn't comprehend why he wasn't laying on the ground next to the Roman. Whatever strength that was keeping him upright dissipated and he felt his knees connect with the floor, and everything suddenly seemed so far away.

What was the point of life if it could be thrown away so heedlessly? Zac had taken so many lives and he could say it was because he couldn't control himself —that it wasn't his fault, that he didn't know—but it would be a lie. He was a killer and a murderer, and he was no better than Regulus.

He was glad to die. And that's why he was so disappointed when he didn't.

"Zac, you're bloody alive!" Nye pulled him to his feet. "Smile or something. If I had confetti, I'd throw it over you."

But Zac couldn't say anything. His throat had closed over in grief and disbelief. All he could think about was Aya...how he'd loved her and left her alone while he came here to die.

"Aya," he croaked. "I have to..."

"Mate." Nye laid a hand on his shoulder. "Tristan's got it. I don't like the guy much either, but he loves her, too. He's got it."

Zac could only manage a nod to that one. "The Three?"

"They'll keep," the spy told him and looked back at Regulus' desiccated corpse. "We've gotta do something about that first." Nye reached into his pocket and handed Zac his cell. "It's not the plan anymore, but I guess this is a call you want to make."

Underneath Highgate Cemetery was a small network of catacombs, full of mass burials dating back over the past few hundred years. A place like London, so full of people and life, it became necessary to store their dead underground because there wasn't enough room above. There were tunnels like these, hidden underneath modern cities that'd been built up over Medieval fortresses all over Europe. Plague, sickness, and overpopulation filled the halls of the dead more readily than anything else.

Where some catacombs had walls upon walls of stacked human skulls, this one was said to have stacks of coffins, and those coffins wouldn't have stood the test of time very well.

After talking to a surprised and relieved Gabby, they'd dumped Regulus' body into a simple pine coffin and brought it across town to South London, where one of its most notoriously haunted cemeteries lay.

They wanted to stick Regulus in the most obvious place and hopefully, he would stay hidden until they could find a more permanent resting place. Once he was secure, they'd contact Aya and Tristan's informants to do the rest.

The night was almost pitch-black as Zac and Nye arrived. The sky was clogged with clouds and little light reached them from the few security lights scattered around the cemetery. Nothing was moving inside the walls, making the looming feeling of death even more intense.

Zac hesitated at the opening of the catacombs, not liking the damp musty smell that seeped from below.

"Defying the National Trust, huh?" Nye quipped behind him. "This place is protected by their flowery red tape and somehow, I don't think they take new burials down there."

"The perfect place to put him," Zac replied. "There's forgotten corners down there that even the historians won't poke around in."

"Do you believe in ghosts?" the spy asked, gravel crunching underfoot as he shifted nervously.

"Really?" Zac's eyebrow rose, his breath vaporising in the air.

"This place is creepy."

"Are you scared?"

"What's scarier than a vampire?" he asked. "Let's just dump him and get away from this place."

Breaking the lock with a twist and shoving the door open, Zac led Nye down into the catacombs and into the darkness. They hadn't gone far when Zac sensed her presence almost immediately. It was so familiar there was no mistaking it.

He bade Nye to put the coffin down and walked forward into the darkness and embraced Gabby, who emerged from the shadows.

"Well, this is an unexpected welcome," she told him.

"Did you have something to do with this?"

"With you being alive? I'd just stepped off a plane when I got your call. Whatever went down, I have no idea."

"Maybe it was the Celestine thing..." Nye said.

"And who are you?" Gabby asked, frowning at the appearance of another vampire.

"Gabby, this is Nye. He's one of us... and the guy who was supposed to deliver the *package*." Zac gestured to the older vampire, who winked at the witch.

"Gabby?" Nye asked. "What's that short for?"

"Gabrielle," she replied, eyeing him.

"Gabrielle is better. That's a real woman's name."

"Well," Gabby laughed, "I can see why you two are friends. You go together like peas and carrots."

"Peas and carrots?" Nye exclaimed. "Who's the pea and who's the carrot?"

Zac stifled a groan and ignored him. Turning his attention back to Gabby, he asked, "What are you doing here?"

"When I knew you'd go after Regulus, I had to be here to make sure. This Coraline woman, she may have given you her power, but I wasn't convinced he would actually die for real. That's why I'm here."

"Ahh," Nye said. "You're here for the autopsy."

"And a little bit of witchy concealing." She winked at the vampire, her disposition towards him softening. "With my help, no one will ever find what's left of him."

"So, let's chuck him in a hole and sprinkle fairy dust over him already."

"It's not that simple," she said, her eyes raking over Nye's face.

"See something you like?" he asked, running a finger across his scar.

"I'm not into vampires."

"What do you mean, it's not that simple?" Zac asked, defecting the conversation back to more important things than Nye's vanity.

"Coraline isn't as strong as Aya. I have to make sure he stays dead."

"Oh, he's dead." He rolled his eyes. "I felt the ash fall through my fingers."

"Regardless, concealing him will take time."

"Fine."

"Down here." She gestured for them to follow, holding up her cell phone to light the way. "It's dark and miserable. The perfect place to stick a dead founder."

"I like her," Nye said from behind.

Stopping in front of an alcove, Gabby pointed to an empty shelf and the two vampires set the coffin down.

"I thought this place was going to be temporary," Zac said.

"I'm not taking any chances," the witch replied. "He threatened my family, too."

"What now?" Nye asked. "This place gives me the creeps."

"I need to watch him for a while," she told them. "I will find you when I'm ready."

"Don't leave it too long," Zac said. "I don't like leaving you alone down here."

"I won't." Gabby smiled, placing a hand on his arm to reassure him. "It's good to see you again."

"And you, Glinda."

She laughed, shaking her head. "What the hell are you waiting for? *Go get her*."

A*ya.*

Zac saw her in his mind's eye, lying peacefully on the bed at the hotel where he'd left her. She'd given herself to him and now he'd made it out the other side alive. He was alive. She'd tear him to shreds when she woke.

He wasn't sure what he was more afraid of, that he'd angered her or that he was still alive... or that she would never forgive him. Somewhere along the line he'd seemed to have done just that—forgiven her.

He ran a hand over his face and sighed.

"Mate?" Nye asked, glancing at him out the corner of his eye. The spy was driving them back to the Ritz at top speed, which seemed to be the only way he drove in the first place.

"I'm fine."

"We're almost there," he replied, flicking the indicator on and taking a sharp left.

Zac knew there was only one other moment in his life where he'd felt this anxious and that was when Victoria had left him dead in their townhouse in New Orleans. The subsequent flight to the manor felt very much like this drive across London, and he couldn't help the feeling of dread in the pit of his stomach.

She was okay, Tristan was there to protect her. She was okay.

As soon as the car came to a halt in front of the hotel, Zac shot from the car and barely heard Nye call out after him as the spy tossed the keys to the valet. He was at the elevator, pushing the button a million times before he could catch up.

"Zac," he said.

"I've got a feeling," he replied as the doors swished open.

The attendant eyed them as they got in. "Four again?"

Zac nodded sharply and they ascended, his stomach churning. With a sense of déjà vu, he pushed through the door as it slid open and strode down the hall, Nye following behind. Without stopping to knock, he pushed the door to Aya's room open, and his heart sputtered and almost died.

The room was trashed. Furniture was splintered, glass was smashed, and there were holes in the walls, but all he could see was that she was gone.

No.

Zac roared in agony and his eyes settled on Tristan,

who was laying in the middle of the floor, covered in blood and very much dead. Not his true death, he wasn't desiccated in the slightest, more the temporary kind. He went to grab the knight from the floor and shake him alive, but powerful hands held him back.

"Settle down." Nye pushed him away. "He loves her too, you know. Don't put this on him. Look at the room, Zac. *Look at it.*"

Looking around, his eyes finally seemed to focus on the surrounding destruction. He saw the splintered furniture and shattered glass. He saw the holes in the wall, and he smelt the knight's blood. Whatever had happened, Tristan had put up a hell of a fight.

"It's not his fault," Nye said. "*It's not his fault.*"

Tristan's eyes snapped open and he drew in a loud, wheezing breath, clutching his chest.

"Arrow," he exclaimed, trying to stand. "*Arrow.*"

"She's gone," Zac said as the knight's gaze finally settled on the two vampires who stood above him.

"No," he said, eyes darting about the room wildly. "*No.*"

"Who took her?"

Tristan groaned, holding his head in his hands. "the Coven."

"How the hell did they know?"

"Witches." Nye shrugged. "How do they know anything?"

"I'm sorry." Tristan grimaced, clutching his head. "I tried to stop them. I tried..."

Nye hauled the knight into an armchair. "I know, mate. You made a right mess. How's the limit on your credit card? The damage bill is going to be huge."

"Shut the hell up," he hissed. "We have to go after them."

"Yeah, we do," Zac said, looking at Nye.

"I have to go," the knight spat.

"I don't like your tone, Tristan."

"I love her, too," he hissed as he stood. "Don't go blamin' me for this. You're the one who drugged her, or have you already forgotten?"

Zac grabbed the front of the knight's shirt and jerked him close.

"Zac," Nye said. "This ain't the time to be fighting over it."

With a grunt, he let Tristan go, pushing him away.

"We've got to work together," the spy continued.

Zac looked Tristan up and down and scowled. "I still hate you."

Tristan grinned wryly. "Better than nothin'."

"How are we going to get into the sanctuary?" Nye asked.

"Coraline," Zac said. "She'll get us in."

Tristan pulled his cell from his pocket. "I have Coraline's number. I can call her."

"Give it here," Zac said, holding his hand out.

Tristan unlocked the screen and dialled the number and didn't hesitate in handing it to him.

Turning his back to the others, Zac held the cell to

his ear, seething as each ring went by, until finally, someone picked up.

"Hello?" came her tentative voice.

"Coraline?"

"Who is this?"

"Your favourite bad guy."

"Zac?"

"We need your help."

"I'm done helping," she snapped. "You know everything I do. I'm not coming back. Not after you crashed a car with me in the boot."

"They have her, Coraline."

"W-what do you mean?"

"What do you think it means? the Coven has Aya."

"Shit."

"Yeah, big piles of it," he retorted. "You need to get me in."

"But you have Celestine blood…"

"We've never tried my blood and I don't want to have to rely on it. Not now. There's too much at stake."

"And what do you think you're going to do against forty witches?"

"Whatever it takes."

Coraline sighed and he could imagine the annoyed look on her face. "You better hope to God I haven't been blacklisted yet."

"You're still in Salisbury? I'll come and get you."

"No, it'll be faster if I get the train from here. They

go every hour and the next is in... twenty minutes. Get me from Waterloo. Two hours."

"Done."

"She'll be okay," Coraline reassured him. "I know them. They won't kill her until they wake the original witch—Aya's power is too potent to waste it. Besides, a ritual like that will take time."

"Okay," he said again, knowing she was right. "I'll be waiting." There was nothing he could do to get her here faster, and Gabby couldn't help with this.

He ended the call and tossed the cell back to Tristan.

"Have we got a plan?" Nye asked. "I don't wanna go into this witchy showdown blind."

"No," Zac said. "I'm going in alone with Coraline. I have Celestine blood and it will fool them long enough so I can wake Aya."

Tristan scowled. "You hope."

"What other choice do we have?" he almost shouted at the knight.

Nye shrugged. "You can let us back you up."

"No." Zac shook his head. "If there's one thing I know about witches, they will peg both of you as vampires without having to lay eyes on you. You'll be good as dead."

Nye scowled. "Are you still so willing to throw your life away?"

"Shut the hell up, Nye."

"No way," Tristan exclaimed. "I mightn't like you

either, Zac, but Arrow is important to me and you're important to her. You should be dead right now, yet you're still here. If that's not an omen, then I don't know what it is."

"Goddamn it, Tristan is right," Nye said.

"And you're important to her, Tristan." Zac scowled at the knight. "And you," he jabbed a finger at Nye, "have just got your second chance. You both know I'm right. I'm the only one who can go into that place and have a hope in hell of coming out alive."

Nye shrugged, looking away. "I still don't like it."

"Neither do I," Tristan agreed.

"It's how it is," Zac said. "Liking it is optional."

"She'll still be out," Nye said, taking something from the inside pocket of his coat. "Take this."

Zac snatched the auto-injector from him. It was a clear, green-tingled liquid instead of the thick, slimy emerald it was the first time.

"It'll wake her up in a hurry, so try not to give her all at once."

"Why?"

"Because it might make her lose control," Tristan said, and from his tone, Zac knew the knight had seen her at her worst.

"It'll be fine," he murmured, looking at the injector, not sure who he was speaking to exactly. "It'll be fine."

CHAPTER 26

Zac stood next to Coraline in a dark alleyway, their breath vaporising in clouds around them on the crisp night air. Coraline's train had been delayed twenty minutes because of ice on the tracks and he was thoroughly wound up.

"Where is this super-secret hideout anyway?" he asked, twitching.

It'd almost been ten hours since Aya had been taken and it made him restless. Who knew what the Coven was doing with her? Coraline said they'd wait until the original witch had been woken, but what if it was already too late?

"Underground. I thought you knew this?" she said, shooting him a withering glare. She wasn't happy in the slightest, was she?

Giving the witch an equally hard scowl, he replied, "Let's just get in and get this done."

"This is the back door," she said, pointing to the

wall. "The main entrance is over a few blocks. I assume this was how she got in the first time."

"It's a wall," Zac drawled.

Coraline rolled her eyes and sighed. "There's a glamour over it, idiot." She pressed her hands against the brick and to Zac's surprise, it wavered like ripples of water across a still surface.

"The wards are gone." She frowned as an image of an old wooden door appeared.

"What does that mean?"

"Either they know we're coming, or they haven't replaced them since the Hunter was here."

"Aya came through here before? On her own?"

"Yeah," she said vaguely, pushing the door open and disappearing inside.

Before he could think twice about it, Zac followed, stepping into darkness. It didn't take long for his eyes to adjust and when they did, he saw the beginning of a staircase spiral downwards. Without another thought, he descended, following Coraline into the depths of the station, the air cooling even more than outside.

The stairwell opened up into a long hallway and Coraline walked down it without hesitation, trailing her fingertips along the wall. Soon they came out into what used to be the ticket hall. It was dark, the only light pooling in from a dozen skylights that'd been set into the celling high above, but the debris that littered the place was as plain as day.

"What the hell happened here?" His gaze ran

over the collapsed tunnel and the broken skylight in the ceiling. At some point someone had repaired it with a strategically placed board at street level.

"What do you think?" Coraline asked. "The Hunter was here, and it didn't go well."

"You're saying Aya caved in the tunnel?"

"Yes."

Zac gave her a look. She was mad. There was no way Aya could've done this.

"You don't know much about the Celestines, do you?"

"So now Celestines can move the earth? *C'mon*."

"Yes, they could and don't give me that look. I didn't know she still had that kind of power."

"I guess there are a lot of things we don't know."

Coraline looked away. "Well, we can't go that way anymore."

"How can we get through?"

"Here." She pushed through a side door hidden behind the ticket kiosk. He would've missed it if it wasn't for her.

"Obviously," he drawled.

Without a word, Coraline led him through to another hallway. This time it looked like a service route staff had used when the station was still in operation. It was dark and cold and obviously saw little use from the Coven, if they used it at all.

"How did you know this was here?" he asked.

"How do you think I got out unseen? They don't know about it."

Zac was having a hard time believing her. "They don't know about a door set in plain sight?"

She rolled her eyes at him. "Forget it."

He shrugged. "Witchy juju spells, whatever."

"We could be discovered here," she said, ignoring him. "There's nowhere to hide, so I suggest you stay behind me and keep the one-liners at a minimum."

He nudged her forwards down the hall. "Fine with me."

As they walked down the passage in the murky light, Zac listened to the surrounding silence. For a network of tunnels, even as built up and habitable as these, the slightest sound would echo, but as they wove deeper into the network, he heard nothing. For a place that was meant to be a sanctuary for an entire coven of witches, it didn't seem right.

"It's a bit quiet, don't you think?" he murmured.

"Yeah," Coraline whispered. "I was thinking the same thing."

Involuntarily, he shivered, suddenly wanting to get out of there as soon as he could. "Can you sense her?"

"I think Alisandra's got her in her rooms."

"Alisandra?"

"The matriarch. Their leader."

He nodded his understanding. "I'm right behind you."

They passed several doors and turned a few

corners, not coming across a single soul. Something was going down. Was it the ritual Coraline told him about on the phone?

"Here," the witch said, stopping in front of him. Her hand was on a door handle and she stood completely still for a minute before pushing it inwards.

Zac wasn't sure what he was expecting, but it wasn't the lavishly decorated interior of the matriarch's room. Past Coraline's shoulder he glimpsed red- and burnt-umber-coloured Turkish rugs on the floor and large landscape paintings on the walls. It was less like a room in an abandoned underground train station as it could be. A Japanese-style folding screen, covered with cream rice paper, had been drawn aside and somehow, he knew Aya was behind it.

Stepping into the room behind Coraline, his heart skipped a beat as he laid eyes on a comatose Aya. She was laid out on a bed, asleep and peaceful. There was no blood or any signs that she'd been hurt, and he stumbled past Coraline, who began rifling through Alisandra's things.

Dropping to his knees beside the bed, Zac grasped Aya's hand. God, what would she say when she woke? He pulled the auto-injector from the inside pocket of his coat and almost dropped it when Coraline let out a surprised cry.

"What?" he hissed, looking back at her.

"It's Alisandra's grimoire," she gasped, snatching it up.

Zac knew enough about witches to know that those little books were like a gold mine and the grimoire of the matriarch of the Coven…? Coraline held the world's weight in uncut diamonds in her hands.

"Aya will need that," he said, watching her flip through the pages.

She nodded, but he wasn't sure she'd actually heard him. She opened her mouth to say something, but her head turned towards the door and the grimoire snapped closed.

"Coraline?" he asked, frowning.

"I can feel something," she whispered, clutching the grimoire to her chest. "I better go check it out."

"You better not be ditching me and running off with that," he said, the warning clear in his voice.

"I'd never leave the Hunter behind," she cried.

He regarded her for a moment and said, "Fine."

Her gaze turned towards the door again. "Hurry. I can feel a buildup of power," she said. "Get her out. I have a bad feeling they're performing the ritual."

"Now?"

"*Yes*," she spat. "If I'm right, then I have to stop it."

"Then go. I've got her."

As she disappeared through the door, Zac turned back to Aya. Pressing the auto-injector into the side of her neck, he pressed the antidote into her system as slowly as he could, remembering Nye had told him that it would bring her back fast. Too fast and it would cause all sorts of problems. Get out and regroup. That was their objective.

When she stirred, eyes fluttering, he put the injector back inside his pocket. Clutching her hand, he caressed her face, rubbing a thumb over her cool cheek.

"Aya," he whispered. "It's Zac. Wake up. *Please, wake up.*"

"Zac?" Disoriented, her eyes tried to focus on his face. "What have you done?"

"I'm sorry," he said, tucking a strand of hair behind her ear.

She blinked hard a few times and looked around and recognition flashed in her eyes. "Where am I?"

"the Coven, they—"

Aya sat up sharply, pushing him away. "What did you do?"

"I drugged you so Nye and I could kill Regulus. the Coven took you before we could return."

A horrified look spread across her face as the words tumbled from his mouth. Standing abruptly, she paced the room a few times.

He reached out warily, but it was the wrong thing to do.

She pushed him hard against the wall, her fingers biting into the skin at the crook of his neck. She was losing it. He could feel the tension coiled in her lithe body even as it pressed up against the length of him.

"I haven't finished with you," she snarled and was gone.

Aya felt her fingers dig into Zac's neck and it took everything she had to hold on to herself. Even as the words left her mouth, she knew it was only a matter of moments before she lost control and she had to get away from him.

"I haven't finished with you," she snarled and left the room in a whirlwind of fury. He drugged her? *He drugged her?*

But she had bigger problems to deal with than Zac.

She felt power thick on the air and it stunk like Alisandra. Her vision slipped into a blurry haze as she stumbled onto the main platform of the station.

The thirteen witches of the Inner Circle were standing in a sweeping arc across the rails, their backs to her with their heads hung low. Behind them were another twenty witches in the same position, all chanting in unison, the indistinct murmur of their voices echoing against the walls.

Thirty-three witches.

She'd never been up against that many at once before. There was no telling who would come out of this, especially since her true end was almost guaranteed.

Breathing heavily, Aya grasped the edge of the

opening to the tunnel and clutched her chest. Her heart thumped erratically and the whoosh of blood almost drowned out the mutterings of the witches. How they hadn't noticed her arrival was beyond her.

Trying to focus on the words of their chant, she tensed and almost lost her balance, finally understanding what they were doing. They were performing an awakening ritual. *The* awakening ritual. And she had to stop it.

Aya let herself slip and all at once, she felt her mind drift away and give in to the beast that lived inside her—her vampire side. Aya knew she couldn't do this any other way. Was it desperation or fear that led her to take this path? She didn't know.

At least she had the sense to go after the Inner Circle first. They were so deep in their trance that she'd ripped through four of them before they stirred, the spray of hot blood coating their clothes and faces. The witch standing directly beside her screamed in horror when her gaze fell on what was left of her sisters, but it was cut short when Aya plunged her hand into her chest and tore out her heart. Tossing it aside as the witch's body crumbled to the ground, her white gaze locked onto Alisandra's.

Aya's head tilted to the side and she felt her bloody lip curl into a sneer, revealing the fangs underneath. This one she would save for later. In a blur, she was on the line of witches behind the matriarch, hands tearing and fangs biting through flesh and sinew, sticky blood coating her face and hands, soaking through her clothes.

She was sure they tried to defend themselves, after all, they were the mighty coven, Celestine incarnate, but even they didn't have the power to stop a hybrid vampire in mid-rampage.

Whatever power they tried to restrain her with didn't bother her in the slightest. In fact, she didn't feel it at all.

Blood ran in rivers down the platform and along the disused rails, it splattered on the walls and coated the world red. Aya tore and ripped everything she grabbed hold of apart, unaware of who or what it was.

Suddenly, she stopped, her hands empty. No one was left except...

Her head snapped up as she heard a muffled sob to her left. There was one pulse of life remaining. Aya lunged towards the sound with incredible speed and her hands latched onto living flesh.

"*No,*" a small voice cried.

Who was that? She felt the reverberations of power through her hands and knew she held onto a witch.

"Aeriaya!"

Aeriaya? So that's who she was.

Alisandra. Matriarch. Kill yourself. End your pain. We don't want to see you suffer. The original witch would make the world suffer.

the Coven was dead.

Gone.

Alisandra let out a blood-curdling scream as Aya's fingers bit into her skin, but it was a sound that was too far away to be heard. Blood ran through her fingers, warm and sticky. Coppery with the tang of something familiar. Home. Mother. Father. Brother. They had seen the bones of her family and what had they done? *Conspired to kill her.*

With a howl of rage, Aya sunk her fangs deep into Alisandra's jugular and tore, blood spurting down her front like a waterfall.

The bones of her family desecrated. Her home had been defiled.

Her fingers dug into flesh and she felt bone.

They'd tortured and murdered their own. They'd manipulated her and tried to kill Tristan. They'd taken her. They'd forced Zac to come here.

Her fingers closed around bone.

the Coven was dead.

She twisted and felt a sickening pop as she tore Alisandra's head from her body.

the Coven was dead.

The dull thud of flesh against concrete was the only sound that filtered through her foggy mind.

Then everything was silent.

CHAPTER 27

Z ac sat against the wall, breathing heavily. He thought he'd seen anger in Aya before, but the rage that'd seeped from her was unbearable.

Annoying sound bounced around the room and he clamped his hands over his ears and sunk his head to his knees. This had all gone so wrong.

He didn't know if it was one minute or twenty that had passed as he sat there shell-shocked, but he dragged himself to his feet and stumbled into the hallway. That's when he realised that the annoying noise was screaming. Horrible, gut-wrenching *screaming*.

One thought passed through his mind before he snapped out of it and ran full tilt down the hallway towards the platform. *Aya.*

One thing was certain, someone was in excruciating pain and when he found them, he knew wouldn't like what he saw.

He steeled himself against the overwhelming stench of blood that was already filtering into the tunnels, but for all his assumptions, nothing prepared him for the scene he was about to lay eyes on.

Skidding to a halt just inside the main platform, he stifled a horrified gasp. Aya stood in the centre of the abandoned station, covered head to toe in dark, sticky blood, surrounded by what was left of the Coven.

At the sound of Zac's boots skidding across the ground, she slowly turned, her hair hanging limply around her face. Her gaze seemed to meet his, but her eyes were white, her expression lax. He knew if he wasn't careful, he might end up in pieces alongside the Coven.

Anyone who saw her now would think she was some macabre devil, but all he saw was a star who'd lost her way.

"Aya," he whispered.

Faster than he thought possible, she was in front of him, their faces an inch apart. With a roar, she threw him clear across the station, his body colliding with the wall on the opposite platform with a boom that seemed to echo on forever.

Zac landed face-first, shattered tiles falling over him as dust clogged his throat. Icy hands flipped him over and he stared up at Aya's bloodstained face, which was etched with a twisted look of pain.

Coughing up dust, he tried to flip her off him, but she buried her fingers into his hair and slammed his head back into the concrete floor. Pain shot through his skull as black spots exploded in his vision. His tentative grip on his control waned and he felt his fangs grow in as blood flowed from the wound on the back of his head.

Clawing at her hand, he groaned in agony as the shattered pieces of his cracked skull pressed into his brain, desperately trying to hold on to consciousness. If he passed out now, then nothing would stop her.

Wrapping his hands around her slender arm, he squeezed with all his strength and Aya let out a roar of anger as her bones splintered under the pressure.

It had the desired effect. Her grip loosened on his hair and he pushed her backwards.

This time, he was on top, holding her arms above her head, trying to restrain her. But she was too much for him and had him flat on his back before he could open his mouth to calm her. Fingers wound around his throat and he knew if she couldn't stop herself, he only had seconds left.

Zac didn't recognise the woman above him, but he knew Aya was still in there. She held his life in her hands, her fingers biting into his skin, tearing into his flesh, but he didn't cry out. He trusted her. She wouldn't take his life. It was already hers.

"Aya." His voice sounded scratchy and very far away. "Come back."

He lifted a hand and traced her bloodstained lips with trembling fingers, hoping to God she could see him through her blind rage. His vision blurred around the edges and the ringing in his ears was almost unbearable, but he didn't lower his hand from her face, trailing his fingers along her jaw, lingering on the spot below her ear. The one he'd kissed right before he'd left.

All at once, recognition flashed in her eyes and she let him go. Jerking back like she'd been burned, she fell backwards off him, scrambling away like a frightened animal. A look of utter horror spread on her beautiful face as she pressed her back against the wall of the station.

Zac sat up, wheezing as he tried to draw in oxygen to his starved lungs, well aware blood was still seeping from the back of his crushed skull.

"Aya." He couldn't manage more than a whisper.

She opened her mouth to say something, but the words seemed to die in her throat. Her gaze dropped to her hands, which were covered in a thick layer or blood and dirt, turning them repeatedly like she couldn't comprehend what they were.

He crawled slowly towards her through the broken tiles, his eyes fixed on her. Her head jerked up and her gaze met his—blue and clear and full of horror.

"Stay away," she sobbed, pressing herself back into the corner.

"No," he whispered, edging closer.

What would he look like now if he just left her here in the middle of this? She'd just tried to kill him, but he knew she'd lost control—something he knew *all* about. He would never forgive himself if he left her now.

Reaching out, his fingertips lightly grazed the skin of her arm and with a sob, she fell into his chest. Zac rested a cheek against the top of her head, his arms wound tightly around her as they sat in the aftermath of the carnage she'd wrought.

"I-I almost..." Her muffled sob was loud in the empty cavern of the station.

"It's okay," he muttered into her hair, breathing in her familiar scent that was tinged with blood and dirt. "You came back."

And what he suspected was the first time since she'd been turned, she cried. She really cried.

He tightened his arms around her and rocked back and forth, soothing her as best he could.

Zac would stay for as long as it took. Even if it took forever.

***

As soon as he was able, Zac took Aya back to the Ritz, where Tristan and Nye were waiting for them. There was no reason to move now that the Coven was gone. They would be safe.

It was still the small hours of the morning, so they got inside the hotel with no one seeing them. Covered in blood and dirt as they were would've needed considerable compulsion.

Aya had clung to Zac like a frightened child the entire way—shell-shocked and numb.

As soon as he coaxed her into the room, Tristan was on his feet. Zac transferred Aya to his arms with a grimace and stood back.

"Got you some clean clothes, mate," Nye said, eyeing him with concern. Zac had texted the spy as soon as he left the sanctuary, letting them know what'd happened and to expect them.

"Thanks." He sighed, watching as Tristan's head sunk into Aya's shoulder. He couldn't help but feel the pang of jealousy that stung his heart.

"Coraline is downstairs at the bar when you're ready," Nye told him.

"She's okay?"

"Yeah. She said she'd wait for you. She's got news."

Zac nodded, glancing back towards Aya. "I'm going to clean up," he said to the spy and disappeared down the hall to the bathroom.

What the hell did Coraline want? Despite their frosty relationship, he was glad she'd gotten out of the sanctuary, but it was over now. There was no sign of the original witch and the Coven was destroyed. Their 'weapon' would stay sleeping and would eventually be forgotten.

Zac made short work of showering, a sickly feeling of dread building up in the pit of his stomach. If she was here to see if Aya was okay, then why did she need to speak with him?

Downstairs, breakfast was in full swing over at the restaurant, but the bar was quieter. Through the floor-to-ceiling glass, Zac saw only a handful of hotel patrons had stopped by for a coffee. Walking inside, he spotted Coraline at a table in the far corner, flanked by a worried-looking Maximus.

She looked up as he approached, sensing his presence, but her eyes said it all. *Something wasn't right.*

Sitting down at the table, he nodded at Maximus. "Good to see you in one piece, Coraline."

"Never thought I'd hear myself saying it, but you too."

"How did you get out?"

"When I saw the Hunter tear through the inner circle, I knew I had to get out or I'd end up right beside them."

"Smart move," Zac told her. "But there's more, isn't there?"

She sighed. "Yeah. When you put her out, did you know what the Coven could do?"

Zac frowned. "What do you mean?"

"the Coven knew how to end her. For good," Maximus said.

"Shit," Zac hissed. Why had he been so stupid? That's why she'd gone off at him like she had.

Coraline shook her head. "I'll take that as a no."

"Of course not," he spat.

"Told you, Corrie," Maximus murmured into the witch's ear.

"Told you what?" Zac asked a little too forcefully.

"He said you were in love with the Hunter."

Love. It seemed such a far-fetched notion after everything they'd done. He and Aya? They were always hurting each other in the name of love. It wasn't right. Zac knew he would have to be the one to pull away if there was any salvaging their relationship. Aya had found herself, she was sure in her love, but he hadn't found what he was looking for, not yet.

"Zac?" Coraline poked him.

He grunted, looking back up at them.

"Is she okay?"

"What she did," he faltered. "What she did was horrific. It'll take time."

Coraline smiled thinly.

"That's good," Maximus said, laying a hand on hers.

Zac sighed. "It's not good. It's the least of the bad scenarios."

"Zac," the priest started warily, "we don't think this is over yet."

"We thought the Coven was trying to revive the original witch," Coraline continued. "We're going to find out for sure. After we went through Alisandra's grimoire, we found a reference to the original's resting place—Brú na Bóinne, in Ireland. There was nothing about who it's meant to be."

Zac tensed, his heart sinking into a mire of dread. He was getting tired of it to be honest.

"What's that look for?" Coraline asked.

"Regulus said it wasn't the witch..." he replied slowly. "He said it was something else. I thought he was bluffing."

"That's why we have to see for ourselves."

"If the ritual was successful, then we will soon know what they woke," Maximus said.

Zac nodded. "And what about Gabby? Have you heard from her?"

"No," Coraline replied. "Last I heard, she was still in the catacombs with Regulus' body. I left the grimoire with Tristan for her."

"I'll go look for her," Zac said. "You better let us know the moment you get to wherever this place is. This time I'd like some forewarning if I'm going to have to fight another ancient psycho witch."

He supposed they'd need all the allies they could gather in case the worst happened. He didn't like it one bit, but he'd have to take Nye and look for the Three. And who knew where they were and even if they were still together. He was sure Pyke would go to the Tower of London, and they'd start there first. He'd hinted he'd spent most of his life there—he was an executioner after all.

"You have my number?" he asked.

"Yeah." Coraline tapped her temple. "And a hard line to Gabby."

That was it then. Another game of wait and see.

"Good luck, Coraline, Maximus." Zac nodded and stood sharply.

Out in the foyer, he pulled his cell from his pocket and dialled Gabby's number, hoping she could get signal down in those dank catacombs.

When Zac could bear it no more, he went to her.

He'd let Aya sleep for a day, alone, while Tristan guarded her like a rabid German shepherd. No one would get past him again, at least, not without a few wounds to count for it. After the knight had apologised for going off at him like he did, Zac's disposition towards the older vampire had softened somewhat. Tristan knew he'd never win Aya's love, not in the way he wanted, but he was satisfied to be counted as a brother.

Nye had kept an eye on the old apartment that once housed the Six, but no one had come back to it and probably never would. Soon enough, they would have to find the Three and win them over to their cause. Once Coraline and Maximus had confirmed the original witch still slept, then they would know what to do next. Either end the threat for good or fight like hell to take her out.

Zac opened the door to Aya's room as quietly as he could, not wanting to wake her if she still slept, but she stood by the window, looking down at the street below.

When he closed the door behind him, she sighed. It used to annoy him when she didn't acknowledge his presence, then suddenly saying hello without looking up, or coming out with some smart-ass comment that took him off guard. He kind of missed it to be honest.

"Zac." Her fingers were balled up into the curtain.

He walked up behind her and pried her fingers away, pulling her against him. "You look exhausted. Have you..."

He felt her head shake against him.

"Your power?"

She shook her head again.

"Take my blood," he whispered and pulled her towards the bed, forcing her to sit in his lap.

Without a word, she eased his head to the side and bit into the skin of his neck as delicately as she could.

Closing his eyes, he relished in the feel of her lips against his skin and the pull of his blood as it left him. When she drew back, he felt oddly cold.

"I've been hearing some outrageous things," she said, laying her head against his shoulder. "I don't remember much, but I do remember coming back to myself in the sanctuary."

"It's okay. I know you're sorry for that. I know."

She clutched onto him like she was afraid he would disappear. "What happened to Regulus?"

"Aya, Regulus is dead. I told you—"

"What do you mean?" The look on her face was confused at best.

"I killed him. Coraline loaned me her power and I killed him."

She shook her head in disbelief. "But the link. He links everyone to him. How?"

"I don't know." He shrugged. "I thought I was."

"You were just going to sacrifice yourself?" she exclaimed, standing up. The look in her eyes was wild and he couldn't fathom the breadth of it.

"Yes."

"I don't know what happened, but you're still here." She pulled him up and pressed herself against him, arms winding around his waist. "Never do that again. Not when I'm here to help you. You have to let me help you."

"It was Gabby," he said, ignoring the last part. "She told me what to do."

"She knew you were going to do this? Did she suggest it to you?"

"Not exactly." He wound an arm around her waist and kissed the top of her head to calm her. "She wanted to undo the link, but she wouldn't have gotten here fast enough. She turned up a few hours after it was done."

"You couldn't wait a few hours?"

"I didn't know."

"Zac..." she scolded him, but he placed a finger over her lips. She knew why he wanted to do it.

"When the Coven took you..." he began, but she placed a finger on his lips this time, silencing him mid-sentence.

"It's done. They're all gone now."

"I'm sorry," he said. "I didn't know they could..."

"I should've told you. I will tell you," she said and he realised she was still stuck on the trust issue.

"No," he stonewalled her. "Don't tell anyone. Not even me."

Even though they'd finally done away with the Romans and the Coven, deep down something was still missing. Something in his heart was still missing and he knew he wasn't there yet. He wasn't the man Aya deserved to love... not yet.

"All this time," she began, her eyes downcast, "I've been counting on myself... All this time I've had to bring myself back from the edge."

"Aya—"

"No, listen to me. After all this time, you were the only one who's brought me back. *You.*"

He wasn't sure what he was meant to say to that. How could he bring someone back when he couldn't find the way himself?

"If you would forgive me, then..."

"Then what?" Zac whispered, already knowing what she was going to say. Then they could be together forever and be each other's anchor? He couldn't do that. Aya had learned to control the wild parts in herself and if he wasn't there, it wouldn't matter. The other way around? He almost had it. *Almost.*

"Regulus is dead. the Coven is gone. Don't you understand? *I'm free.*"

"And what about the Coven? What if they awakened whoever it was?"

"Then we'll fight it," she told him, "like we've fought everything else."

He turned his face away, not wanting her to see the pain that flashed across his features. "You'll always be fighting something, and maybe I'll always be fighting my demons."

He'd descended into something terrible again and again as a coping mechanism. He'd turned to the only thing he knew, and that was being a true vampire. He turned into a monster to cope with his pain. It was so wrong on so many levels. He needed to do this on his own.

"Zac." She turned his face back to hers. "What's wrong? There's something else, isn't there?"

"I'm tired of fighting." He always thought it would be Aya leaving him in the end. She'd already set the precedent for it. Had she felt this way when she'd told him all those horrible lies? It seemed like such a long time ago and so much had happened since then. "Aya, I will never love anyone else like I love you, but we can't do this." As the words left his mouth, he felt his heart breaking. "If this is what it does to me... What it does to you... Then we can't do this."

"You can't be serious," Aya exclaimed.

"I need to learn how to live on my own again. I relied on you to the point where I couldn't function without you. And you..."

"And I what?" She narrowed her eyes.

"This isn't you, either."

By the way her expression crumbled, she knew he was right.

"You were right when you said it was a dream." He sighed, looking away.

Looking back, it often felt like their love had been the ultimate fantasy. They both wanted to feel for someone, and Zac had always felt like he'd been waiting for something to break it apart. To wake up or feel a sharp pinch that told him it was just that—a dream.

But now here she was pleading with him not to leave. This dangerous thing would push them over the edge to their destruction. They had different paths to take.

"How can this be wrong?" She placed a hand over his heart. "After everything that we've been through, how could it be wrong?"

"We've hurt each other so much all in the name of love. You see nothing wrong with that?"

"Zac, don't do this."

"Aya." He sighed, struggling with his words.

"Without you, I could never have found the path I was meant to take. I need to find the person I'm meant to be on my own. It was never wrong... just the wrong time." It was ironic that now the tables had been turned. Aya couldn't let him go. They would never be even. "If you truly love me, then you'll let me go."

She let her hands drop limply from his face, her expression pained. Smiling at him sadly, he knew she understood. "I love you and I know you love me. I'll be here, no matter how long it takes."

"I can't ask you to wait for me."

Running a hand down his face, she smiled. "You're closer than you think, Zachary Degaud."

Leaning in, he kissed her deeply, savouring the taste of her lips. Who knew when or if he'd be able to do it again. "Goodbye, Aya. We'll see each other again... someday."

He didn't look back as he walked out the door. He couldn't.

Nye was waiting for him in the hallway, leaning against the wall with his arms crossed. "I'm sorry, mate," he said, frowning.

"Save it, Nye," he drawled. "We've got work to do."

"Do you really think we can convince them?"

Turning, he looked at him pointedly. "Without a doubt."

"Then where do you want to start?"

Zac grinned. "The Tower."

Gabby sat in the darkness of the catacombs underneath Highgate Cemetery, her coat and scarf drawn tightly around her. The only light was from her cell phone, which she had opened a torch app, shining it onto Regulus' coffin. Enough time had passed since Aya had ended the Coven. How she knew was still a mystery to her, especially since she'd had no contact with anyone since Zac and Nye had left her. There'd been a buildup of power, then nothing.

But a simple phone call from Zac had confirmed it all.

Walking over to the coffin, she shuddered, knowing who was inside. There was no way he was waking up anytime soon, not without a little help anyway.

Opening the lid, she gazed down at Regulus' desiccated body. If Aya knew what she was doing... God, if Zac knew, she'd be in a lot of trouble.

Suppressing a shiver of revulsion, she reached out

towards the Roman and placed her palm over his heart... or the deceptive pile of ash that was his heart. The glamour really was quite lifelike. If she didn't know it, she'd think the Roman was truly dead as well.

His evil, black heart still sat intact in his chest and what she'd done made her gag. What she'd put Zac through... He had every right to be mad with her.

The Roman had brought her to London days ago. She'd undone the link when she was bidden and orchestrated Coraline's escape. When she knew Zac had been given the witch's power, she cast the complicated glamour over Regulus. She'd had no choice in the matter. The lives of her family and friends had been threatened and she had no way of protecting them all.

If Regulus was going to make her play his games, then she would give as good as she had to take. Sending a sharp jolt of energy straight into his heart, his eyes snapped open and slowly rolled to meet hers. They were bloodshot and tinted a sickly grey, but they were very much alive.

Scowling at him, she pushed another burst of energy straight into his heart, this time not holding back. *Let the bastard suffer*.

Regulus sat up sharply, gasping for breath as life crept back into his body. "God, Gabrielle," he wheezed. "You could have been a little more gentle about it."

"Now why would I do that?" she sneered, leaning against the wall.

"Because I could kill you right now," he said and lifted his hand to grab her, but much to his surprise, it stopped in midair.

Gabby tilted her head. "You were saying?"

He climbed out of the coffin, his jaw set. "I'm breathing again, so I take it Aeriaya did what she was meant to."

"the Coven is gone," she confirmed.

"Good. And what of the ritual?"

"They believe it was interrupted, but the priest Maximus and Coraline have gone to Brú na Bóinne to make sure."

"And the link?"

"Severed."

"Zachary is still alive."

"Yes."

"*How heartwarming.*"

"Why do they need to think you're dead anyway? It doesn't make sense."

Regulus laughed. "I am the last original vampire. There are things only I can do."

"You went to a lot of effort to orchestrate your own death."

"It had to be believable."

"To whom?"

"The Coven and in case they succeeded, to their little friend."

"Don't make me regret helping you, Regulus," she said sharply. "I want answers."

He snorted, leaning forwards, "Gabrielle, there's a hell of a lot at stake here. I need all the people on my side I can get. I may be the only vampire alive who can stop this thing."

"What is it?"

"Everyone stupidly thinks it's the original witch. None of you have one iota of intelligence."

"What do you mean? It's not?"

"Let's just say that Aeriaya is not the only hybrid I've been hunting these past two thousand years."

Gabby's face paled and she swallowed hard. "What do you mean? There's another? A hybrid with what?"

Regulus smiled wryly. "Are you ready for a wild ride, Gabrielle? You better pray to your God that the Coven didn't succeed."

"Why?"

"Because if they did...? It will be the end of the world as we know it."

THE AWAKENING
(The Witch Hunter Saga #4)

A buried monster. A secret alliance. The battle that could see the end of all things is just beginning...

Witch Hunter Aya swore to protect the Earth, no matter the cost.

But after thousands of years searching, the Coven has finally awoken an ancient horror. One that has the power to control death itself and bring the world to its knees.

With an unpredictable supernatural force unleashed, Aya, Zac, and their friends face the fight of their eternal lives.

They thought the Romans were the first vampires, but there are older and more evil things in the world. Things that should have remained buried and forgotten. Things that should have been left alone.

The epic battle that could see the end of all things is just beginning.n*The Original has awoken...*

The Awakening is the fourth book in The Witch Hunter Saga, an Urban Fantasy series like no other... Vampires, witches, and fae abound in this thrilling new twist on an ancient myth. You haven't read vampires like these before.

The Awakening is OUT NOW!

ABOUT NICOLE

Nicole R. Taylor is an Australian Urban Fantasy author.

She lives in the western suburbs of Melbourne dreaming up nail biting stories featuring sassy witches, duplicitous vampires, hunky shapeshifters, and devious monsters.

She likes chocolate, cat memes, and video games.

When she's not writing, she likes to think of what she's writing next.

Follow Nicole Online:

Website: nicolertaylorwrites.com
Facebook: facebook.com/nrtaylorwrites
Newsletter: nicolertaylorwrites.com/newsletter

www.ingramcontent.com/pod-product-compliance
Lightning Source LLC
Chambersburg PA
CBHW060732190726
48285CB00001B/172